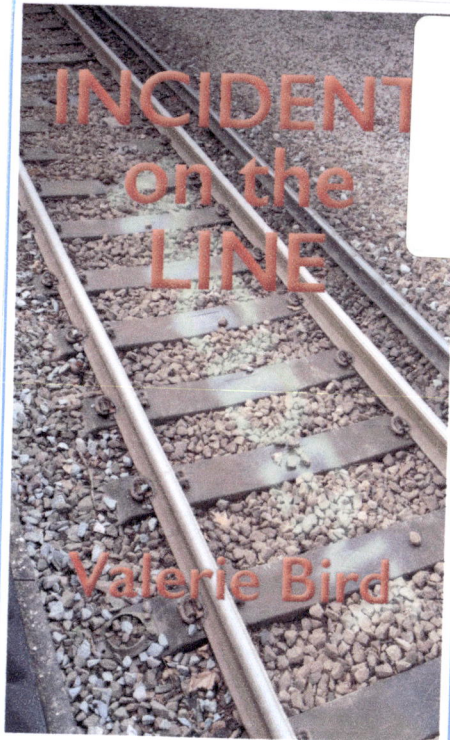

INCIDENT
on the
LINE

Valerie Bird

t on

ine

**Thank you for taking time to
read 'Incident on the Line'.**

If you enjoyed it, please consider
telling your friends and/or posting
a short review on Amazon

http://bit.ly/vbiolrev

Word of mouth is an author's best
friend and much appreciated.

If you have finished with this copy,
I would be more than happy for
you to pass it on to someone else
to review.

Thank you
Valerie Bird

*ens
for you
proofreading*

Valerie x

ISBN: 1539649318
ISBN-13: 978-1539649311

The right of Valerie Bird to be identified as the author of this work has been asserted by her in accordance with the Copyright, Designs and Patents Act 1988.

This is a work of fiction. The characters, incidents, and dialogues are products of the author's imagination and not to be construed as real. The author's use of names of actual persons, living or dead, and actual places is incidental to the purposes of the plot and is not intended to change the entirely fictional character of the work.

Cover design Valerie Bird and Drew Westcott

Published by: Drew Westcott
www.drewwestcott.co.uk

Dedication

For my sister with love and admiration

This is the way it is

Life concertinas back and forth, time compressed in the fluted bellows of memory. Each pleat an instant, an event, a point in time that stands out, makes the everyday different, plausible or implausible, bearable or unbearable. Breathing in and out, tuneful or discordant, this is the way it is.

I laughed when my editor suggested that the time was ripe for an autobiography. Yes, crime still topped the charts but life stories were up there alongside. I've no history, I said, am too young and innocuous for a tale of revelation and invented misdemeanours. I've no need to traipse the tracks back to ancestors, to peer back into dusty records; the past delved, rummaged, poked and pinched in the hope of what; royalty, infamy?

This is the way it is, and private. Or was until the unlikely, the incredible, the improbable possibility came to haunt me, crept up my spine, clouded days, crowded nights with interminable questions. The bellows at full stretch or squeezed in tight, back and forth to search out what had been and how to go forward. Lottie, Gerald, Roger; these impossible connections? I flounder under a litany of metaphors; language and life losing all harmony.

2002

We should talk

'Greta Salway. But you won't remember; so many years ago.'

I had to speak to him. Leo had dragged me across, me, the prize author to be introduced to another mêlée of academics, damp handed men, sharp-eyed women. I was the escapee from their inner sanctum, the coterie of learning. And there he was amongst them, the fallen star, attempting to mingle with his former herd. How odd. I felt no frisson of fear or pleasure.

Leo looked on with interest, ears and eyebrows cocked for what he'd say later was my 'back story'. One I never wished to share.

'Well, well, if it isn't one of my sweet girls!' Gerald clicked his heels, and with a pretentious bow lifted my hand to his lips. 'One of my protégés. When was it, tell me, when?'

He made it sound as if he'd spread his realm further than the UCN, the zenith of his career, before a stint in some faded American university and then back here and to Bournemouth. I'd picked up rumours at the beginning, fuelled by curiosity and anger. Then nothing, the relief of nothing. Yet here he was, thirty years later, in front of me, the curls thinner, limper, the grey merged in amongst the mouse, wearing a jacket that revealed the worst of time's ravages.

'1970, the Creative Writing BA.' I wasn't going to remind him and the rest of the company that I'd had to leave after my second year and by the time I returned to resume where I'd left off, he'd gone.

'Oh, that would have been before I went to America.' He looked at Leo thinking to impress, and then turning to me, excluded the rest of the room. 'What are you doing here at this God awful gathering?' I might have responded but he left no space for an answer. 'Can't think why I came, all the old hacks, few of my contemporaries.' He laughed, raising his glass; 'Age catching up, better for wine than for men.'

Surely this isn't the man that I'd loved?

> You called me at midnight
> to say we should talk
> words blurring along a line
> the air frosted.

America would have suited him well in those days. The flower power man in corduroy trousers, shirt of Liberty cotton, a watch with hands that told the time, hour, minutes, seconds, on a brown leather strap. He wore sideburns, showing pinches of grey; an aura of distinction rather than the ageing process. He was thirty-five. We all admired him.

Not at the beginning. I was bored and cross during the introductory lecture by the Principal of the College who made a tedious overture to the courses and lecturers, giving a stern but jokey discourse on the dangers of plagiarism; 'Honouring the other poor sods who've laboured before us is vital, they need our recognition as you will require the same of others in years to come.'

Each lecturer was introduced in a playful tone, as if we were children who had to be cajoled into believing the courses were going to be fun. Or, as I learned, the principal liked practising his wit, sure of a laugh. I didn't.

'Gerald Porter, Senior Lecturer and Course Leader in Creative Writing,' the Principal simpered, 'will be carrying you through to the heights of esteemed rhetoric, casting aside any baggage you might have acquired in your earlier education.'

Sitting forward awkwardly, knees and toes together, heels wide apart, like a cockeyed dancer, his fingers and thumbs joined to make a triangle, apparently deep in thought, Gerald neither smiled nor snarled; I wondered if he was listening. The Principal called his name twice before he rose and walked to the microphone as if in a stupor. I was not impressed.

Leo said; 'You know she's won Crime Writer of the Year?' A necessary intervention, he wanted acknowledgement for his trophy writer.

'Really?' Gerald frowned indicating that there was something troubling about this piece of information. 'Who's sponsoring it these days?' The question was only half directed for my attention and I didn't bother to answer. Leo muttered a reply sensing, as he would, the rudeness of the response. Leo is after all my dearest agent, has been for years, a lovey with nerves of steel when negotiating a book deal, and never lost in the snappy jargon of a pseudo social scene which this was.

Did I want to talk to this man, Gerald, so long ago my lover?

> I called you in the morning
> to ask for a place,
> an entry in your diary,
> the air fragile.

'Leo, be a dear, get me another glass of wine while I put this man in the picture.' Whatever he thought of my raised eyebrows, Leo sauntered off taking my empty glass without offering Gerald the same courtesy. I needed to confront this intrusion alone. Alcohol-fuelled bravado or revenge.

4

1970, I was nineteen, greedy for this chance to hone my skills as a writer, convinced that I was destined to become great. I wanted to knuckle down, be told what to read that I hadn't already read, to absorb it all like a sponge. To garner all his learning, his knowledge, his craft; not to take the relationship as far as it went.

Perhaps it was, in that moment all those years ago, as Gerald opened his mouth to speak that it changed, my hostility evaporated. 'I'm grateful to the Principal,' he said, his voice a low tenor, 'and to all of you for taking this BA in Creative Writing, one that I'm proud to teach, as are the rest of the staff on the Course.' He surveyed the hall, as if gathering us in, his private circle which, of course, many of us became. We waited as, for a moment, he faltered, overwhelmed, it seemed, by the sight of our avid attention. This was his trick, I came to believe, an air of shy unease in lectures, to make us hang on, alert for what he would say next. In seminars it was piercing clarity, work savaged apologetically. The soothing voice, his passion for verse, 'words plucked, cajoled, sited or spurned'; there was no escaping his reverence and knowledge; Donne, Clare, Wordsworth, Edward Thomas, on to The Waste Land, though not much beyond. You couldn't fool him, couldn't slate any author without a damned good reason for your censure. And then he'd look at us with a shrugging smile and say; 'Yes, that's interesting.' We all believed that his was the Holy Grail and that is something I'll not demean.

An individual tutorial was a joy; he may have torn your essay to pieces with his green pen, yet criticism was couched in terms that gave you possibilities, somewhere to go for the next assignment. He was good at that. I cannot fault his teaching, his ability to zone in to your strengths and weaknesses, to give you the encouragement and space to do better.

> *You called me at noon*
> *to tell me that time*
> *glances across the sundial,*
> *the air floating.*

'How was America, Gerald?'

'I do remember so well, Greta,' he looked down at his empty glass, and then up, straight at me; the hazel green eyes hadn't changed, despite the jowly cheeks, the ropey neck. 'I couldn't say anything in front of Leo. He's your agent?'

'Leo French, the best in the business, I should have introduced you,' I said, cross that I hadn't. I repeated; 'Was the job in America as exciting as you'd hoped?' I wanted to say - and your wife, how did she find it? And even thinking that made me angry; any envy and resentment in those far off days was hardly relevant, little reference ever made to her existence. 'We live on this other plain, Greta; you and me, our passion, the bliss of our beings, above the chaos that churns around us,' was one of his declarations.

'What would you believe?' he was now saying. 'I wasn't fooling, Greta, when I told you that you were my most perceptive student.' I waited for more, a real answer, that went beyond, 'something like that,' the perfect distancing tactic, his favourite phrase which had always paralysed me with annoyance. 'It was a shambolic department, narrow minded, and they didn't really want some English gent telling them that or changing the syllabus in any way. I was trapped in my own vanity. There, you have it, an unvarnished assessment. And you can imagine Laura loathed it, moaned for the entire five years we were there.'

Surprised at this honesty, I said; 'Am I meant to sympathise?'

'No,' he laughed, 'I treated you badly. You could accuse me of running away.'

Hell! I thought, this is not what I want. What does he mean, what does he know? Not about Lottie, he cannot know about her.

I said; 'I'd never accuse you of that, certainly didn't at the time, if you remember. Bon voyage and all.'

I called you in the evening
to talk about lilies
growing in a garden deep
the air fragrant.

'I heard you had a child.' His words rang round the room though with all the noise, so many packed in, voices rising higher and louder in order to be heard, only I could have registered what he'd said. He was looking at me with real regard, as he'd done all those years ago. That first time we'd stood so close, glasses raised to celebrate the publication of my first poem in some wordsmith's journal. A high wire was our firmament, at thousands of feet above the earth. He'd handed me his glass, taken my face in his hands, gently, softly, bending to touch my lips and then again and again until the world slowed, stopped and I drifted off into space, whirling in a treacherous light with no ability to touch reality. Romantic nonsense from this distance but I cannot deny the madness that overtook me.

'I skipped a year,' I said without expanding. 'And now crime's my business. Met a tame police inspector and it took off from there.' A twisted truth of which I was unashamed; I wasn't trying to impress Gerald. Or endanger the solid veneer built up over all this time. 'Thirty years, Gerald, twenty of them reasonably successful. And you, your writing? I must admit I haven't been studying academic journals. What's been happening?'

Leo returned at that moment with two glasses of warm wine. Gerald looked as thankful as I, took a couple a gulps before swaying slightly and mumbling; 'Publishing poetry's become a damned difficult market.'

I introduced them though Leo had obviously been acquiring an update on my companion as well as the wine.

'Someone told me you'd submitted a large tome on your career,' Leo said, 'teaching creative writing as an art form? Was that it? Any success?' And it wasn't Leo being snide; he doesn't operate in that way. Open and shiny as a buttercup; I once said that to him to which he replied; 'Until the sun goes down and then I close up to process all the nasty bits and pieces of the day; you'd be surprised at how beastly I can be in my head.' Me too, I should have said.

Gerald started on a rambling explanation of the things he'd written but not bothered to publish; 'All philistines, these days,' I heard him say but I tuned out, I didn't want sad explanations from this man I'd once believed exceptional.

> You called me at midnight
> to whisper that love
> is freedom and loss
> the air swollen.

The panelled walls, hung with flattering portraits of past masters, bounced back the rising tempo of conversation. I looked around without bothering to identify anyone; clusters of heads deep in two or possibly three stroke conversations, exaggerations, excuses, bits of gossip. 'Did you know he's not had an offer for ...' 'The advance was totally out of their league, I recommended an auction but ...' 'Teaching absorbs all your creative juices, don't you find?' None audible, but I knew it all. There had been too many of these 'dos', all part of the publicity machine, and being in Cambridge had been a big draw. I turned back to Gerald and Leo. Two men smoothing each other's ego, and I didn't want to listen. Leo threw back the last of his wine, grimaced at which Gerald laughed, a laugh I'd known and loved. Always I'd wanted to make him laugh, to see him happy. Make him happy.

> *I called you, I called*
> *to offer the truth*
> *that winter comes before spring*
> *the air leaden.*

How could I have let that happen? The physical approaches shouldn't have been a surprise to one as blasé as me. Me? It was us then; for a good six months that is what I believed. And for a further six months fooled myself that I was the one who was different.

What didn't I know about life by then? Not innocent, well over the age of consent, so why was I ready to risk the hurt after the leap over the precipice? And yet my cynical have-it-all self, I'm in control of the bungee rope, left me that moment in his home study. The light searing through long curtains, white splodges of bright blue, drawn across the French windows, a tasteful sanctum. I remember the slight lift and whisper of the heavy cloth as a breeze through the open door to the gardens added to the elegance; blocking the view from inside and out. We were away from the world, closed off from prying eyes.

Did I love him? Yes, I loved him and did for a long time after, beguiled, bewitched. He liked chocolate cake, assumed I did too, 'our treat' he'd say. Why didn't

I tell him, no, it's not to my taste. But the rest of him was.

'Haven't we had enough of this?' Gerald was saying. 'Who wants to be surrounded by the smell of success and stench of failure?

'Speak for yourself, Gerald,' Leo said. He was glowing, his aquiline nose agleam, his slick black hair sprang like a raven's wing from his brow. 'This is my trade remember; warm wine, bitching and pitching, and remember I'm hosting this lovely lady.'

I couldn't have put it better myself, but I also couldn't bear the look of chagrin on Gerald's face. Long lost love turning to pity. Leo may have noticed but he was having none of it. 'We've quite a bit more schmoozing to do before supper time.' And then before I could contradict him, even if I'd wanted to, he said; 'Join us later if you're free. We'll be at the University Arms.'

'Except,' I began but Gerald wasn't going to listen to me. Whatever he wanted, and perhaps it was admiring company, I don't know, he gave one of his stock gentle nods of the head, the sanctified poet, and slid away, brushing closer than necessary, a hand lingering on my shoulder.

'Odd bod,' Leo said, as soon as he was out of earshot. 'What on earth did you learn from him?'

1969

You shift the earth

I said; 'I'm pregnant.' Not that I'm carrying a child in my womb, or that I'm expecting, just the blunt medical fact. It had been five months crouched in my belly, a free wheeling roly-poly creature that had come to home with me. A love child it would be, not illegitimate, no bastard, but my beloved. By all the runes of social norms, I ought to have been distraught, at my wits end, to find that in one unguarded moment an egg spun into the path of a tiny heat seeking missile and was exploding into a glorious human being. I never thought it a mistake, a foolish act, a wrong; it was given by all that is good in our amazing universe. And has nothing to do with him. It was my infatuation, not his. Other people, if they'd known, would have accused him, the usual suspect, the culprit; abusing his privilege, his duty as teacher and tutor. I think, thought, that's such a lazy way of describing how it happened. Even how they, Joy and Jim, my Mum and Dad, would react didn't trouble me; or that my great ambition to become a world class writer would be put on hold. And this wasn't the euphoria of crazed hormones. Merely pride. The practicalities would be grasped, my life would go on a different route. Another journey. I was up for this, my grand opus.

Joy brought a pot of tea, the teacups rattling the saucers, a plate of macaroons on the tray I'd made in woodwork. School was where I learned to gobble life up; words were my pleasure, my fascination, and that they led to other learning, to the 'how to' of life was all I needed. And them; Joy and Jim.

'Sweetheart,' Jim took the tray from Joy, 'a child?'

Joy stood, her arms as if still holding the tray. 'Who?' she said.

I shook my head. 'It's unimportant,' for I knew what she meant.

She stared at me, the bluest of eyes, her hair crinkly with the latest perm. Doreen, her sister, would have done it, as I did once. The vile smell of the lotion I plastered on before winding the tight curls. So close we were, the only daughter, the only child. Now she said; 'For you or for him?'

In the garden of the council house in Waterbeach which was home, one of a row with pebbledash walls which they'd enlivened with honeysuckle and roses, we sat, side by side on a wooden bench encrusted with lichen. That day in March, my birthday, the snowdrops were peeking from dark corners, a few daffodils shouting from sunny spots; the warmest day of spring.

'A baby,' Jim said, tasting the idea as if rolling a boiled sweet around in his mouth. 'Is that definite?'

'Of course, I wouldn't have brought news like this if I wasn't sure of my message.' A severe response but I was smiling, the glow of motherhood radiating from me. 'It is what I want.'

'Determined,' Joy said, though there was no sweetness in her tone, 'that was always your way. They said that on your first school report and then many times after.' She wasn't cross, nor acquiescent, and there was more. 'Stoical, a thoughtful child, will go far. That's what they said. And you wanted to go far.' Neither of us had moved. 'Now? How?'

The sweetest parents, you can hear it in their names, Joy and Jim. Married late, a child later; Joy was thirty nine, Jim forty two. 'Best time to have little ones,' I remember him telling me over and over. 'Settled in to the beauty of life, able to tackle the snags head on.' He ran the local hardware shop; it was in the days when you could buy one screw, ask advice, borrow a tool, have straw delivered. As manager, not owner, it was all hours and not a huge wage but it was steady, as he was. Everyone liked Jim Salway. His family had lived in the town since way back but I've not bothered to do the family tree, and he certainly wouldn't. 'You may not think it, girl,' he'd say, 'but we've come up in the world. All labourers before me, all good honest labourers.'

Joy had blown in from a small town on the Wash. We went back for a caravan holiday; Cromer, facing the North sea, the sand dunes bristling in the wind, a wind that cut down from the steppes of Russia. A beach for sand castles, gritty sandwiches, windbreaks and jumpers; that's what we called them in those days, jumpers. Joy's knitting, wool I wound from skeins which Jim held with his hands wide apart, told our family story. A small family but as warm and patterned as you could wish; no simple knit-one-purl-one, we were cables and ribs, stripes and figures. My favourite jumper was sandy yellow for the desert, halfway blue for the sky with the dark silhouettes for palm trees and a camel train walking across my chest. It was a marvel and back then in the fifties my friends were envious.

The whistle of a train, the line to Ely going north, Cambridge going south, broke the air, called time. Time for me to make it clear. 'It's immaterial. It was my carelessness, and there is no one I want for a husband or a father to my child. Please believe that.'

What was I asking of them? Their youth was taken up by war, a blitz on everything that had been solid when they were born, and then the slow climb out of austerity. Nothing swinging or free; love and courtship were a careful progress from handholding to an honourable wedding at the registry office.

'A grandchild,' Jim said though it was more of a question. 'When is it coming?'

'The beginning of August, a Leo child.'

'And what does that mean?' Joy was sitting beside me on the bench, all our hips touching, the warmth of each of us pressing in.

'Fierce and fiery,' I said though I wasn't a horoscope believer. Later, for a while, it amused me to think of this prediction.

'How will you live?' Joy said again. 'It's a scholarship you're on; will they take that away?

'No, it's all fixed. I take this next year out though still doing research and writing, and then go back for my final year. They're happy with that, and so am I.'

'And this baby, where will it live and be happy while you're studying?'

'She'll do it, Joy,' Jim leant forward to pour from the cosy-covered teapot, 'and we'll be grandparents before we're too ancient to enjoy a little one.' His eyes caught the glint of the sun and I wondered if he might cry. That is one thing he did which went against all the manly power he presented as father and husband, supporting his wife and child. Christmas carols, Nat King Cole's 'When I Fall in Love,' or 'Abide with Me' with no one even dying, brought tears to roll down his cheeks and a handkerchief pulled from his pocket to blow his nose.

Avid film goers, Joy and Jim, the cheapest seats. I was Greta after Garbo whose mystique and beauty they both admired, and what he interpreted as part tragedy and part nobility when she went into graceful retirement from public life.

'Jim, dear, I know our daughter's a miracle but there's practicalities. Neither you nor I can give up work to help. Where would you live?' she said to me.

'Haven't I always found a way? You've said, it's our motto, nothing is impossible if you want it enough.' I was leaning into her, looking out across the little lawn to the apple tree which separated the flowers from the veg. That was another of Jim's sayings; 'Keep them apart, let them know their place; flowers, fruit, veg. Who wants to see rows of Brussels from your bedroom window?' The grass was so green.

Joy shifted; I felt it, that tiny sideways move closer to Jim. Was that the first moment I recognised the unravelling? The adored, adoring daughter was asking too much.

'Shouldn't whoever this man is, be asked to contribute to the child's upkeep? Isn't it his right?'

No, no! I wanted to shout, he must never know, and it's what I so firmly believed all the way through to Lottie's death and beyond. And I believe it to this day; I couldn't explain then though I can now.

At the time I was amazed that Gerald never questioned whether it might be his child, though I was vastly relieved. It hurt that he must consider me a promiscuous slut and that it of no importance. I had kept the news of my pregnancy from him for as long as possible, avoiding any private contact, but that he never enquired, or made reference to who might be the father, only added to my conviction that he was a cad, with no rights to parenthood.

'Please, trust me,' I said to them. 'I'll be a good enough mother for my child never to need anyone else.'

And it's still there, that moment, I can hear the held breath, the inaudible gasp at the cruelty of what I'd said. I would always need them and that's what they needed me to say. I was pushing them away in denying them knowledge of someone I wanted to forget.

Had I ever been an easy child?

At school I'd been teacher's pet, solid student, clever enough and eager to please. As an adolescent there had to be a bit of rebellion: paragons aren't popular. I became the hard nut, promiscuous on my terms; boys at the church youth group, at school dances, if it suited my purpose. I wanted the power, to show that I was more than a blue stocking, the feared insult of most girls in those days. There was the crush on a teacher which went too far, too late realising that the line between admiration and intimacy is easily crossed. Nothing abusive, nothing to harm me but I cursed my naivety back then, removed myself from danger, but did nothing to warn anyone else. Viewed from a distance I'm ashamed that I ducked the responsibility of the victim, but can I really blame myself at fourteen?

So why was I vulnerable to Gerald's advances, why hadn't experience taught me? No, I was as guilty as he.

Joy and Jim would have known none of this. Joy was a nurse, State Enrolled not Registered. 'We're just not allowed to give them their drugs. But most of them value a well-made bed, a bit of a chat, a bedpan or a hand to the toilet, more than medicine,' she'd laughed. Proud, she was, of what she could do for her patients, and I was proud of her. She explained to me the facts of life in the same matter of fact way she would show me how to cook sponge cakes. Joy had made sure that I wasn't ignorant. Contraception was a necessity, I was given all the information. Which must have made the fact of my pregnancy harder for her to condone.

I went back to Norwich until the end of term. I was fit as a fiddle, well-tuned and blocking out any other songs of longing or love. Mini skirts and bell bottoms were in fashion and I must have been determined to follow the trend letting a huge gusset into the front of my jeans and denim mini, elasticating their waists. I bought a couple of large men's shirts to wear over the top, as proud as any other plump pod. Or was this all bravado to hide the hurt? I know that I was rigid in my determination to be independent, to forget Gerald and that he had any connection with me and my child.

'You're avoiding me, Greta,' he said. 'Are you worried that I'll disapprove?' He'd summoned me to his study to say 'farewell'. The sky was ablaze, a red pall threaded pink and orange across our campus to the flatlands beyond. I turned away from the window, the beauty too hard to bear. I wasn't going to stay in this room, a bleak affair in one of those purpose built fifties blocks, which had once been a haven, a place of excitement, of adventure, where I'd been shown how good I could be and had bartered my gullibility for his approval. I looked across at the battered sofa where we'd curled up together, a grimy chintz.

'As if I would, Gerald,' I lied. 'Too much to do; work and exercise. Got to keep healthy and focused.'

'I miss you; our little tête a têtes; but I know you're best off without me.' The pathetic tone was almost genuine. 'And next year — well, I don't know what to say. It's such an exciting venture for me. You do wish me well, don't you?'

That sky was scorching the back of my head, the ice around my heart was melting. He stood over me, his head bent to mine, his forehead almost touching. 'You're such a special person,' he said and I craved a strait jacket, anything to stop my arms from reaching up, my face turning towards his mouth, to want his hand to lift my chin. His smell, animal overlaid with fabric softener and aftershave, drained every nerve-ending impulse. The world was a dumb ball and my baby kicked me into touch.

'Of course,' I said.

Did I cry when I got out of there? Did I curse and swear, rant and rave, kick trunks of trees, toss cricket balls through the chapel windows? Of course not. I took my lovely secret, held my belly, and wrote a bad poem.

> *You turn over stones*
> *lifting an edge*
> *to peer under*
> *wondering if*
>
> *the flat complaisant*
> *dull to the day*
> *undiscovered innocence*
> *offering the same face year to year*
>
> *may hide some other*
> *organism to flatter*
> *your polished ego*
> *a rare specimen.*
>
> *Your disturbance is acute*
> *light pours in on half formed*
> *sickly white shoots which*
> *prise from their pressed underworld*
> *aching to crawl for the sun.*
>
> *You expose beneath*
> *the darkened place where*
> *grubs and woodlice eat away*
> *roots and stems leaving only decay*

cultivated by the predator.

*You shift the earth
and walk away.*

It was August 15th when Lottie was born in a maternity hospital in Cambridge where they pretended I was a widow rather than a wanton woman. Joy and Jim had bought me a ring, a modern silver and gold band which was so unexpected and given with such deference to my taste rather than theirs, that I knew it would add further cruelty if I refused to wear it as they wished.

Going back to Waterbeach and our home was bliss. Her cradle was in my old bedroom and a cot ready in the tiny spare space under the eaves. I took a short course in typing; it was before the age of computers. I found work typing up and proof reading other people's dissertations and the odd article and publication. A lot of that sort of thing happened in Cambridge, those few miles from Waterbeach.

Jim treated us like precious jewels or more precisely as pieces of priceless porcelain. Unmarried mothers were the butt of sniffs and avoiding glances on our estate or had been. Jim was having none of it. He'd take Charlotte, as she was christened, out in her pram on Sunday afternoons and in the evening when daylight extended at the end of March. By then she was sitting up and fixing any passersby with a fierce gaze; she didn't smile at strangers. 'A haughty child, you have there, Greta. Thinks she's aristocracy, that's what.' Mrs Pollard, the verger's wife, told me and I knew she was fishing for clues as to the father. Not aristocracy, I could have said, merely an ordinary lecher who I want to forget. A philanderer.

1970

The wicked witch

Dropping stitches, letting the ladder run down, neglecting to go back and pick up, to make amends, this is one of the hardest parts to confess. I didn't want to use or abuse them, Joy and Jim, though they never said I did. No, that isn't the guilt I carry; it is that I could never tell them, withholding such vital information hurt Joy more than she'd ever admit and more than I want to plead even now. But I do. Oh my dear mother, if only I could have explained; I so nearly did.

'What will you put on the certificate?' Joy asked straight after the birth. 'You ought to let her have that bit of knowledge even if you won't let him be involved in her upbringing.'

'How would that help her?' I said, cross and weepy from another set of hormones either invading or leaving my body. 'A name on a piece of paper seems worse than nothing to me.'

· 'Isn't it her right to choose to know or not know?'

'No,' I said, sunk beneath a slab of misery. To say, to rehearse the shame that he hadn't wanted to know, had pretended that he was not involved, allowed the presumption that I was a careless slut sleeping around, was unthinkable, for I believed, and still believe, that the admission would have diminished me and Lottie. I had to hate him and yet I mustn't for Lottie was part of him. I can see to this day the lemon yellow voile covering her basket cradle, the hard summer light cutting across a tattered nursery rug. The silence hurt.

And then with the instinct of the good mother she was; 'I'll come with you, love,' Joy said, meaning to the registrar's office, softening on seeing my distress. 'I don't want you to be unhappy.'

Charlotte Emily Salway; I let them help me choose. We talked of the Bronte connection; that C E Salway would sound splendid if she wanted to become an author too, as we were still in the days when it was better to disguise that you were a woman when offering work for publication. I began as G E Salway. Greta Elizabeth. A film star and a princess.

Joy leant over Lottie's little body, clad in the christening robe I'd once worn; 'Do you think her father would like those names?' Jim, who cradled the baby, looked up at me, apologetic, as if the remark pinched him as well as me.

'More than probable,' I said, 'not that he'll ever know.'

'Has he children of his own?' she said.

'That's enough, Joy,' Jim said kindly but with a definite full stop. 'Isn't she enough on her own?' And he wasn't referring to me.

'My father was a terror,' Joy said cutting the lavender from our next door neighbour's hedge as if continuing a conversation. 'He'd come in reeking of drink, shouting my Ma's name like she was his slave.' Her scissors snipped each stem, quick and regular. 'It's not good that I hated him, not good that I saw her for the fool she was.' Snip, snap, lavender ready to tie up and dry for the tiny bags she'd make for the church sale of work. 'Scarred we are by our parents. I'm glad they'd gone before you came, that you never knew them.' It was a balmy day in the September after Lottie was born. The Michaelmas daisies buzzed with bees, butterflies sucked on the buddleia bush, not a time for harsh tales. I was sitting in the shade of the apple tree trying to feed my reluctant baby. 'Though knowing where you come from is important,' she went on, 'you can think not to make the same mistakes as them.' The scent of lavender so sweet, so old and calming; I breathed in. 'Will Lottie be thankful she didn't know where she came from?' The snip, the snap of the scissors. Lottie's eyes were closed, food ignored and that father the last thing she and I needed to be thankful for.

Each reference to this unknown father was a barb, a small stab to a wound whose scar tissue was hardening. Too proud to be seen as the naïve student; my mantra that I could never blame Gerald. I preferred to keep the secret of the blissful days listening to his voice, to absorb every nuance of what he knew. He never hid the fact that I was not the first and wouldn't be the last. Thinking back, it's difficult to credit the careless throwing aside of all caution. And now with all those years gone by, all that has past, I can affirm that he had no right to be her father and dread to think of his reaction had I told him.

And for my child, Lottie, even during the struggle to work and look after her, there was no regret, never any regret. Only for one brief moment after she died did I wonder and fear that without a father she'd lost out, which could have been another cause to add to the terrible quest for reasons why.

I should have said sorry, so many sorries when the probes and the obscure questioning confronted me. If I'd believed in a god, I could have asked for supernatural guidance. Some people find the confessional an escape; I always thought it a cop out.

Joy and Jim weren't strictly religious; church was a habit, a comfort and a social duty. Friends were made at those events that take us through the year's calendar; Mothering Sunday with daffodils, Easter and lilies crowning the altar, Harvest Festival which you could be forgiven for thinking was an allotment competition; the grotesque size of much of the fruit and veg the pride of the parish. The supper gathered everyone in to eat, drink and sing some hefty songs. The pretty church in the Fens, a good vicar, the order of hymns telling us the seasons, music embedded in one's psyche even without any belief in a god. Joy wanted Lottie to be baptised. 'Whatever you think, it'll give her a sort of passport with these kind of people; and the church has lots of nice tunes and sayings.' And that was surprising coming from my mother who was straight up and down, no pretence; it was never worth attempting a lie, she'd always know. A look would come on her face, as if a bad smell had hit her nostrils and she'd turn away, blocking any further discussion, explanation, excuse.

Which is why she could never accept that I was choosing to cover up what, in her opinion, was paramount.

Such a solid family, a happy childhood that allowed me the freedom to go off on my own and meet friends, time to learn how to look after ourselves. I had a bike which I knew how to maintain; nobody else need tell me how to mend a puncture, fix a chain, adjust handlebars or seat. We didn't have fancy machines in those days, the sort designed specially for mountain biking, not even a racer. Mine was a ladies' bicycle with little style but I'd strip it back to give me the best speed or I'd borrow one from the boys, thinking it classier. How fortunate we were to have no fear of traffic or the danger of perverts, it being before the time when newspaper sales increased with exposés of abduction and murder trumpeted across their front page. We were free to go off for whole days, roaming anywhere we wanted. Our only directive was to avoid strangers if carrying sweets. Trusted to come back at whatever time we were told or when hungry, there was little need for sanctions. And more times than not I'd be away on my own taking a book to write in or read.

The cemetery was a favourite place. The yews, vast and ancient, guarded the entrance, their red berries holed to house a black seed, poisonous to touch. In spring the snowdrops massed and shook out their skirts; the collapsed graves, moss covered stones, gold engraved black marble, were all fodder for the aspiring poet.

> Sparrows dare to chatter in the yew
> gossip to gossip relentless talk
> chitter and flitter fluttering out
> when the black crow rises;
> teasels' dark brown wizards' wands
> waiting for the witch
> to gather up the dead.

Little did I know then that I was destined to make many more visits to that sad sanctuary, riven by grief.

How much we loved Lottie, the wide-eyed child who let us laugh at her more than she ever laughed at us.

'Don't you eat any more, they'll give you tummy ache,' Joy would say as Lottie helped her shuck the peas. I can hear and see them to this day. A line of washing, shirts followed by vests, frocks and diminishing sizes of pants and knickers, the night-time nappies, a uniform line pegged to flout the wind. It was June and Lottie almost two. The apple tree with tiny fruit setting, half hiding poles lined up for runner beans led

24

to another place for Lottie to inspect. We watched her toddle off, determined and unsure.

'She's a clever child,' Joy said, 'takes after her mother, and possibly her father?' And yes, there was a question mark and the direct look, hard and challenging.

'And wily too,' I pretended not to take her meaning. 'Look,' I said, 'see what she's done?' And up the path Lottie came, her knickers bulging from the pea pods she'd picked and stuffed away for future consumption. We laughed, hugged and kissed her, sharing a precious child with no one else.

'I have to work,' I said, 'to find a proper job.' It was the Christmas after Lottie's second birthday. Existing on the pocket money that came from typing and proof reading wasn't enough. And I needed to start a proper career. 'We'll have to go to London; there's a publishing house looking for sub-editors. I think that means the ones who do the photo-copying and make the tea, but I have to begin somewhere.'

'What do you mean, 'we'?' Joy had her feet up on the sofa, a glass of mulled wine in hand, her cheeks assuming its rosy red.

'I'll find a flat; Lottie can go to a child minder, or even a nursery school. It's time she mixed with other kids.' This came off the top of my head.

'London, strangers, all in one swoop? And with her chest?'

Lottie's colds were a constant source of concern to Joy; yes, she coughed, she wheezed but she always recovered. 'All children suffer at this age.' I was usurping her position as if I knew it all. 'And aren't the Fens famous for their damp air?' Flippant, cruel, I may have been but underneath panic rose, a box of birds pecked at my brains. I needed to let them out.

'You've never said that before,' Joy swung her legs to the floor, pushed her stockinged feet into slippers as if getting ready for a fight.

Were we drawing up battle lines? Women's rivalry? No, Joy wanted only the best for us. But I said carelessly; 'Fledglings have to learn to fly from the nest.'

Joy looked across at Jim who was peering at us over the top of his spectacles; the television switched off.

'We'll come back to you at weekends.'

A small publishing house, 'exclusive' Brendan would say, Brendan of Brendan and Barker; I was there at the bottom of the ladder, back on track, where writing happened, was recognised to have happened, and was soberly pleased. Nothing would trip me up as I climbed to the top, not this time, I thought.

Lottie didn't mourn for her grandparents. Our flat was mean and often as dank as those flat lands of East Anglia, but we could look out over roof tops to the lights on bridges crossing the Thames, see the great majestic hulk of the deserted Battersea power station. From our vaulted window we watched the tiny people scurrying below, miniature ships passing along the ribbon of river, hardly hearing the distant sounds of a land far below. For two years I was intensely happy and I'm sure she didn't suffer..

Lottie was four, Joy just turned sixty and Jim a sprightly sixty seven when I was offered the chance to look after two of the firm's clients, new but well received authors. 'Ambition runs through you like that stuff they sell at the seaside, Greta dear,' Brendan threw the work he wanted critiqued across his desk. 'Prove it, be savage and conciliatory. I've seen you do that, see myself in you.'

I walked out of his office on a magic carpet, floated through the rush hour crowds, jumping on and off buses which appeared as if whisked up by some genie. But I was late. Lottie was sitting on the stairs of the child minder's house dressed up ready to come home, guarded by the woman's husband. And he was livid. 'What time's this!' and it wasn't a question.

'So sorry,' I began but he cut in.

'Not the first time, is it?'

'I know, and I ...' but there was no placating.

'Yea, your job - what about Lindy? She's done enough overtime for you, and she's got her own kids to think about.'

Lottie was crying; she was old enough to know the row was about her. Darkness blanked off the rest of the house, the single light bulb glaring down on us; Lindy's bright welcome, the toy strewn floor I'd left that morning vanished as if a once seen mirage.

'It won't happen again ...' I tried, but, 'No, it won't,' he said, 'I've told her not to put up with it any more. Put upon. It's easy for people like you.' I'd scooped Lottie into my arms, slung her bag over my shoulder.

'School, my kids parents' evening,' he was saying, 'and I should be there too. Our kids come before ...'

But I didn't let him finish. I knew I was wrong; I'd been pushing the boundaries too wide. 'You're telling me that I can't bring Lottie here again?'

He'd opened the front door; 'Yes.'

I looked up at him standing in that rectangle of light. I said; 'Please tell Lindy, I apologise, and you're right. She's a wonderful woman, your wife.' Lottie was snuggled in to my shoulder, her weight more than I could bear but there was no putting her down.

'I'll tell her that,' he nodded, all anger gone. 'She needs protecting,' he said. And for an instant I was envious.

'You're not to give it up,' was the first thing Jim said. 'Bring her to us, we've got time and you know how we love her.'

Me, too, I could have said, but it wouldn't have helped.

So in we walked that day, drenched with November rain, Lottie a bedraggled waif who ran to warm her hands at the familiar fire, as if from the wicked witch.

'I've retired,' said Joy, peeling the wet clothes from my daughter's back. 'It was time to give those bedpans a rest. We'll be all right.'

1974

A Tame Police Inspector

'Give it over, Frankie.'

'I ain't got nothin'.'

'Tosh.'

'Nah, ya got it wrong.'

'No, Frankie, I got it right. Hand it over before you get more trouble on your back.'

'Fuck orf.'

I was in the ladies toilet, overhearing what wasn't meant to be heard; I was sure of that. Voices, somewhere close, one of authority, one wheedling and whining. I hadn't seen them when I came in.

'Frankie, I don't want to hurt you, that's not our deal, is it?'

'I ain't got nuffin.'

'I said, give it, or we'll take a little walk. What's it to be?'

'Get orf!'

They must be in the gents, I thought, the wall between merely plasterboard. I washed my hands, let the water gush longer than needed, wanting them to know I was there.

'Give us the stuff, a word in my ear, and you can go. Scuttle back to your rat hole and no one's going to know, just you and me.'

'It ain't on me.'

'Tosh. I saw you got given it, know who gave it to you, and who gave it to him.'

'Fuck you!'

I had to leave, but did I want them, whoever they were, to see me? I inched the bolt across with both hands, and slid out of the cubicle, flattened against the door. The passageway was dark after the neon of the toilet cubicle; the walls shiny with pock marked paint, the smell of bad drains and a faint whiff of escaping gas. A place to do bad business. To the left a square of light edged the door back to the bar, to the right a lit exit sign and that's where they were, not in the gents, but at the end up against a door marked, PRIVATE; nose to nose, two blokes squared up. The big man had one hand closed around the other man's throat; the ghoulish green light above them was enough to make out shapes, their actions.

The other man, Frankie, I presumed, wasn't small or without any fight in him. He jacked up his knee aiming for the big man's balls, but missed and was yanked up to hang from the hand round his throat, his legs dangling, toes barely touching the floor.

'Get orf! Let me go!' a strangled cry.

'That's better, Frankie. So, is it in your pocket or stashed up your arse?'

Neither of them saw me as I stood, back against the wall, transfixed. Drug dealers seemed the obvious explanation.

'Give it up now or I take you down the station and give it out on the street that you've squealed.'

'Get orf!'

I needed to escape. My raincoat was black, my shoes rubber-soled wedges, I'd no flashy jewellery to catch the light. And what did it matter if they saw me; I wasn't the one committing a crime.   I turned and walked back into the pub.

I'd still got half a glass of gin and tonic on the table where I'd been sitting just past the fruit machine.   It had seemed the least conspicuous place when I'd come in; business deals aren't best done in public. I thought, was that another business deal I'd witnessed? The rain was falling in shards outside.

I wouldn't normally have been there, a pub on the Old Kent Road, but I'd met up with one of my authors; he'd got his copy back with my notes and gone.   He wasn't keen on being edited, especially by a woman. That's why we'd met in this pub, his local he'd said. Working class, tough man of the street is the image he wanted to portray, none of your wine bars or posh cafés.   He'd refused to come to the office, said he hadn't the bus fare. I wasn't sure whether he was an uncut diamond or a lump of dross.

Behind the bar a dolly-bird was still polishing glasses, slowly, deliberately, holding them up to the light. The men in front of the bar were turned into their drinks or up to the oversized television screen on the far wall. I sat down again to finish my drink, be an anonymous part of this scene, not the one back there. This, I thought, is a film set waiting for the arrival of the cowboys to come in for the shoot out. I decided that whatever the weather or whoever might be outside, I wanted to go home.

A couple of minutes earlier and I would have been out of the place but as I stood up to belt my coat he came flying through the bar from the toilets, the smaller man, Frankie, skidding against the chair where my umbrella was propped, felling said umbrella which caught against his shins, tripping him to land flat on the floor a couple of feet short of the door.

'Huh! Thought you wanted to leave, Frankie.' The big man called out; he was already at the bar. He raised his eyebrows in my direction. ' Nice one, lassie. I'll be wanting to thank you after this little runt has found the exit.' And Frankie was up and gone.

The big man shook his head; 'Sorry, about that folks; our little drama's done with.' No one else seemed to have noticed or even heard him. 'Sharon, pull us a pint of lager, and what'll you have, lassie?'

Sharon flashed her eyelashes at him not moving a muscle on the rest of her face. I picked up my briefcase and slid out from behind the table; 'Thank you,' I said, 'but I've finished here.'

'No, a drink? Come on, let me buy you a drink. If not for you, at least one for your umbrella.' Whoever he was with the bushy, black eyebrows, the huge smile, he was someone to reckon with. Had he seen me back there, knew that I'd been listening?

'No, no problem,' I said, 'I've to be off.'

'On a night like this? It's pissing it down out there, if you'll excuse my English, but then I'm a Scot so it's of no consequence.' He was laughing, possibly one of the happiest looking men I'd seen in a long time. 'Let me buy you just one; what's it to be?' He'd come across, was already picking up my glass to smell the dregs. 'A gin and tonic for the lady,' he called across to the dolly-bird. 'I'm Angus,' he said, holding out his hand for me to shake. 'It'll ease up out there shortly so you'd best stay for a chat.'

'As long as you're not going to frisk me,' I said, 'I'd be pleased to accept.'

That was how I met Angus, my 'tame police inspector' who was a constable with the CID.

'What are you doing in this godforsaken pub on a night like this? Can't see it being your local.' He'd sat across from me, hunched forward, arms on the table, both hands circling his pint. And apart from that drink I was the focus of his attention; he wasn't putting on a show for the other drinkers.

'I didn't catch your name,' he said.

'Greta Salway,' I said.

'Well, well, a Garbo lady.   Not a recluse, I'm thinking.'

'You neither,' I said.   'The station, I heard you say. I'm hoping it's police not railway.'

And there was the big smile again, infectious. 'Nice one, lassie. Detective Constable Angus Macpherson, CID. Off duty, you might say, I caught a bit of business.' He drew on his lager. 'And what's yours?'

It was easy to talk, to explain, though I kept it spare. He'd not shown me his ID by then but I was prepared for an adventure so when he offered to give me a lift to the tube station I didn't refuse. And I was pleased that he didn't try to take me any further, despite finding out that I lived in Battersea. He dropped me off at Borough on the Northern Line. He didn't ask me not to repeat what I'd witnessed, or ask if we could meet again.   And I'll admit to being a touch disappointed.

So when he phoned the office a week later and asked to speak to me, I was pleased and intrigued. That I'd mentioned the name Brendan and Barker and that he'd remembered, flattered me.   And I needed some excitement. I was twenty six without a boyfriend, and apart from a very brief affair with a turnip from a rival publisher two months previously, I'd been celibate since Gerald. A sad state which needed fixing.

Angus was the answer to a maiden's prayer.

'I thought you wanted to be a writer?' he said.

'I am.'

'Poems? Who's going to read that stuff?'

'It's not about being read, it's about being inspired, having a voice.'

'Tosh! You need to be heard if you've got a voice and poetry isn't what real people read.'

'True if no one writes anything worth reading.'

'Okay, lassie, I'm sure your poems are special but they're wee. How many are you going to have to write and get published to make any money?'

'Don't call me 'lassie', Angus. I'm not a teenager or a dog. Greta's the name and G.E. Salway is going to make it in that elite world of poetry.'

'When?'

And, of course, he was right.

We weren't living under the same roof but he spent most nights when he wasn't on duty at my flat. I liked him and he was a great lover. For a big man he was remarkably gentle and fierce at the same time. He always made sure that I had a good time too. I wasn't in love and nor was he. We sort of agreed that without putting it into so many words. He'd a small daughter by a previous relationship so we had that in common, though neither of us talked about our children. Kith and kin, I sensed, were for him where trouble began and ended. I went back to Waterbeach most weekends and he went somewhere else. Neither of us pried into our private lives.

'Crime. You'd make a good crime writer.'

'How come?'

'You've got me.'

'Pardon?'

'I reckon you'd make as good a detective as any of us. I'm often thinking it's my job you're after, always on at me to dig the dirt; you're like a ferret going at me with your frisky paws.'

He always made me laugh.

It was his idea and he was right. I was fascinated by his world, the slippery nature of it all and yet the obsessive following up of minute pieces of information. And he was a maverick. My first knowledge of that was the incident in the pub; acting on his own, taking short cuts, keeping the dark side close, perhaps too close at times, was his way.

'I get results, lady. That's what they want. Make your enemies your friends is what my Dad preached.'

'Your Dad?'

'Yes, a drug pusher who turned to the Lord. A miraculous conversion before I was born so it was all fairy tales, the drugs and the God stuff; but it's potent and I'm not going to believe or disbelieve any of it.'

That was as much as I got of where he came from, what influenced him to be the guy on the right side of the law. And I do know that is what he truly believed.

'Results. Swill around with the scum and they'll lead you to the sharks, the right dirty bastards who often look super clean on the surface. Rules are okay when you're dealing with the little guys, but I've got to operate between the tracks for the big boys.'

He liked Chinese food, cartoons and classical music; it was Angus who took me to my first concert at the Royal Festival Hall. And it was he who said; 'What about a lady DI? You may never be one, lassie, but I reckon you could write like one.'

I said it was the last thing I'd be able to write. 'It's not a genre I'm familiar with.'

'Genre? What's all this posh tosh again? You'd be different. There's only Miss Marple I can think of. And that's not the sort of stuff I mean.'

I laughed; 'You're mad.'

'A Scottish lady detective. What about that? Young, chippy, got to keep her end up with the blokes she works with. There, I've given it you.'

And he had. We went off on a trip to Glasgow and decided Paisley was where she came from.

'We can do this, Greta; crime's the same all over but I reckon her being a Scot gives us a bit of an edge. A female dick; that's what you've got to write.'

He fed me what he'd always off-loaded; the wheelings and dealings of his day to day world. There were never any names, he was careful like that, but it was easy enough to create my own character and to a great extent she took on many of my own frustrations and fixations. Let's face it, the 60s gave us the pill and so-called sexual liberation but it didn't bring equality in pay or promotion and as for abuse, there was and still is plenty of that about. Just because I hadn't suffered didn't mean my characters wouldn't.

'We publish literary fiction, Greta, you know that as well as anyone.'

'I'm not asking you to publish me, Brendan, that would look like nepotism.'

'No, darling, not nepotism; much as I love you we're not related.'

'Favouritism then, and that's what I don't want. Just read it for me and tell me how bad it is, or not.' I would have said 'crap' only Brendan was very old school and no one swore in his company.

'But how could I tell you?'

'Then find me someone who will, please.'

'I suppose I could do that.   But I'm fearful that I might lose an excellent editor to popular fiction.'

'Dirty words in your dictionary, I know, Brendan, but I have to try.'

'But my dear child, the poetry, where's the poetry in that?'

And I think that was the moment when I was finally released from Gerald's spell.   Where is the poetry, I kept saying to myself all the way home on the bus. Bits of life are poetry but most is dodging and diving, never letting too much hurt stick to your back.

I did miss my little daughter, believed that I was selfish and sensible in equal measure, was jealous and thankful all at the same time. Lottie was flourishing in Waterbeach with Joy and Jim and they were too. It was the same solid, happy childhood they were giving to her as they'd given to me. Which is why I think that Angus was such a tonic, he was so far from what I'd known before.

'This pains me to say it, Greta, but you're good.' Brendan slid the manuscript on to my desk a week later. 'I read you to the end, and didn't want you to finish. So I've sent you to Larry Goldman; crime's his business, he's the best, and he's promised to get back to me before Christmas.'

Three years Angus and I were together, and in that time Morag Maclachlan came to life.

We went back to that pub on New Year's Eve, took a couple of bottles of champagne, ready to order more. It seemed fitting to celebrate Morag Mac's beginning, where we had begun. It was my idea, I'm the one to blame, but Angus didn't say 'no'. It was 11.30 and we'd come from a rowdy party on the South Bank.

The pub had, as we'd expected, an extension for New Year's Eve but from the sad atmosphere it didn't seem to have been worth it. There was tension from the moment we walked in the door. Why had I thought it would be any different? The crude lights of the fruit machine blinked, the television was showing some programme with dancing girls and some old codger singing; the sound was turned off. A musical medley of Top of the Pops tunes of the year was blaring from speakers above the bar; I remember hearing Abba's 'Dancing Queen' and Queen's 'Somebody to Love', two of my favourites which, briefly, I felt were chosen specially for that evening.

Everyone in the pub, and it can only have been twenty at most, turned to check us out as we came through the door, noisily I admit, each clutching a bottle of champagne. Angus went straight up to the bar.

'It's drinks all round on us.' He used his bottle in a universal gesture to include the entire pub. 'We're celebrating, the lady's to be published.'

The dolly-bird, Sharon, had been replaced by a scrag of a man who was ready to argue; 'Can't bring your own booze in here, mister.'

'No, fair enough,' Angus smiled around at the assembled company who were anything but that. One small mixed party, a pair of women, the rest loners who'd got nowhere else to go, all waiting for the end of the world. Not a smile from any of them, a cursory sour interest and they turned back to their drinks.

I should have told Angus that we ought to leave but I just thought one drink and we'd be off to find somewhere better. I'd not been to this place since that first day and naively, I never asked Angus whether he'd been back. I guessed he must have.

Angus, who had managed to squeeze a small space beside the bar, was still easy, off duty jokey, ready with his wallet, the bottle of champagne standing beside him on the counter. I hadn't joined him, was hovering beside the table where I'd originally sat, holding my bottle close to my chest, my arms wrapped around my body, already feeling the need for protection.

Angus brought a couple of glasses of lager across to me, shrugged his shoulders and went back to collect his wallet and the other bottle. And that's when it all exploded, including the bottle he was carrying. Someone stuck out a foot to trip him, as my umbrella had once felled that other man, and as he lay sprawled on the floor two others grabbed his wallet, kicked him in the guts before picking up the shattered bottle and cracking it over his head. And were gone.

It was a long time after before I could bear to taste champagne or lager.

1976

Morag Maclachlan

The landlord must have rung for an ambulance. Someone else put him in the recovery position. I knelt beside him, my face close to his. I wanted to cradle his head in my lap, kept telling him he'd be all right. My dress was stained with his blood that flowed too freely. I was sure he was going to die. No one spoke, no one asked who I was. They left us alone, those that had stayed; another incident best ignored. The fruit machine flashed, the television at full pitch, the floor frayed wood planks. I called the police as soon as we arrived at the hospital.

'Tell us again exactly what happened.'

I couldn't tell them anything useful. The picture was vivid, a slow motion action film, the three men were criminals. I mustn't make them up.

'There were three, you said. Height, age, clothes, anything, miss?'

I'm a writer, can create people like them, but their reality was a blur. Had they asked the other people in the pub, I wanted to know, but they were cagey, brushed that aside. Did they believe me?

'All white, and they didn't say anything? At the bar were they when you came in? All three?'

Why on earth had we taken those bottles with us? Angus wasn't a fool; he'd have known we couldn't drink them in the pub. Were we so drunk?

'You say it was a celebration?'

The blood was stiff on my skirt, brown on blue; my leather jacket nothing against the cold, my feet frozen inside black patent boots. Did I look like a tart? I said he was my boyfriend. We'd been together for three years. I didn't tell them I was a newly born author. My name was all they needed. Greta Elizabeth Salway. He is Detective Constable Angus Macpherson, CID. I kept telling them.

In hospital for a month, two months sick; his head and his guts; he wouldn't talk about it. I visited every day to start with but the incident came between us. I was scared and he was a blank wall. Was it his pride? Would it affect his career?

'You carry on, lassie, Morag's good, you're good.'
'And you're not.'
'I'm getting on. No one kicks young Angus out of the game.'
'I shouldn't have suggested we go there.'
'Did you?'
'Why did we go there?'
'Why not?'
I forgave the 'lassie' and accepted that's all he'd ever say.

Gradually I gave up going to see him as often; all he wanted to know about was my writing. I should have been pleased; men, in my experience, rarely want to discuss someone else's success. But, of course, Morag Maclachlan belonged to him as much as me.

'I've got someone else for you, Greta.'
'Someone what?'
'An advisor. You need to move on, lassie; I've not got any more stuff for you. And Mick's a good bloke, an inspector and all. I'm moving you up in the world.'
'Why?'

'He took the exams. Think I'm going to do that. Stuck here I might as well look at a few books.'

'I didn't mean that.'

'No, but I did.'

And that's how Mick Parsons, Detective Inspector, came into the frame. A wary, pernickety man I never warmed to; he, I'm sure, agreed to be my consultant only as a favour to a sick man. A solid, married man who went on to become a Chief Superintendent; I wasn't going to have an affair with him. When Angus was out of hospital, we met in the Royal Festival Hall café occasionally as he said that being close to music was the best aid to recovery.

'Angus, I can't keep Morag up in Paisley.'

'Why?'

'I don't know enough about the place. Without you it won't be authentic.'

'Ask Mick. See what he thinks.'

'No, you're the one to tell me.'

'Greta, let me go. You've got to move on.'

'Could she be seconded to another police force?'

'You're the author, lassie.'

And that was one 'lassie' too many. Morag moved down to the Norfolk Constabulary operating out of Norwich. An affair gone wrong, beaten badly by the ex-lover, a spell in hospital, the town gone sour, they transferred her to a backwater where she could lick her wounds. How wrong they were; Norfolk is alive with the illicit, the illegal, the impermissible from incest to murder and all stops along the line. I owned my character as Angus predicted, and I gave her a sidekick. A second novel was taking shape.

'You look all in, love,' Jim said.

'It's been a difficult week.' I hadn't told them what had happened two months before. We were past Valentine's Day but Jim's card for Joy was still in pride of place on the mantelpiece. Was that the trigger for the despair that kicked in and swallowed me up? Angus had been a friend who'd needed no explanation. But the truth was more than that; through him I'd been given a new career, a way to write that I enjoyed, with success. 'A writer without all those frills and fancies, that's you, lassie.' he'd said. How could I deny that I'd loved him?

Joy and Lottie were making Simnel Cake for Mothering Sunday. 'See how good she is at rolling up the balls of marzipan? Perfect.'

Lottie's eyes were bright with the praise.

'Chip off the old block!' I laughed.

'What block?'

'Your Grandma's block; it's just an expression meaning you take after her, you're like her.'

Joy looked up sharply. 'And it's a good thing I can teach her something. There's lots of other things she needs help with.'

'Such as?'

'Not what I can talk about now. We've to get this damned cake in the oven.'

Joy never swore, or so rarely that I knew there was trouble and I was too weak to deal with it.

Tucked up in her bed, I read Lottie a favourite bedtime story from 'The Wind in the Willows.' So many times we'd shared this together, snug in the little room under the eaves. Sometimes Lottie wanted the part where Mole is fed up with spring cleaning and comes out to find the wide world and Ratty. We'd been in the Wild Wood many times with the fear and relief of finding Badger's door scraper before entering his safe underground lair. Toad made her cross and the battle with the weasels needed to be won before she would go to sleep.

'Did you ask her to read any of it to you?' Joy said when I came downstairs.

'No, should I?'

'Well, that's the thing. I went in to her school last week and her teacher says she's struggling with her reading.'

'But she's been able to read since she was really little. When we were up in London ...' I stopped.

That had been four years ago when I'd given up responsibility, left my daughter in someone else's care.

'It's numbers she likes. Jim'll spend hours with her going through all the maths he knows. She laps that up.' Joy was proud to tell me. 'And you can see she's a real dab hand with cooking and I'm teaching her to play the piano.'

'Wonderful,' I said. 'But ...'

'She's just not interested, doesn't want to read stories; tells me it's boring.'

'But she loves me reading to her, she loves the books I bring.'

'Of course, because you're giving her time. That's what she does with you; she'll not share it with anyone else.'

I was wretched that night, tore myself to shreds, sleep beyond me; I cried the tears I'd needed to shed for weeks, months, maybe years. It all flooded in; the child minder's husband saying; 'My kids parent's evening, and I should be there.' I'd not even known, not thought to be there for my child. And that I denied Lottie the knowledge of a father. It was all my fault. As was my suggestion that Angus and I went back to that pub on the Old Kent Road. And where had that other bottle of champagne gone?

'Tell me, are you Mole, or Ratty, Mr Badger or Toad?' I asked Lottie next day.

We'd been to a Mothering Sunday service in the church and Lottie was given a bunch of daffodils to take to her mother. She brought them back to the pew, crept in beside us, not knowing what to do. I whispered to her; 'Give them to me, Lottie, and I'll give them to Joy, my mother, and yours most of the time.'

As we walked back down the aisle towards the old wooden doors welcoming what was outside, a shaft of sun lit the stained glass window above us painting a bright red pool on the floor, dust motes swirling before me.

'What sort of chap is the Mole, Lottie?' I said.

'He's friendly, he's shy, and he's often scared.'

'And the Rat?'

'Oh, Ratty's like you. He's always busy and he knows everybody and everything. He has lots of good ideas.'

Where had she got that from?

'Okay, that's interesting,' I said. 'Tell me about Mr Badger then.'

'He's a bit like Granddad, very wise, but he's sometimes a bit gruff and Jim's never that. And Toad,' she went on without being asked, 'is stupid, lazy and too proud of himself. I'm never going to be like him.'

'Who do you want to be like, Lottie?'

'Granddad,' there was no hesitation.

'And Grandma?'

'Oh, Joy's the one who makes it all happen. She must be the author.'

'Brendan, I want to work from home more often. Can I?'

'What's this about, Greta?'

'Spending more time with my child and my writing. It'll make no difference to my work for you.'

'Little Lottie, how old is she now?'

'Nine.'

'And where will you live?'

'That's it. I could live in Waterbeach and travel to London, daily if needed.'

'Oh dear, popular fiction; I knew it was corrosive.'

No, I could have said. It's my daughter; I may be corroding her childhood.

Was that a good idea? No, I missed London, often stayed overnight. Picked up another boyfriend merely for the use of his flat. I can't say my time with him was memorable. We met in a pub in Old Compton Street; Colin was his name. I thought he was interesting material when I first came across him. He worked for Customs and Excise, had a father in the Ministry of Defence. Gleaning plot lines overtook all my relationships at that time.

Inspector Mick Parsons did not fail me, though he wouldn't write anything down. I tried sending him questions: how soon before the body would be cold if this or that took place? For how long can you hold this man in custody? Would firearm officers be called if so and so happened? I had to go to him for my answers at a time to suit him. He would book an interview room where he'd go through my sheets with a red biro. I always remember that red biro. In my mind I was the criminal, even though I was the interrogator; across the table he'd say yes or no, and I'd have to prise extra information, desperate for any grubby details, tit bits of what they were working on. I couldn't do with him what Angus had done; re-enact a scene to check the entry of a knife or bullet. Poor Colin became my stooge though he never took it seriously. Mick, though, took it all very seriously and I was sure that the information he gave me would be accurate. When my second Morag Maclachlan novel was published eighteen months after the first, Mick was the first to congratulate me on its authenticity. He put that in writing; I've kept the letter.

Lottie let me help her to read; nowadays they'd call it dyslexia, such a common problem for many children. It was vital to move her forward. Writing was more of a problem; to make up a story was of no interest to her, even to retell something she knew had happened was a struggle. If the spelling wasn't right it didn't matter, but she hated me saying that.

'It has to be perfect. Nothing's right if it isn't perfect.' It became her mantra which must be one of the reasons why eleven years later we were dealing with tragedy.

'What will she do if she doesn't get through her 11+?' Joy and I shared the same worry.

Jim told us we were ridiculous. 'She's way ahead for her age; how to handle numbers is what fascinates her. She'll sail through the arithmetic test.'

How good a mother was I then? I proposed a private school if she didn't get in to the grammar.

'And who'd pay for that? Her father?' Joy couldn't stop herself, and I was so low that I almost confessed, told her about Gerald. Fortunately Angus had rinsed and wrung that man right out of my hair. The thought quite cheered me up.

'The Fenland Murder' was published when I was pretending to live in Waterbeach. Much as I loved Joy,

Jim and Lottie, I needed to be on the move. I took Lottie with me to visit Norwich and the Fens for research; we all took a holiday on the Norfolk Broads. The strangeness of those rivers, broads and canals, locks and windmills, pale skies spread out as if the whole world was encompassed there, enchanted me. It was eerie and peaceful and I tried to write poetry again. I said to Lottie; 'Tell me what you know and we'll put it all together.

> Oulton, Sutton, Barton and Hickling Broad,
> Rivers Bure, Thurne, Ant and Chet,
> Wensum, the Waveney and the great Yare
> from spring to sea, wind a wayward course.

'Is that poetry?' she said.

> Who named Horsey Mere or Breydon Water
> Wroxham Bridge, How Hill and Potter Higham?
> Sky meets water, reeds and sedges, dykes and
> marshes, dragonflies, and the swallowtail.

'It doesn't rhyme,' she said.

> The peat was dug, canals were cut to drain
> the land of sea, for sheep to graze as wind
> turned sails to grind the miller's corn for bread
> that fed men born when Athelstan was king
> before the Normans crushed the people's peace.

'That's all jumbled up,' she said.
'Yes, we need to work on it,' I said.
'Why?'

I didn't give up and nor did she. Come eleven she won a scholarship for her arithmetical ability, donned a posh uniform and strode off into the abstract world of numbers.

I sidelined Morag in my third novel. Her sidekick was far more interesting; ambitious and canny, craving the bright lights and dark underbelly of London life. Augus would have said; 'Like you, lassie.'

Two years after the incident I met that awkward author, who was not only averse to a woman editor but also an inverted snob, in that same pub on the Old Kent Road. By now I'd decided that he was an uncut diamond, and he'd recognised that I was suitably hard and sharp to take his work to print. He would have come to the office, he'd enough of an advance to afford a taxi but I perversely suggested we meet there. The place hadn't changed; dolly-bird was back behind the bar. I wanted to ask her; 'Sharon, have you seen Angus lately?' but I didn't. Was I trying to eradicate the memory of a man I didn't want to forget but who needed to be forgotten?

I drank gin and tonic, tried to ignore the flicker of the fruit machine or the drone of the television set, imagined the brown stain of blood on the floorboards. We did our business but before leaving I took our glasses back to the bar and there it was, amongst the other memorabilia of Millwall rosettes, photos of past patrons, a darts trophy; my bottle of champagne.

1981

Little Max

Whether I should, how I could, and what to tell Lottie about her father came to a head in 1981, at the time I met Max. It was Max who knew about mothers who made no apology for absence and fathers who forgot. Now, all these years later I hear that riff, 'I know who he was. My father.

'You are the most interesting woman in this room,' he said from behind my back at one of Leo's parties. I was alone out on the terrace of Leo's roof garden, olive trees in silver pots and white hydrangea, and like the crowd of us there, the others inside, supping on champagne and homemade goodies, nothing on sticks. 'Where's the old queer been hiding you?' he said.

I turned on my Manolo Blahnik heels to find this man assessing my neck.

'He's little Max, darling,' Leo said later. 'Only in stature, of course; his intellect is to reckon with; an astute critic of anything theatrical. Maximilian, the greatest and most generous donor of free tickets to the best shows.'

'You are?' I said to this man's face.

'Max Bretcher,' he held out a hand. 'And I know that you are Greta Salway, one of Leo's creations.'

'Pardon?'

'One of his authors?' he cocked his head to one side; I thought canary rather than parrot.

I took the offered hand; 'Leo is my agent,' I said. 'And what is your role in life?'

He smiled, a golden smile, and I was partly mollified.

'Director, actor, improviser, company manager. Take your pick.' His expression suggested a bowl of cream and licking of lips.

'Interesting,' I said. 'Should I know you, I mean in any of those roles?'

'Possibly not. Most of my work has been abroad. But I'm making something over here at the moment which I think is taking shape. Just need the funding confirmed.'

'Sadly I see little theatre,' I said.

'Oh dear, we'll have to put that right.' He seemed delighted as if I were another project.

'I've had my nose to the grindstone, no time for much fun; deadlines are a curse and a blessing.' I didn't need to explain that I was new but not new enough.

'Would I have read anything you've written?'

'I've no idea. Do you read crime novels?'

'Give me a title.'

'The Black Bureaucracy' was my last,' I said.

'Can't say I have. Need to put that right too,' which wasn't a false promise as later he did read all that I'd written.

That evening I wanted to move away, suspicious of a man so eager to hold my attention, but I didn't. Max's trick or his gift, as then, is to focus solely on the person he's talking to; his eyes following the movements of my mouth, appraising, appreciating, the rest of the room didn't exist. It was heady stuff and despite my cynicism, I loved every minute of it, knew that I'd like more.

'Perhaps we can meet again,' he said. 'I'm a bit swamped at the moment, like you; lots of scripts, the good, bad and the why did they waste paper, ink, and postage.'

'I know what you mean,' I said. 'I was an editor once, still am occasionally when Brendan twists my arm.'

'Oh? Brendan? Brendan and Barker?'

'Yes, you know him?'

'Know of him. Does he publish you?'

I laughed. 'No, of course not. He sent me to Larry Goldman. If you know Brendan, you'll know that popular fiction brings him out in a cold sweat.'

'You do yourself a disservice. Being an editor on his payroll is very impressive whatever his views on the value of the modern novel.'

Max might have broken my heart if there'd been one left to break.

The pedestal he'd place me on was what I needed at that time. I'd had my three book deal, though they weren't called that in those days; 'The Paisley Priest' with Morag Maclachlan, 'The Fenland Murder', and then 'The Black Bureaucracy' with my new DI, Lisa Battle, the sidekick who'd been promoted to London and was on the Hackney force. My fourth was proving more problematic. I'd moved back to Morag in Norfolk.

Larry said; 'You need character loyalty, Greta. Readers don't want to keep switching their affections.'

'But they know Morag, and they took on Lisa happily enough, didn't they?' This was true, sales had been excellent, but I wasn't going to stamp around with Larry. Brendan had told me once; 'Writers should know, whether they're writing first class literary fiction or popular trash, never to offend their publisher.'

Larry said; 'And this backwater, Norfolk, is it? I wasn't happy with that before.'

'But it worked, Larry, and I believe it will this time too.'

'A bit literary, isn't it? All the emphasis on this place in the back of beyond, descriptions of the landscape, as if it's a character, or something.'

'Yes, that's it. The effect of the place on the people and how they react to the murders and the police investigation; that's its strength. They're not churned out cop penny dreadfuls.'

Larry squinted at his pen, twirling it as if focusing for an eye test. I thought, you'll make a useful character one day; good cop, bad cop, maybe villain?

'Devil's Dunes'? Kind of medieval isn't it?' he was saying.

'Larry, it's highlighting the struggles of a woman, Morag, battling on her own. Aren't readers of crime mostly women? And supposedly it's the age of women calling the shots. Mrs Thatcher?' Larry was a true blue Conservative, already smitten with the handbag lady.

'You're a cunning vixen,' he said, and publication went ahead. But I knew I was on trial for my next pitch. Leo even suggested we find another publisher but Brendan's values were an influence that I couldn't shake off; I was too nervous to reject his advice, his recommendation.

The inspiration for 'Devil's Dunes' came from that first holiday in Norfolk. Going back there two years later to Wells-next-the Sea, Lottie eleven, and the weather was kind, the sun trailing us along the silver sand, the tide rushing in and out, sculpting the saltings, the wind gentle from the west across the Lincolnshire coast. Dunes formed by wind and tide, hillocks anchored by maram grass, held a wildness. The haunting uncontrollable nature of land and sea; the wide expanse of wetted sand visited every six hours by the force of another planet, the cool moon, thrilled and scared me.

We'd hired a cottage and a beach hut and although it was often 'cardigan' weather, Lottie, Joy, Jim and I enjoyed the normality of a relaxed family. 1979, 'The Black Bureacracy' had been published meaning that I was away on a series of publicity stints at the end of that year and into 1980. I'd also moved back to London, taken a pokey flat in Islington having broken up with Colin and therefore had no bed to share during the week. I needed to make amends to my family. Or at least that's how it felt. That we had such a happy time was particularly important.

Leo sounded me out after his party; he's an incorrigible matchmaker. 'I like to see people sparring with their own kind. Nothing worse than a couple who've nothing left to fight over, nothing left to sink their teeth into.'

'I wish you weren't gay,' I told him as I stacked glasses into his dishwasher.

'Heaven forfend! I'm the happiest bunny in my present state,' he looked at me as if over a pair of specs, 'though physically, darling, I'm a total wreck.'

'So you say,' I said.

'Now Max is worth the odd row,' and standing watching my efforts he delivered his punchline; 'Such a shame he's heterosexual,' followed by an exaggerated shudder.

Max certainly was well worth the attention I gave him. I'd rarely been to the theatre before meeting him. And Leo was right, he may have been working abroad for the past five years but his contacts in London were wide and varied. This was in large part due to his background and education; a top public school, Oxford and a famous actor father, long since dead. A winning combination even without the prettiness and charm.

'Greta Salway? It's the man from Leo's party,' Max phoned three weeks later. 'I have two tickets for 'The Magic Flute' at the Royal Opera House. Are you up for it?'

I could have said 'which man' but was too pleased with an invitation befitting a popular author. The little black dress came out again and although I toyed with a pair of flat pumps, I wore the vampy stilettos.

He'd asked me to meet at a pub in Covent Garden where he was holding court with two couples, each of whom were hanging on his every word. I was greeted with great extravagance; 'You have to meet this beautiful woman, from the Leo French stable. Greta Salway meet …'; I cannot remember their names. I later protested that I was an author in my own right and didn't need Leo, Larry Goldman or Brendan to give credence to my career. He heard me out gravely, apologised profusely but, as so often when a whiff of criticism passed my lips, I wasn't convinced of his sincerity.

And the style of our outings never changed; meet in a pub, Max entertaining friends, already into the booze. I don't think we ever went anywhere entirely alone, the two of us. It never mattered though. I loved the casual adoration extended to Max by the people we encountered from the pub to the entrance hall, in the bar and auditorium at the Opera House; he was this special person who everyone knew or wanted to know. "Hi, Max! Let me introduce you to…" became a kind of battle cry. Which is why, stupidly, I took on the role of the sidekick, the gangster's moll. My entire time with Max was spent in trying to rid myself of the little woman tag, the country bumpkin, the amateur.

Perhaps it was his intellect, his knowledge and analysis of work, theatrical or artistic that dented my self esteem. I was fascinated by his ability to act as critic to his own and other people's work, quickly and honestly, even when I didn't agree. He was a sweet and attentive lover, a considerate companion and he was fun; there were outrageous trips which he organised on a whim; a weekend in Timbuktu, New Year's Eve in someone's castle in Scotland and there was all that posh theatre. Lets face it I'd come from an East Anglian backwater, amateur Gilbert and Sullivan and children's theatre for Lottie. The few concerts I'd been to with Angus didn't seem to count. I was in my early thirties, a tender age for most women; it was crossroads time. I steeled myself to accept the other enterprises and women who took his time. Years before that I'd vowed that jealousy was unbecoming, an insult to one's self. A sentiment easily trotted out when time has eroded the memory of phone calls promised but forgotten, meetings arranged but ignored, and without apology. My time with Gerald gave me that firm grounding.

Mostly though it was his vulnerability that snagged me, caught in those brief moments when his guard was down; I became the woman wanting to save, protect, reform; the mother figure. None of which he asked for and would have sneered at; he disliked any advice I came near to giving, particularly on the subject of drink. Max never played the poor-little-me card.

Lottie had won that scholarship to a grammar school in Cambridge soon after I met him; her world was shifting. Pleased and excited as she was, it required a long bus ride to and fro, a whole new set of friends and a different curriculum. I hated and feared that I was the absent mother; I needed to give her extra support. When I was in London I called her each evening and, as it was pre mobile phones, I frequently had to find a public phone box at the appropriate time.

'What's all this clandestine mania for phone booths, Greta?' Max asked one evening six months down the line. 'Is there a husband lurking, or merely other lovers you need to satisfy?'

'A daughter,' I said stung by the amused tone.

'And she lives with her father?' he said.

'She lives with my parents.'

'I can't imagine you being married,' Max said. 'Who's the father?'

'That's something I never discuss.'

'Oh, a secret! I like secrets that are kept. I'm never interested in prying into other people's affairs.' He was already into the second bottle of wine. Sitting in the garden of his aunt's house in Greenwich where he lived, and she didn't, we were alone.

'Good,' I said.

I remember the child's swing hanging lopsided from an old apple tree, the rope long since frayed and broken, a relic of a time long since played out. Was Max the child who had swung to and fro, ridden it to the sky, leapt off at a daring point to leave it bouncing aimless and abandoned? It was at the far end where the wilderness of unkempt lawn gave way to a small orchard. September; if I wandered down there I would see the apples rosy and ready to pick, plums fallen and riddled with wasps and rot.

'But you have told her?' Max was saying.

'Pardon?'

'She knows her father?

'It's not relevant.' I lay back on the extended wooden deckchair he'd set out on the veranda. 'These,' I said stroking the faded canvas stripes, 'make me feel I'm in a Twenties' movie, the Great Gatsby, perhaps.'

He sat up and faced me. I was invisible behind sunglasses but I could feel his watching, examining me.

'Would your aunt have given parties like that?' I said. 'Was she a flapper?'

'Still is,' he said, 'in her head.'

Late afternoon, the sun hot enough for a bikini, the days when I was still crazy for the all-over tan. In this garden, though, I never sunbathed topless, not prudish because of Max but of the ghosts who haunted the house. I loved the place, wanted to own it myself even with the 'other occupants'. It's possibly another reason I stayed with Max so long. Even, dare I admit, momentarily wanting to be his wife. This house with sashed windows, French doors leading to different parts of the garden from three of the rooms, invited light and secreted dense shadows. Definitely not burglar proof,

'A father must be relevant,' he said.

'I said it was not for discussion.'

His father was dead and ever present. He'd drunk whisky to the point of extinction; Max worshipped him. 'The greatest actor that ever lived; Olivier hammed it, my father breathed it.'

Max turned the bottle up to find the last dregs and sat, still observing me.

'What?' I said.

'A father has to be known even if dead.'

'Why?' which I knew was a stupid question. How often had I fended off Joy's pleas? Here was a stranger calling me to account.

'You know Lewis Home?' he said.

'The producer you hate?'

'The unhappiest bastard in the business, yes.'

'So?'

'He discovered at twenty-one that he wasn't the son of the man he'd always known as father.'

'And?' Where was this leading? Max rarely gossiped about other people; another trait of which I approved.

'It bugs him, constantly, and that his mother wouldn't tell him who his true father was, even on her death bed.'

None of this was triumphal. He was concerned, even that last inch of so of wine was untouched.

I said; 'Lottie knows where she comes from – someone whom I loved once.' I sat up and took off my specs. 'I've told her that we didn't intend to have a child together. I knew he wouldn't want to be tied to me and I didn't want to be tied to him.'

'Is that fair?'

'To whom?'

'Lottie and him.'

'Why are you quizzing me, Max? I've lived with this for eleven years.'

'Provenance is all important.'

'That's pretentious rubbish!'

He got up, swigged the wine from his glass and left me, his Noel Coward dressing gown swinging loose behind him.

I looked at my watch; in an hour I was due to make that phone call to Lottie. Should I leave now, find a call box on the way home? I pulled a baggy tee shirt over my head, screwed the lid on the suntan lotion and gathered up the rest of my belongings.

'What are you doing?' He was silhouetted in the doorway, arms wide with a bottle and corkscrew offered to his audience, his blond body beautiful against the red Chinese-patterned silk of the robe. 'This was my father's, Greta. He was useless as a Dad, never there, egotistical, his career was everything, but I know who he was. And I have this.' I knew he meant what he was wearing, possibly the body that he was proud of, but I saw the drink too.

'I have to go.'

'Why?'

'To call Lottie, I told you.'

'Use the phone here. You don't need to go anywhere. Please don't go.' He came to stand over me, put the cool bottle to my cheek, and gazed at me with the troubled eyes of any Mills and Boon hero. My hackles raised for battle, I knew that I had to stay. There was a conversation to be finished.

Max left me alone to call Lottie in a study at an exquisite writing desk and a phone that reeked of the days when dialling zero brought the operator to put you through to Mrs Cholmondeley or Lady Astor.

Lottie said; 'Are you with the Max man?'

I told her about the house, what I knew of the aunt, trying to make it sound fun and spooky. I listened to her triumph in riding her bike to the station in Waterbeach and going on her own to Cambridge and back. She said; 'I can see why you like being independent. It sort of gives you a gutsy feeling.'

I laughed at my bright child but those words live on with me too; was she forced to think that she too had to take off on her own?

Max cooked supper; a frittata of left overs and a tomato salad rustled up from plants in a decrepit greenhouse.

'Do you grow these, Max?' I asked.

'No. There's old Mr Pearson who I think may have been one of the retainers when there were such things, and he's forgotten that there's no one to pay him.'

'Don't you?' I said.

'I never see him.'

'Then how do you know it's him?'

'He left me a note in the handwriting of a man educated to the age of twelve. "Mr Daniel," it said. "Your dear aunt left a little money and was as kind as to let me use her garden for growing vegetables while she's away. I hope you'll have some, there's too much for me and Mrs Pearson. Yours obediently ..." I have it still.'

This was the Max I cared for, a man who despite his air of precocious authority, was rooted in a childhood of loss. I had to tell him about Lottie.

'She hasn't asked to know more than I've told her. She has three parents rather than two, all loving her intensely, she's safe.'

'I don't know,' he said. The third bottle of wine was empty. He still wore the robe with tee shirt and shorts underneath; he'd tied the sash. 'I had a shower of nannies, a matron at school or my mother's acolytes poring over me and retreating when the moon was up, or was it down?'

'It's Lottie's father that I don't want to tell,' I said. 'He knew I was pregnant but assumed in his off-hand manner that it was nothing to do with him. I didn't want to enlighten him.'

'Heavens! Was he such a bastard?'

'Yes, Max,' I said. 'But I loved him and he didn't love me. That had to be the end of our story.'

Max said nothing more; pity was not what he offered and from then on I knew that there would be an end for us too. I'd admitted to baggage and heartache, none of which I wanted to share any further.

Looking back on those three and half years I have no regrets; he taught me as much as Gerald about the vagaries of a woman's heart but perhaps added too much more to my cynical attitude towards men.

Gerald was the rocket that seared into the sky, burst with the biggest bang and thumped to the ground leaving a massive crater; Max was a firework but his blaze and shower of sparks fizzled before they reached earth.

I knew that I must talk to Lottie.

1983

The facts of life

Dora said; 'You wait till she asks.'

'And if she doesn't?'

'Sure to.'

'Is that your only advice?'

She tugged open a packet of peanuts, offered them to me before tipping a handful into her own palm. 'Okay; you got to grab something to start her off, an ad., tele, you know, one of the soaps?'

'What?'

'Yea, there'll be something. Best in the car, driving.'

'Why?'

'No eye contact, you don't have to look at each other. Funny that, being able to say outrageous stuff when you can't see the other person; secrets shared when the lights are out, love affairs broken off down the phone.' Dora screwed up her face, eyebrows raised to her scraped back hairline.

'Is that what you did?' I said.

Dora was a good friend found in 1982. Max was into yoga, body and brain. I joined up at a separate class knowing I didn't want anyone trying to get inside my head; meditating was not for me, but exercise would be good. Dora started at the same time, a thoroughly subversive influence. Apart from the many times she decided to 'lie this one out', she considered the 'booze up' at the pub afterwards more valuable than all the 'cobras, cats and shoulder stands' we attempted. I kept to myself my new-found ability to mould my body into unusual poses. I didn't want to boast or share how invigorating and relaxing I found the two hour sessions. I enjoyed her company too much.

'I told Lance and Charlie when I was driving them home from my mum's one evening last month,' she said, 'it was after she'd let them watch Coronation Street.

Dora worked full time as a clerk in an accountant's office, had done since she left school. 'Numbers might fool you to start with, but they've got to add up in the end.' Her present 'man' was a 'doll' but there'd been plenty of 'slippery customers' on the way. There was a son from a teenage relationship, Brad, and the twins were her second brood, and then Charlene and Cheryl, the 'little princesses' with her present partner; they'd recently started school. The 'yoga night' was her only time out.

We had one thing in common and plenty of angst to make each other laugh.

'Lance said; "Why does he want to get into her knickers?" right out of the blue. We'd just come up to the junction with Holloway Road and Canonbury, a tricky turn that, and he knew it was nothing to do with cross dressing. His uncle's trans.'

I laughed. The pub was full, smoke swirling, ashtrays full, and Dora's voice carried. Older couples sat silent at the next table not bothering to chat, the company enough; the men sniggered, the women smiled and looked away.

Dora went on, oblivious to our neighbours. 'That's a dodgy right after the traffic lights like I said, specially in the dark and I wasn't feeling my best. Johnny's all over me these nights, I think it's the new moon, and then when I've lumped him off, he snores to take the roof with him.' She sighed at the memory and swigged the last of her wine, set her glass down firmly and gathered in a few more peanuts. 'But I knew that was the moment so I said, you know where babies come from and there was a chorus of 'out of mummy's tummy'. She carried on crunching and saying; 'So I said "and it's how they get in there that you need to know". There was a quiet in the back, like they knew this was a punchline, the nuts and bolts of it.' She picked up my glass, empty too and said; 'Why don't we make a night of it, get a bottle? What do you think, treat ourselves?'

I said it was my round then, she was giving the tutorial.

'Whatever! Chardonnay, Greta love, and make sure it's chilled.'

This was sixth months since we'd met. It had been immediate, that liking, finding an ally. She with her ponytail tied with red ribbon; proper Lycra leggings that were brand new and red too. There was nothing disruptive about her; none of the other eager, dedicated women were offended by her lack of effort and our teacher made every attempt to cosset her. There was no extra fat on Dora; tall and with a big bosom which she carried proud. I asked why she'd come to yoga. 'Wanted something for myself, where I could relax, and it sounded posh. None of that sweaty stuff where you don't know whether you're on your arse or your elbow.' And she certainly did nothing to make her perspire in that class. A hard face with her hair flat from her forehead but she has a generous heart and a beguiling view of the world.

'Okay, so what did you tell them,' I said.

'Well, something about liking someone a lot, and men's willies and women's bits feeling like they fancied each other, getting excited and wanting to rub together, sort of. And then it's only when you know that you love someone and want to be with them and take care of them and he wants to put his thing into her whatsit and she wants it too … what are you laughing at?'

'Sorry, it's good, even with your coding.'

'Well, no, I did use the proper terms as well but I didn't want to go shouting about penises and cunts in here, did I?'

We both spluttered into our wine, caught the giggles and like a couple of ditzy teenagers dissolved into uncontrolled laughter. Dora was a tonic and still is though I've neglected her recently.

'Did they ask any questions?' I finally managed.

'Well, Lance said is that what I did with his dad which was tricky as I can honestly say I hate the bastard now, the way he's treated us, but I could say I loved him back then.'

'So what do I tell Lottie?'

Dora and I had bonded like the best of sisters. Our backgrounds were so similar and so different. My hard working country people to her hard working city folk but the initial support we were given, both for our ambitions and our early pregnancies, was completely at odds. She'd been told to get a job; staying at school wasn't going to do her any good. And the baby was considered a disgrace for which she had to suffer. 'Not that they were horrible to me, it's what other people would think of their slut daughter that they minded.'

'What have you told Brad?' who I learned was the twenty year old son.

'Well, that's not been a problem because his father stood by me for a while before he went into the army.'

'Didn't you want to marry?'

'No. Mum and Dad tried to persuade me but he wasn't what I wanted, and he didn't want to be tied.

'Was he young too?'

'Sixteen like me. A careless bit of fun, it was. He used to come and see Brad often, remembers his birthday too but he lives in Germany now, married a girl when stationed out there years later.'

I'd told her about Lottie and Joy and Jim soon after we met. She was so easy to talk to, mull over women's worries and bits about my personal life; she became someone to trust. I didn't bore her with my work; 'That's really too intellectual for me, if that's the right word,' she told me. 'I never can settle to a book, there's too much to do, people wanting stuff, and the bed's somewhere to sleep when I'm not having to pleasure my man.'

I'd only recently told her about Max but I hadn't mentioned Gerald even though I was sure she'd understand. If I let it out to anyone, I always feared it would creep insidiously like blotting paper pulls ink until it's saturated. The stain would be huge and visible.

'So you've done the facts of life?' she said.

'Yes, in a broad, science lesson type of conversation; the facts.'

'And she didn't want to know how she happened?'

'No. Every time I start a conversation about sex, periods and so on, she says; "Yuk, that's enough. I've done it in school."'

'Hmm, so she's not ready.'

'For that bit, but Max saying; 'I know who he was,' about his father, the emphasis that it was important, has got me worried.'

'But if Lottie's not asked, what's your problem?'

'Except one day she will and either I lie or say I can't tell her.'

'Not good either way, Greta love. I see where you're coming from.'

That October, 1983, was a miserable time; strikes, riots, for which I felt sympathy. Greenham Common Women's Camp had been set up two years before and I was itching to be part of it. Dora said;'I've enough on my back without carrying other people's problems. "Look after your own" is what my dad always says and he's no bigot.'

Lottie said;'One of the girls at school said they're all lesbians as if that's bad. She is_wrong, isn't she?'

'Yes, that is wrong …

'Grandma said that too. They're all sorts of people, some of them mothers.'

'Yes, they were desperate at what was happening and began to march from …'

'I know. And Grandma says she ought to have gone with them to Greenham but Grandpa can't be left on his own.'

'But, that's not true either,' I said. This was my opening, I thought. 'A lot of people are prejudiced, that's …'

'I know what prejudice is, like when you believe someone else is bad without any proof just because you don't like the way they look or behave.'

'Yes,' I said, 'and Grandma and Grandpa …'

'I know about them, they're only really happy when they're looking after each other, and me.'

'Yes, and it's the best sort of marriage but …'

'Oh, you don't need to talk about not being married and about divorce. Lots of the girls at school have parents who are divorced and most like it better. Nichola told me it was horrible when they were together, her dad always shouting at her mum and her mum shouting back.'

'Yes, that must be …'

'No one shouts here.'

We weren't in the car with my eyes on the road and hers on my back in the rear seat. She was sitting with me at the dining table in my new flat busy with a project for school - at least, I thought it was for school - on the development of the nuclear bomb and how to protect ourselves if it was dropped on Britain. She'd insisted we go to the offices of The Times newspaper for articles recently published as the subject was high profile. Joy and Jim took the Cambridge Evening News to keep up to date. 'It's very difficult sometimes when I want a broader view on the world,' Lottie said. A large picture of that mushroom cloud was her front cover.

'Your father and I didn't shout at each other,' I said. 'He was a nice man but I knew he didn't love me properly, not enough to stay with me and look after us both.'

'Oh, right,' she said. 'Have you got any more glue?'

'He was a clever man too, but I didn't want to share you with him.'

'That's all right Mumma. Nobody asks who my father is. I just hope he supports nuclear disarmament.'

What else could I have said?

I reported back the next time after yoga.

'Well, if she's happy with that, why are you worrying?'

'I know, but at some stage oughtn't she to know his name?'

We went round in circles, Dora determined to come up with a solution.

'What about writing a letter with his name and where he is for her to open at a certain time?'

'I don't know where he is.'

'Okay, but she'd have a name, and you could put a bit more than he's nice and clever.'

'What if she did find him and he rejected her?'

'Well, I don't know.'

All the laughter had gone, the bottle of wine too.

'Was he such a bastard?' Dora said.

'Max asked me that.'

I went home that evening chastened. I knew I had to think this through, work out what was true for Lottie. Was he such a bastard? Arrogant, selfish, egocentric were traits I could have attributed to him, even then. But truth is sometimes too cruel.

Remembering back to Lottie at that time, I see this fizzy girl, full of projects, things to do, things to achieve, she didn't need a father.

'I have to pass my Grade 5 piano exam before I'm thirteen,' she said. I'd managed to buy a second hand upright which Joy and Jim fitted into the living room by moving out their old dresser. Nothing was too much trouble for their little Lottie.

'Grandpa's helping me with my wildflower album,' she said. 'See!' Pressed flat and dry, stuck into a scrapbook with tiny, neat pieces of sticky tape, and labelled with Latin and common names, she displayed her specimens, pages and pages laid out before me. 'The next thing I want to research is what were the old beliefs for their healing properties. Did you know that the library will order books in for you if you ask?'

Reading was no problem now when it involved research, facts.

What joy she gave, how did I deserve her?

At a parents' evening later that school year, I asked whether all the activity at home was causing her school work to suffer. The rather frosty response I received, not being famous enough or an alumni of a

Cambridge college, was that; 'Lottie is achieving well above average as you will have read in her report. There is never too much that a child can attempt. Please make sure that encouragement is always offered.'

I amused Dora with this conversation when we met soon after.

'Snooty cow!' she said. 'Mind you she's got a point. Wish Lance and Charlie went to a school like that. Football is all they think about.'

'Football's good. Fresh air, exercise.'

'And you sound like Johnny. Says it's not done him any harm.'

Johnny's a bricklayer or 'brickie' as Dora always called him. She wasn't demeaning him; she made it clear that he was skilled, much in demand and 'would bust his gut for his family, and that's all of us.' It was at times like that when she spoke of him with affection and a sort of reverence that I wished for something more. But then, I thought, who could I accommodate in my life, dedicated to that 'room of my own'? I loved writing and needed to work, needed to make a living. Or, I thought, perhaps I was addicted to men on the side, no commitment.

I examined my fear of Gerald knowing about Lottie, and vice versa, one bitter day in January 1984. I was stuck on Norwich station, trains disrupted by ice on rails, the dark sky glowing with the false light of thousands of streetlights, shops and homes. The stars obliterated by humanity's terror of blackout. That's something Gerald would have said; it may even have been a line from one of his poems. I felt miserable. What if he came along now, I thought? What if his slightly stooped figure dressed in anorak and cords sat down on the seat beside me? Fourteen years on I didn't know where he was. America might be over and he could be anywhere. I looked around; so many people waiting, stoically reading evening papers, chatting, strolling to and fro. Strangers.

I was ashamed, that was it. Gerald and Max in different ways brought out my inferiority complex, my need to hero worship. I hated my lack of control. To have admitted my pregnancy to Gerald would have shown me up. Always wanting his admiration, his approval; he would have been disappointed at my carelessness in conceiving his child. That he might pity me, or deny his involvement, I couldn't bear. And he had, of course, never considered the possibility all those years ago, why would he want to now? I'd been right not to tell.

But I was wrong to be ashamed, I ought be like a fury, wild for his blood; he was a weak, self-absorbed blaggard. Lottie was a daughter to be proud of; and I was more than pleased with what I'd achieved since her birth. I stood up, physically stood up tall, took a deep breath, and laughed.

'You're right, Dora. A letter for when she's eighteen or twenty one,' I told her after the next yoga session. 'I'll name him then.'

'You sure?'

'Yes.'

'And if she does ask before?'

'I say what I always said, and explain about the letter.'

Dearest Lottie
I want you to know that I loved your father very much when you were conceived and for a long time afterwards. He was my tutor at university and technically he shouldn't have been in a relationship

with a student. But in those days people turned a blind eye.

Gerald Porter lectured in creative writing, was a poet with several small anthologies published when I knew him. There is nothing I can say to detract from his personality; the problem apart from his age – he thirty-five when I was twenty – was that he was married. I knew nothing of his wife or life outside the college. And that was the reason I did not tell him about you, as well as the large part of me which wanted to keep you all to myself.

I don't know where he is; he left for America before you were born and I had no wish to contact him. If you want to get in touch now, I am sure he would receive you well. I hope that he won't be angry with me for keeping you from him for all these years.

You know how much I love you – remember those times we wanted to find the most we could love – 'more than the whole universe' – you decided.
Mumma alias Greta Salway   1984

The letter is still lodged with my solicitor. Though knowing what I know now I am thankful that it never came to light. A travesty of the truth.

Dora and I continued to meet up though less frequently. Yoga had given us up after three years; the usual problem of lack of premises, the community hall sold for housing development. I found somewhere else but it was too far for Dora. 'Johnny wants me to go with him to the gym. Can't say it's what I want but he's keen and the twins are old enough to babysit the girls.'

After Lottie died and I was tearing myself apart with guilt, trying to find where I'd gone wrong, what I had done to cause my child to want to kill herself, Dora talked sense.

'Mothers feel guilty all the time for what we've done or not done for our kids. But they don't see it like that, not if you've loved them good and strong, and you certainly did that for Lottie.'

1982

Romeo and Juliet

Lottie said; 'I wish they were our neighbours because I'd be able to go and see them everyday. He's so clever and she's so wise.' Would that wisdom help me today? How would they unpick and resolve my dilemma? Roger was their friend.

They were our stalwarts, a reassuring deep bass beat in my life from 1982. Already acknowledged for their assistance with research in 'Death of a Consul' published in 1983, Douglas and Audrey Soames were a source of gracious support until their death a year ago.

How formal that sounds but to some extent it's fitting. Neither of them came from a privileged background, yet they believed in service to your country and the social niceties which at times seemed at odds with their political views.

'Douglas is organising a meeting with our local member of parliament.' Audrey 'phoned soon after we met. 'He wants to get a debate going in the town on nuclear disarmament. I know that you're a supporter of CND, dear.'

'Yes, and a debate sounds interesting. When?'

'March, but no date yet. We hoped you'd be able to come. Add some weight to the debate.'

'Audrey, I've strong views but …'

'Come and have lunch. We've old friends from Pakistan coming next Tuesday. Any chance?'

And that's how it was, constant invitations to tea, lunch, parties, peace events, poetry readings; I loved them a lot. As did Lottie.

Colin knew them through his father. Douglas was a member of the British consulate, recently retired, and ambassadors from many countries were their friends. Nothing boastful as everyone was judged, or I should say appreciated, for their contribution to peace in the world.

Colin had said; 'If you want the dirt on cocktail parties and ambassadorial junkets the Soames might be worth a call.'

This was before he and I broke up and at the time it seemed a useless contact. But as the idea of a body in Camden Lock involving a foreign diplomat began to niggle, I took up his offer. And got much more than I deserved.

'Audrey, I'm taking Lottie to the demo at Greenham Common next week,' I told her some time after that debate. 'Would you be able to come with us?'

She laughed. 'Well, yes, dear. I don't usually do these things without Douglas but it's women only isn't it?'

'Yes, and Joy is coming too.'

'Oh,' I heard the deepened interest.

'We'll be driving down from home, Waterbeach, and could pick you up at Newbury Station, save you bringing the car.'

'So kind, what a lovely thought. Let me talk to Douglas.'

Lottie told me many years later; 'If Romeo and Juliet had lived, hadn't taken sleeping potions, hadn't drunk poison, hadn't stabbed themselves or anyone else, they'd be them.'

'Who?' I said, thinking she meant Joy and Jim.

'Douglas and Audrey. We're surrounded by them, aren't we; Shakespeare's best lovers?'

'Are they the best?'

'You can't count any of the others.'

'What about Hermia and Lysander, Beatrice and Benedict?'

'Stupid quarrels even at the beginning. They'd never have lasted.'

'But Romeo and Juliet certainly didn't.'

'Different.' Lottie was determined to be right.

'Othello and Desdemona, Antony and Cleopatra, Hamlet and Ophelia?'

'Point proved.'

I didn't argue.

Is it comforting to remember that she held such firm views on love? At the time, it was amusing and reassuring. Her influences, the examples in her life were heartening. But in hindsight I see her view was too rigid, there was no allowance for shading. If she'd met her father, if I'd let her see that love is pain, rarely bliss, would she still be with me?

Douglas drove Audrey to the camp and though keen to stay and be part of it, reluctantly took himself off to Newbury. 'He's got a picnic, dear,' Audrey said. 'He'll find a river and take a walk.'

Lottie said; 'I don't see why it has to be a women only thing; Douglas or any man should be allowed to show their support. I mean, he's been campaigning for ages. It's a shame.'

Audrey said; 'I think the organisers want it to be seen as the women of the world uniting against this dreadful bomb.'

'Yes, but …'

'Women have been seen as the ones to be protected in the past whether they wanted it or not.'

'I know that. I've just read 'Middlemarch'. Sickening!'

'Yes, dear, I agree and that's why this is a particular show of our power and solidarity,' Audrey finished triumphantly.

We tied a bunch of yellow jasmine to the wire, joined hands, sang, 'We Shall Overcome', ate two picnics, ours and Audrey's and parted late afternoon, at a time arranged for Douglas to swing past the camp like an errant knight to pick up his lady.

Lottie said; 'Was he a fighter pilot in World War II?'

'No, I'm afraid nothing as glamorous as that,' Audrey said. 'Something in Intelligence. But we didn't meet properly until it was all over.'

Later when we learned that they had been part of the human chain from Greenham to Aldermaston earlier in the year, Lottie was deflated.

'Why didn't she tell us? Why didn't they ask me to go?'

'We didn't know them properly then. They wouldn't have realised that you'd want to. And they never boast.'

'I told the girls at school about going to Greenham. I wanted to give a talk to the class, perhaps even to the school, but Miss Browne said it wasn't appropriate.'

'Well …'

'No, not well, wrong. I can't think why I'm at this school. If I went to the comprehensive it would be different.'

Joy and I looked at one another. Conspirators in believing that 'this will pass.'

When did all it all start, Lottie's need to take up causes? Why her vigilance on the rightness of what went on in society?

She was seven when she found out about the NSPCC and her fury and horror that children could be treated badly by anyone, let alone their parents, meant it was something she had to stop.

'Why don't they take the children and give them to someone who will love them?' she wanted to know.

Joy explained that it wasn't as easy as that. 'The children don't want to leave their parents however awful they are, and there aren't so many people who would want to take on someone else's child.'

'You took me.'

There was never a satisfactory answer.

Lottie organised a sale in the church hall to raise funds for the charity, at least she bullied Joy and Jim into taking that on too.

We were proud of her. As were Douglas and Audrey.

'Douglas has no head for fiction, I'm afraid, Greta,' Audrey said. 'But I think your novels are wonderful. My WI ladies can't wait to meet you since I put them on to your books.'

'Douglas told me,' Lottie said, 'his favourite authors are Montaigne and Shelley.'

'Yes, philosophy and poetry,' Audrey said.

'I can understand people wanting to know the way to think about things, what it's all about, life and us, but poetry? It's so sloppy.'

'Tell that to Douglas.'

Which, of course, she did. This was Lottie at fourteen.

Douglas and Audrey lived in a village surrounded by the South Downs; beautiful countryside where Douglas would lead us on walks as if he were charting his own territory. The nearest station, Haslemere, was on a direct line from London.

I asked Douglas; 'Should I mind that Lottie is so absorbed in what is wrong with the world and in believing that she needs to put it right?'

He laughed; 'That lively mind!   No, no, she's an example to us all.   She hasn't been polluted by the constant drag of knowing that, well, we're all pinpricks in this vast world of greed and ignorance.'

'Oh, don't say that!'

'Difficult not to feel it. But I won't tell Lottie.'

And he didn't.

'Douglas and I have been discussing humanism,' Lottie said. 'Why did you never tell me?'

'Well, I …'

'I'm going to join. It fits in with what I think.'

'I'm sure Joy and Jim would agree too,' I said.

'And thank goodness, he's explained about Shelley and his radical views which he was condemned for. It's why he admires him, not just the poetry, which is a relief.'

'What's so wrong with poetry?' I said.

'Mumma, it's no good explaining to you, like it wasn't to Douglas. Why make something complicated, hidden meanings, etcetera. It's not necessary, is it?'

'But it's the beauty of the words, the rhythmic form, the clever …'

'Blah!   Sorry, and I didn't say that to Douglas. Evidently Shelley said that poets are the unacknowledged legislators of the world.'   Her eyebrows were in danger of disappearing into her hairline. 'I just don't get that.'

It was good, I thought, and still think, her individuality, her ability to take other people's ideas and fashion them to her own. Until that moment when something somehow tipped her into needing poetry to express how she felt; but it wasn't enough.

Douglas and Audrey never asked about Lottie's father and she never mentioned the subject to them. I didn't know them well enough when Max shamed me into thinking more clearly about Lottie's need to know. I'd almost forgotten the letter that I'd written and given to my solicitor.   But when Lottie gained her place at Cambridge University to read mathematics, I knew that I ought to tell her that the letter existed; she was eighteen.

'Okay, that's fine,' she said. 'If I ever fancy knowing.'

'Nobody else knows, Lottie,' I said.

'That's all right, Mumma. I don't need anyone else in my life; whoever he was, you knew he wouldn't be right.'

Was that too glib?   I wanted to ask Douglas and Audrey. They'd come up to London for the launch of my 1988 publication, 'The Missing Minim'.   It had originally been called 'The Missing Crotchet' but Leo pointed out; 'They'll either think lacy ladies with aspidistras or the sacred contents of my underpants. Change it, darling, quick!'

Douglas and Audrey became the star attraction at the party.   Leo said; 'Where did you find these gorgeous people with manners to die for.   Utterly charming.   I'm angling for an invitation to their downland idyll.'   He looked longingly across the crowded room.   'I didn't know people still drank sherry; had to dash out for a bottle.'

They left at an appropriate time having worked their way around the assembled crowd with the ease of seasoned party people.

'Come and have breakfast with us tomorrow at our hotel,' Audrey said. 'I want a little bit of gossip. You will come won't you, dear?'

Douglas said; 'Splendid evening; publishing is a different world.'

'What a delight your agent Leo is!' Audrey told me next morning. 'He's promised to come for one of our poetry get-togethers next weekend. You have to come too, please, and Lottie, if she's available.'

Douglas said; 'We mustn't push our luck, sweetheart. I wouldn't put it past the child to stand up in front of our party and proclaim that poetry is obtuse and old fashioned.' He was laughing; I knew that he adored Lottie, they both did.

'You are so kind to us both,' I said. 'Lottie looks upon you as her other grandparents.'

That was the first time I'd thought of that and it shocked me. I'd deprived Lottie of other possible relatives; there should be other grandparents, half brothers or sisters. I tried to squash the thought immediately; I knew nothing of Gerald's extended family; had he ever mentioned a son or daughter?

'We're the ones who are honoured,' Audrey was saying. 'Such a clever girl; she gives us enormous pleasure. You both do, dear.'

It seemed the right time to tell them of my recent dilemma, the letter I'd written to Lottie, but I couldn't. And I think I was right. They never intruded into what had gone before; I was the one who'd pressed Audrey into telling me about their time in Pakistan or Paris or New York, and all their other postings. And even then the tales were of the 'delightful people' they'd met, and not the ones invited to cocktail parties. It was only at Audrey's funeral that I learned of their only child who had died at the age of two from leukaemia.

When Lottie died I didn't know how to tell them. I took the coward's way out and asked Leo to go with the news. By then he'd been 'adopted' too and I knew would be the best person for that terrible task.

It was four weeks after her death that I went to see them in person. Audrey greeted me at the door, folded me into her arms; Douglas stood behind, tears trickling down his cheeks, put a hand on my shoulder as if to impart some of his strength.

'Let's remember, Greta,' Audrey said. 'That's what Douglas and I've been doing. Going over and over all our memories of her lovely self.'

And that's what we did over tea and Battenburg cake.

'Battenburg cake,' Lottie would say, 'is so delicious and elegant, just like them.'

But I never told them about her poetry, love posted on a wall, which I'd still not found.

Douglas died of a stroke on July 31st 2002 and Audrey a heart attack a month later. I knew that if Lottie had been alive she'd have said; 'Of course. Romeo and Juliet, they couldn't live one without the other.'

And it is through them, Douglas and Audrey Soames, that I met Roger Harlow for a second time.

1985

Paul the photographer

I was with Paul in Paris when it happened. We'd gone over for a photographic exhibition, were due back the following day. Mobile phones were a rarity which neither of us possessed. Our hotel was up in Montmartre and we'd left early in the morning, spent most of the day at the exhibition or sitting in cafés where Paul liked to 'observe'. He was constantly quoting his hero, Henri Cartier-Bresson and I remember him saying on that particular day with great pomposity; 'Photography is nothing, it's life that interests me.' I was amused and annoyed but couldn't disagree with the notion of people-watching as a great source of material. How else would an author operate? Later we'd met friends and happily wined and dined in one of the many good restaurants so that it was midnight before we got back to our hotel and the message. Lottie was dead.

Before that moment when the world rocked and shifted out of orbit, Paul was a good companion and partner, though in retrospect it was a lightweight relationship; lopsided was Leo's verdict. We had been together for five years, shared quite a swanky flat which I'd bought recently in Bloomsbury. It felt like the zenith of all I'd wanted to achieve; the place where those early 20th century pretentious intellectuals had met, where Virginia Woolf had cried out for 'a room of one's own'. Thinking that a piece of property in London would be in Lottie's best interest I know was only partly true; my centre needed to be in London and I was determined to keep it like that. I was paying the mortgage on a home of my own that I could share with Lottie, an insurance for her future. It hurts to think of that even after all these years. But that's how it was.

Lottie was fifteen when I met Paul; bright and dedicated in her enclosed world of calculus, taking 'O' levels that year with the prospect of one day going to Cambridge University.

'May I take a photograph,' is what he said.

'Pardon?'

'You,' he said, 'there, as you are.'

A cold day at the end of February 1985 and I was sitting in Bloomsbury Square Gardens, contemplating the new project. A glittering sun picked out the peeled bark patterns on the plane trees, the frail catkins shivered on a silver birch, while the traffic inched past on all sides of that green oasis. I was wearing dark glasses, absorbed in this first sign of spring, content. I wasn't pleased to be disturbed.

'Paul,' he said, 'I'm a photographer.' He held up his camera, which did look professional, and for a brief moment I thought this might be a publicity stunt. The paparazzi, as they came to be called, followed the famous, the flaunted, not people like me. 'I'm trying to get a portfolio together, my own stuff. It's just that you looked like Greta Garbo sitting there.'

Lanky, a puppy not grown into its frame, was my first impression of him.

'Do you mind, just as you are, and then over by that tree, the motley one. Okay?'

'I'm afraid …' I began, expecting crestfallen, pleading, some sort of negative reaction but not at all. He grinned, his square face split by a big mouth as in a child's first drawing,

'Sorry, sorry, that was far too abrupt, but the light, your profile, your clothes, and yes, those specs.' He skipped around me, long legs doing their own jitterbug, a pierrot. I often thought of Picasso's paintings when looking at Paul.

'Where are these photos going? Is this commercial?' I didn't really know what I meant. Did it matter; I was trying to work it out. My publicist, my publishers; Leo; did this affect me professionally? And, of course, I was intrigued by the Garbo reference; he didn't know my name.

'Into my portfolio,' he said. 'You see I'm desperate to get an agent. I know I'm good, first class degree, an MA, but I need something to wow them in the commercial sector.'

'Anonymous?'

'Oh yes, no problem, I'd prefer that. I like to think my shots are representations of the world at large, a universal world.'

'Oh, yes?'

'It's roughly what Cartier-Bresson said, that photographers deal in things which are continually vanishing and when they've gone there's nothing we can do to make them come back; well, something like that. And this is such a moment. Please.'

I shrugged and let him snap away. I sat on the seat, stood by that tree like some ingénue model, until he finally heard my pleas that it was enough. And then he gave me his card, thanked me profusely, shook my hand, promised that I was his saviour. I watched him lope off and was about to leave myself, the moment of quiet reflection gone, when I saw him rushing back, that camera banging against his chest.

'I should have said, please, come to my show; Thursday next week. Here,' he fumbled in his rucksack to bring out a crumpled flyer and thrust it at me. 'If you can, if you can that would be marvellous.' Another face-splitting smile and he was gone.

That weekend in Waterbeach I remember was especially happy. Lottie and I went on a trip to Cambridge which was different from our usual visits for shopping or the bits and pieces of culture I'd thought essential in a child's upbringing.

'Lets go and explore like we're tourists,' she said. 'I just go to and fro to school. I want to see it through a stranger's eyes, get a feeling for what it'll be like as a student too.'

I can't say I really knew what she meant until I found she'd acquired a map, highlighted sites, and had our itinerary already planned. We took the train and then I followed her, on foot, into most of the colleges, some of the gardens, though it was too early in the year for the glory of flowers. But as she pointed out to me, the structure of the buildings was all the beauty we needed along with the symmetry of the well-kempt lawns. We sat outside The Mill pub with ginger beer shandy and crisps, watching the water pulled from the upper reach over the weir, the gush and bubbles dissolving into the mill pond. We contemplated taking a canoe up to Grantchester but, fortunately, due to the cold, that could be saved until the summer she decided. We explored the Fitzwilliam Museum exhaustively, would have taken in the Kettle's Yard art gallery had time allowed, and collapsed at an Italian style restaurant before catching a train home after ten.

'What about Paris next?' she said. 'I don't get on with French but it would be good see all the buildings. The Pompidou Centre, that looks fantastic.'

That is how she was, my daughter, and I loved her.

'You came!' Paul rushed at me, arms wide, a glass of something in his hand spilling over as he leapt forward to take my hand. 'This is brilliant. I'm so honoured.'

I drew back from the spillage; I'd come in on my way to the theatre, was wearing a best frock. Max, who I was with at the time, had tickets for Covent Garden to see some obscure ballet. Soho was almost on route. 'Thank you,' I said but Paul was already dragging me over to a table where the drinks were being doled out. The room was tiny, the photographs hung with little space between from floor to ceiling. In fact, a ladder had been provided for those who wanted to view the top row.

'Gosh, you look nice,' he said. 'Red or white?'

I was going to ask for something soft, even water, but then remembered that Max would already be 'merry and bright'. I'd given up commenting on his drinking habits after he turned on me with; 'Isn't it better to be the life and soul?'

'I thought I should come and see what a man who has the cheek to take my photo can produce,' I said. 'Are these all yours?'

'God, no!' He introduced me to a Norwegian friend who owned the studio and two fellow artists. 'Photography is art whatever those priggish so-called purists say,' I was told. And I was pleased I'd come. His work was good, even to my untrained eye. I could see the influence of his idol; he had an intriguing way of treating light.

'I'm interested to see the photos you shot of me,' I said when I'd taken in the whole of his show. 'After seeing these I feel flattered that you chose to pick me and that place as subjects.' I was sincere but not wanting to make anything more of this fleeting relationship. Besides I was late for Max who was far too much of a complication in my life to take on anything else.

'Oh, that's great, thanks, yes, please.' From the dancing pierrot he slowed to a graceful harlequin, grown up. 'Here's my number,' he offered a card which I dutifully took. 'I'm so grateful to such a graceful lady as yourself …'

I cut in; 'That's too much. Save it for your girlfriend.' And I was pleased that he was able to laugh though there weren't many times when he found me amusing after that.

Paul was older than I first thought, thirty to my thirty five when we first met. I can't remember his family clearly, having met them once only at another of his shows, or think why he harboured such a resentment of them. And that is, maybe, too strong but there was certainly an awkward streak to him, the need to be an outsider, to take a career path that was very different from theirs. His father was some sort of manufacturer, money no problem, and 'conservative with a capital 'C'. My mother is to the right of Genghis Khan,' Paul told me soon after we met. As I recall she was a tidy women in neat skirts and flamboyant brooches.

'They've supported you financially for more than ten years, Paul,' I once said. 'That seems remarkably generous to me.'

'What else would they do with the money? My sister's married a banker and needs nothing.'

'But does that mean you have to be so ungrateful?'

'Oh, Greta, gratitude doesn't come into it. Yes, I am thankful, but I can't bear to be tied.' The sad face, the pouty mouth followed by the wide grin and a gathering of me into those long arms. 'I'm just scared of being swallowed up.'

One of his friends recognised me from the back cover of one of my novels and, coincidentally, I had a book signing at Foyles about a month after his show, so there he was in the queue, clutching a book, the engaging grin staring down at me as I looked up for the next customer.

'Greta Salway,' he said, 'I'm a great fan of yours, would you kindly sign my copy.' I think it was 'The Dragon's Underbelly' with Lisa Forrester, my Hackney DI.

'Paul the Photographer, how good to meet you again,' I said, and I meant it to a great extent. I'd just split up with Max for the umpteenth time and needed to focus elsewhere.

'How long's this going to take you?' he said indicating the queue snaking back through the shop. '6 o'clock; dinner? Meet you at the corner of Old Compton Street.'

Dinner was vegetarian in a rather seedy dive in Soho; Paul was a dedicated 'veggie', his term, who not only cooked a range of good recipes to follow his passion but always smelled of pulses. Even when he shared my flat and my unguents, a faint odour of garlic and old sacks clung to his clothes, or was it his skin? That evening we parted at Charing Cross tube station but he'd prised my phone number from me and invited me to a performance by a new theatre company, the director of which he knew. Max had been the showman, who knew the up and coming, believed that only he could judge what was worth seeing in the world of theatre and music. It had been hard for me to have my own point of view. Paul was refreshing in his eagerness to support any event which might be termed 'alternative' and, even better, to ask for my opinion. On that occasion it was the Finsborough Theatre and a taut play which any half decent feminist would applaud. I certainly did.

We came out on a high and Paul began to jive down the road towards Earls Court tube station before bounding back to swing me round and plonk a puppy dog kiss on my cheek. 'Thank you, thank you,' he said whilst gazing down at me. 'Can I kiss you, please, Greta Salway.' I didn't say 'no'. I had the flat in Bloomsbury by then where he followed and surprised me as a competent and more intelligent lover than I'd expected.

I've never had girlfriends with whom to share the intimacies of my love life, not even Dora; never wanted them or to do so. If I had, I'd have told them that Paul was easily roused but able to control his climax, trying hard to meet my expectations. Perhaps they'd think the perfect lover. 'You're my muse, Greta, my sexy muse,' he'd say. 'You've taught me like no other woman,' which wasn't meant to make me wonder about those who'd gone before. No petite mort for him, no turning over, the last gasp eclipsing any sign of life or interest in his mate. He would sigh and stare sloppy dog eyes at me, me who was still revelling in the last trembling triumph of orgasm, a sweaty mess, and say; 'You're a miracle, Greta, you and me, a miracle.' It was very satisfying at the time.

Waterbeach had been off limits to all my male friends before Paul. Angus, Colin, Max and a couple of short term relationships, never wanted to be part of that other bit of my life, and I didn't encourage it. Separate and different, no complication, no navigating unwelcome questions or explanations; it worked well. I wasn't ashamed of my family or of those men. And I wasn't worried that Joy and Jim, or even Lottie, might think a man in my life would be a rival for their affection. Joy asked occasionally, usually on my birthday or after a book launch, as to whether I'd ever find a husband. 'I know it's fashionable not to be married, love, and it's not always a bed of roses; it's a give and take, the thorns and pricks, but with the right man, it's worth a try.'

But Paul was very good at ingratiating himself. Barely three months after we met he'd moved in to my flat, originally staying the odd night and then, inevitably, the flat in which he was renting a room was being sold and tenants were no longer wanted. And it wasn't long before he was angling for an invitation to Waterbeach. 'The flat lands, the drained and ditched, the big skies. I've got to come. I could borrow your car. I'd be no trouble.'

And he wasn't. Joy and Jim accepted his childish enthusiasm and he could be charming, listening at length to stories of the 'old days', some of their finer tales of East Anglian myths. Lottie liked him, she even allowed his overtures to becoming a photographic subject and I do, thanks to him, possess heartbreaking portraits of my lovely child. 'It's the puppet, Grandma' she'd say to Joy. 'Don't stand still for too long or he'll shoot you.'

That I include Paul in my saga is because he was there, that he captured the physical essence of Lottie for eternity, and to record and remember how other people react to someone else's grief. Poor man, he wasn't equipped. His proposal was crass and I was beyond comfort.

1990

Paris

'There is a message, madame,' he said. 'Please to phone Joie.' I stared at him, not the usual late-night receptionist who knew no English and rightly didn't care, this was the owner of the hotel who prided himself on his communication skills, a courtly man who plied his guests with anecdotes, offered ideas of how they might enjoy their stay in Paris. 'It is urgent, please.'

'When did she call?' The first fist of fear clutched my stomach.

'It was 1 o'clock, madame, that is our time; 12 noon in Angleterre, I think.'

I looked up at the clock above the counter; half past midnight; Joy and Jim would be in bed.

'What else did she say?'

'It is urgent; she said to phone as soon as you are back to the hotel. Please, come to my office?'

A balloon blocked my throat, air sucked out of my chest as he led the way. Paul must have been behind me or at my side but I have no recollection of his presence. This stranger with the grave and gentle voice, who already knew before I that there was bad news, that's all I remember.

He gestured for me to use his seat and drew the telephone closer to where I sat. 'You would like a glass of water, perhaps, or tea?' His solicitude was alarming. 'To dial out,' he said, but I shook my head; I didn't need the code for where I should have been when the call came through. He left me alone as I punched in the numbers for the connection across the channel, listened to the miles of ether travelled as the insistent burr waited for an answer. In this cubbyhole, enclosed in black and brown and sepia, as if the subject of a Cartier Bresson photograph, I held my breath.

'Joy, what is it?' I called out as soon as I heard the click of the receiver being lifted. But it was Jim.

'Greta, thank goodness, they've found you. Greta you must come home, come quickly.' His voice gulped and wavered. 'It's Lottie.' And then the sobbing and Joy behind him saying; 'Come, darling, come. Our little Lottie.' And the break in her voice, the dissolving to a violin screech of; 'Come quickly.'

'What's happened, Joy? What's happened?' but all I could hear was the sound of their weeping. I raised my voice; 'Joy, Jim, I'm coming, tomorrow. I'll be with you tomorrow, no, I mean today.' I sounded strong, the person in charge who would sort out whatever it was, when I was merely part of this horror, airless, weightless, terrified. 'I'll be on the first flight out.'

Jim barked, the only solid sound he could make; 'We can't do anything, she …' but that's all he said. Not the words that I have to say, they were never said by them. Lottie is dead.

Lottie and I had been in Paris a year before, in April, her holiday prior to first year exams at Cambridge, when she was willing to give up a weekend away from swotting. We didn't stay in Montmartre but in a tiny family run hotel near the Comedie Française, sharing a huge bedroom, going up in an ancient lift and through winding uneven corridors to 'our palatial suite'.

Lottie said; 'This is the scariest place I've been; like in that film 'Thoroughly Modern Millie', remember? Can't we take the stairs?'

I thought she was serious and began to climb to our third floor room.

'Mumma, you're so funny; you don't seem to know when I'm joking.'

That disturbed me, the part-time mother; was I so out of touch? I spent that day like a snail with my antennae primed for innuendoes, remarks that might not be appropriate, and even that she detected.

'You're trying too hard; it's okay. Mothers shouldn't understand their children, particularly teenagers. We need to be mysterious, even to ourselves.' She was nineteen.

From then on I relaxed, took with a pinch of pepper - her expression – comments on The Louvre; 'The gloomiest place I've ever been to,'; the Monet Waterlilies at the Musée d'Orsay; 'Repetitive, but I suppose he never thought he'd got it right'; but the cemetery up on the hill at Montmartre she adored. 'Death is so peaceful, or, at least, being dead.' Should I have paid more attention to that flippant remark? But then, I agreed. We wandered for an hour around the various gravestones, the ostentatious tombs. 'I'd like to be buried here, wouldn't you?' she said. 'To be in such illustrious company and at night you could climb up to the Sacré Coeur and see out for miles. Perhaps I ought to brush up my French.'

We drank wine together as befitted a young woman blossoming to maturity. Although a little gawky still, her hair shone like a field of corn in high summer. As we sat in the Café de Flore, a treat for both of us, I was so proud. And when she said; 'You're like a friend as well as my mother. Is that how it was for you and Grandma?' I glowed but had no idea how to answer or what I ought to feel. I feared a reply that was glib, would both dishonour Joy and the compliment Lottie was paying me.

'Thank you, Lottie, that's the best that I could ever hope to hear. And I've been so lucky that Joy has mothered you too.' That wasn't a whole answer, if one at all. Fortunately a waiter arrived to ask if we'd like a dessert and we chose a Crème Brûlée to share. But I knew I must make a better attempt. 'Joy has been the best mother anyone could have and I've been the luckiest daughter. But a friend? I'd never thought like that.'

'I suppose you never had her to yourself, like I have you. Granddad is her friend, her best friend, so I suppose she didn't need any other.'

Heavens, I thought; such perception but where was the conversation going? I helped myself to another glass of wine. The coward needing fortification, unready for what would come next.

Then, 'It would have been different if I'd had a father,' she said, 'though I know you didn't want him hanging around. *He* obviously wasn't a friend.'

I know there was a lot of red in the restaurant's décor, but at that moment the whole world flushed crimson, blood flooded my brain and those special feelers retreated for fear of what I ought to say. I'd always been honest in telling her that he was a mistake, but she wasn't, that he didn't love me or I him. That the last part wasn't the whole truth didn't matter, but that I didn't consider him capable of being a good enough father was, which is why I didn't tell him. I'd never asked what Joy or Jim might have said to her, but thought they'd passed that on as a question for me. Her analysis of the whole affair was the best, the honest truth.

'No, that was the trouble, Lottie,' I said, 'he wouldn't have been a friend. And that's essential for happiness.'

And then she talked about Paul. 'He'd be a useless father. I like him but he's a sort of puppet, and you can see his strings which is quite funny.'

I laughed so much that I choked and the waiter came over to ask if I'd like some water.

'Oui, s'il vous plait, un verre de l'eau,' Lottie said surveying me with amusement and superiority. 'I'm right aren't, I?' she said. 'You couldn't marry him either, could you?'

Paris, a different hotel a year later, I was a cardboard cut out, flat packed, the air folded from my lungs. I sat staring at the telephone, the white numbers against the black, the arms of the leather chair scuffed and squashed, brass studs missing, the grey functional filing cabinets from a different era. I focused on a photograph above of a hotel dynasty, the generations ranged and poised, a proud print of someone else's family.

What had happened to mine?

'Is everything all right?' Paul said as I came through to the reception desk.

'I have to go.'

'What? What's happened?' His voice was amused; crises didn't happen to anyone else, only him.

'Monsieur?' I spoke to my hotelier who was still there, concerned, awaiting my instructions. 'Please can you make out my bill. I must pack and go to the airport.'

'Why?' Paul stood over me, his strings far too limp. 'There won't be any flights till the morning.' I was already on my way to the lift. He trailed after me. 'Why the rush?'

'I don't know what's happened. It's Lottie is all they could say. I need to go, now.'

'But the airport will be closed, none of the flight desks available for booking.'

'You don't have to come,' I said, 'it's my ...' I couldn't finish and he knew not to argue. Silently we packed our separate bags; it didn't matter what he did or didn't do.

A taxi was waiting for us; the hotelier had put the bill in an envelope which he handed to me. 'There is no need to pay me now. A cheque when you are able.'

I thanked him but settled up. A few minutes more of this early morning weren't going to make a difference to the rest of my life. What came after would; I already knew that.

Looking back I see that too many of my associations with men were tinged with an ulterior motive. Would I have continued to meet Paul in those early days if he hadn't been a photographer? A plot line; the possibility of finding another method for my criminal to kill the victim? 'Potassium ferricynanide? Oh yes, poisonous as hell as it produces hydrogen cyanide gas. You make sure the room is ventilated, that's all,' he told me. And he was a relief from the corrosive effect of Max. Such flimsy reasons; there must have been something else. From this distance, though, it's impossible to remember.

And Lottie was right; I never intended to marry Paul. Soon after he first wheedled his way to Waterbeach, I took her to an exhibition of Picasso's work at The Courtauld. It was one of my many attempts to give her what I thought of as a wide cultural education when I was probably doing what would have pleased me when I was growing up. Joy and Jim wouldn't have had the time or money or thought it necessary to take me to ballet, theatre and art galleries. I hadn't resented it in any way but, like the father who has always yearned for a train set which he imposes on his indifferent son, I'd kidded myself that it was good for Lottie. She never grumbled, neither did she show much enthusiasm. Her greatest find and reaction was to one of the paintings in that collection; 'Les Deux Saltimbanques'; the harlequin and his companion. 'That looks like you and Paul,' she said. 'When he's having one of his grumps and you're fed up with him.' She delighted in her observation, bought a postcard copy of the painting to take and show to Joy and Jim.

Les Deux Saltimbanques

There is a question mark around your ear,
Harlequin, wound into your companion,
melancholy
shared with Pernod and Perrier.

We contemplate the two faced problem,
Picasso's pink period capturing the
orange of her dress,
and the bill as yet unpaid.

Has the circus folded, or are you caught
at the wrong time of the month?   Or,
should we be wondering
what you have said to Columbine?

To say he was quixotic is too flattering. He was rarely optimistic or idealistic. His bright and cheery moods, his ability to charm and play the enthusiastic pet were interspersed with periods of bad temper and childish sulks. That I was successful and continued to be so annoyed him although that is something he wouldn't admit, even, I think, to himself. Most of the time it didn't matter. I was busy trying to keep on top; a new title every year is what my publishers wanted. Novels to print will never be easy and this was possibly the best of times, but I needed to be fresh, scurry around doing the research as well as sitting closeted with words to be written on pages. 'Why do you have to be so dedicated?' he'd say lodging against the door lintel of

99

my study. 'I need some excitement, inspiration. Can't we go to Margate?'

There were variations on this theme and my response of; 'Go by yourself, you don't need me,' met with blank disapproval and hours of disgruntled shuffling around the flat. Most of the time it was the car he wanted, my car, and as he'd achieved too many points on his licence two years into our relationship, it was me, as driver, that he required. I was the glass half full until 1990.

There was nothing he could say on that journey back from Paris, the taxi driving us to Orly airport, the hours waiting for dawn, for a flight. My terror blocked out all thoughts other than desperate scenarios; Lottie with glandular fever, a road accident, meningitis, all images of her in intensive care. Death I would not contemplate.

Paul tried; 'It'll be all right, Greta. There's no point in worrying,' as we took our seats on the plane. My anger, bordering on hatred, was irrational and made worse because I knew that he'd never worried about anything in his life bar himself. 'She's a plucky kid,' he ventured as we recovered our baggage in London, 'whatever it is she'll pull through.' There was no suggestion that he'd come with me to Waterbeach and he had to say; 'I'll go back to the flat.' We parted and later I wished that it had been for the last time. I was numb, a stripped-out husk, and that was before I knew the full horror.

'Why does Grandma want you to get married, Mumma?' Lottie had asked soon after I met Paul. I loved that she called me Mumma to my face but spoke to Joy and Jim of Greta. 'I can't imagine you walking down an aisle like a frosted cake,' she'd said.

I ignored the raised eyebrows, the eyes rolled skyward, and replied honestly; 'Joy wants me to be as happy as she and Jim; she can't understand anything else.' And I added; 'Someone to take care of me, perhaps,' which brought an explosion of laughter, a moment that I hold incredibly dear.

Paul came to Waterbeach for the funeral. A glorious spring day when the grass is a green that you believe never to have seen before, the blue sky and puffy clouds painted as for a chocolate box, and the church massed with primroses, violets, boughs of cherry blossom, her coffin covered in fresh picked flowers. I was rigid, knew that I mustn't cry; dignity and holding up Joy and Jim were my main focus. There was nowhere to collapse, no one upon whom to lay my head, to weep and rail, no person who would have the strength or nerve to approach me.

So his proposal, a fortnight later when I returned to London, was beyond sense, crass in the extreme. 'I thought we might get married, Greta. Would you like that?'

1990

Suicide

There was no crime to solve with Lottie's death, no one to accuse even if the three of us carried guilt and blame as lifelong backpacks.

They said it would be distressing, her body was badly damaged; they meant mutilated. Their term was 'too disrupted'. What else? Lying on a rail track with an express train travelling at seventy miles an hour, perhaps more, coming through a small station, not stopping. What chance would her lovely soft body have against that?

They told me that she would have felt no pain after the first blow, the first contact with the train would have killed her; she would have been dead before the pilot beam, they called it 'the cow catcher', gathered her body to drag it along the track, tearing her, shredding her to pieces.

I wasn't needed to identify her. They were able to use dental records, fingerprints, and, if necessary, her possessions in the room she shared in college. But I had to see her. I wanted to see her, my beloved daughter.

They had tried to put her back together, gathered the bits to attempt a reconstruction, the head, the body, the limbs, but she was barely recognisable. Her face smashed, scalp ripped, hair matted with blood and dirt. I stared at my child as they held the sheet away from the horror of her death, to display what was essentially their handiwork. I had to keep looking, not turn away, to take in and hold the sight of her body with life gone. My child.

'Can I touch her?' I said.

The pathologist shook his head; 'Not until after the autopsy, I'm afraid,' and the police officer, a woman, came closer as if she'd need to pull me back, pick me up. Someone said; 'I'm sorry.'

'Lottie,' I said, not to tell them but to speak to her. 'Lottie, Lottie,' I kept saying, not crying, not pleading, over and over her name as if to restore the tangled mess, for it to be her again. The girl with the corn coloured hair, an arm with the birthmark mole on the underside of her wrist, the blunt toenails she hated that curled up at the edges, that scar on her knee. They were there even with her face taken from us. The pieces not joined but placed, waiting for me to stitch her together. If only I'd learned how to sew.

I nodded. 'It's my daughter.'

Joy had said; 'You can't go on your own,' but there was a lack of certainty in her voice and I'd been relieved that she hadn't insisted. I'd done this. I'd brought Lottie into the world, wanted and loved her, but let so much responsibility rest on them. I had to do this alone.

At the mortuary they offered me tea, kept saying how sorry, that I must sit down, there were a few details it would be helpful to have and a signature. How was I travelling home, was there someone they could call? And the young policewoman offered transport and said; 'How brave!'

Who? I wanted to say. Me or Lottie? I was only upright for her, this I had to do for her; I'd flunked so much. Even if she didn't know or want me now, I had to be brave for her.

It was a late spring day. Outside the mortuary, daffodils were strident in the flower beds under a vivid blue sky. Spurts of young green leaves on trees, grass fresh and cut clean, the satin white petals of a gifted magnolia shone in the April sun. I screamed at the thoughtless, the cruel obscenity of spring that day.

I sat in my car, a husk, a hole, a void. How was I going carry on living? I stared through the windscreen and saw nothing but a whirl of activity that was utterly pointless. I was outside all that, or inside with nothing to make me want or able to get out. I hurt, every part of me hurt, a numb hurt, but I had no right to hurt. And I had to go back to them. Joy and Jim were waiting for me.

Grief should be shared they say, ease the pain with the solace of other people. And yet I felt so far from anyone; I needed a hole to dig and climb into, a hill to drag myself up and hunch breathless at the top. I wanted to cry out to the earth and sky, I wanted to weep the pain out of me for ever.

'Let's have a cup of tea, Greta,' Joy said.

I nodded.

'Sit down, love,' Jim plumped a cushion but our eyes couldn't meet. 'Is it her?' he said.

I nodded.

We sat, the kettle wailed for us, and we drank wordlessly. The air was tight with all the questions, the answers and the horror of what we knew and didn't know.

'The funeral,' Joy said. 'When can we have the funeral?' It would be something to do.

I shook my head. 'We have to wait for the autopsy, the coroner's report, before they can release her body.'

There was no note. I spoke to her roommate, Maeve, who'd moved out to share with someone else.

'We weren't exactly friends,' she said. 'Lottie was dedicated, working hard, had little time for talking. I'm a bit of a party girl I suppose you could say.'

Red hair, a pre-Raphaelite girl, wearing Doc Martens, I knew nothing about her. What had Lottie told me? I couldn't remember anything that she'd said except; 'I've somewhere in college this year but I'll have to share.'

'Who were her friends?' I asked this girl.

'Don't know. Except perhaps the people she was in the pub with.'

'Can you tell me who they were?'

'Not really. Didn't the police tell you?'

'Did she talk about her other friends, her work?'

'No, like I said, we weren't really chatty. Came in went out at different times.'

'Where did she work?'

'Sometimes in the room, lots in the library; she always went to lectures, though there weren't many this year, well, not for me anyway.'

'I know this is difficult, but was she different this year, since Christmas?'

'Don't know. You see I didn't really know her before.'

We sat opposite each other in the college cafeteria, polystyrene mugs of tea. She wanted to get away, she didn't want to enter into any more of the grief, be contaminated by someone else's desperate actions.

'Thank you for talking to me,' I said. 'It's …' but I couldn't finish the sentence.

'It's okay. I'm sorry, very sorry.' She couldn't look at me.

'The room is incredibly tidy, the room you shared,' I said. 'Was it always like that?'

Maeve nodded, her face a blank slate, there was no hope of help from her.

'Thank you again,' I said. 'If there is anything else you remember about her, or what she did. It's memories I want. Do you understand?'

She looked at me then. Furtive pity; can that be a description? It's what I read. I stood up and held out my hand for her.

'Did you find the poems?' she said.

'What?'

'Poems. Since Christmas she's been writing poetry, stuck them all over the walls. Love poetry; some of it was good.'

'They're not there now.'

'No? On bits of paper, they were handwritten.'

The police had established that there had been no foul play, nobody else with her, no one to push her, make her lie on the line. The evidence was that she had ridden her bicycle from a pub in Trumpington directly to Foxton where the rail line from Cambridge runs down to London. The station was unmanned and deserted when the last express train hurtled through. Her bicycle was found parked and chained on the railings at the entrance; her rucksack laid on the platform close to the place where she had climbed down and spread herself along the southbound track. The post mortem established, despite the mangling of her body, that she'd consumed a considerable amount of alcohol and had been smoking cannabis.

'Seven miles from Cambridge,' Joy said.

'From Trumpington,' I corrected her. 'Five miles.'

Joy looked at me; this unpicking, this deciphering of motive amongst what was done on that night or the days or years before, dragged us down. Or maybe it gave us something to do, to alleviate the leaden grief.

'She didn't drink,' Joy said.

'Not with us.'

'Smoking was a 'dirty habit'.   Do you remember when Old Griff from the pub used to sit on the seat by the bus stop and Lottie would go and lecture him on the dangers of smoking.'   Small memories briefly lifted us.

Again the look from Joy and I knew to say. 'Yes, it was her, no one else.'

'She was happy at Christmas, wasn't she?'

'I think so.'

'She didn't come home too often after that,' Jim said.

'Too involved with work, that was what we thought.'

'Joy, she was twenty.'

'What's that got to do with it?'

'We weren't meant to know what was going on in her head. "I am capable of doing anything I want," she'd said. Eighteen, she was, when she told us that.' It was terrifying to be reminded of her pronouncements, which sounded normal and precocious before but sent us further into the discovery of our ignorance, how little we knew about her.

I'd emptied her room where there was no sign of those poems. I didn't tell Joy and Jim what Maeve had said.   There was no need to raise any more unsubstantiated theories of what she had or had not shared with us. I could imagine their response; 'But she hated poetry!'   Alone I put all her possessions into cardboard boxes. They were piled in her room in this house, in Waterbeach.

'She was one of a crowd of us,' the boy said. 'We didn't know her that well.'

Tom, Rick, Harry, Freddie and Debs; 'We've always done things together, the five of us' the girl said, the one who'd agreed that we should meet. 'We came up at the same time but it was only recently we gelled.'

'Lottie was a new recruit, sort of,' Tom was the other spokesperson. 'She was keen to become part of the Anti Poll Tax demos in the autumn term. That's something we were organising in Cambridge.'

'She came on the big London demonstration in March, and then sort of stayed with us,' Debs said.

'It's been since Christmas.'

'Not all the time. Lottie was a worker, she was always working,' Tom said.

I'd asked them to meet me in a pub. 'It's not an interrogation,' I'd said. 'I, we, want to have all the memories that we can gather of Lottie.'

Tom introduced each of them. Harry and Rick could not look at me, drank quickly, wanting to be anywhere other than sitting at that table. Freddie watched all our movements and me, watched and said nothing.

'I'm pleased to know you, to learn more about Lottie, just to know. It's a harrowing time,' I said.

'It's terrible,' Debs said, clutching her glass with both hands. 'It must be dreadful for you.'

There was a murmur of agreement round the table. These clever young things, apparently so articulate, struggling for appropriate words where there are none.

'Yes, it is,' I said, 'and incomprehensible.'

I'd chosen a pub in Grantchester where on this May morning we could sit in the garden. Honeysuckle climbed through a trellis behind us, the scent and the buzz of the first bees another reminder that I had to remember life moved on.

'We were surprised that she'd been drinking,' I said. 'Did she often come with you to a pub?'

'Suppose so. I mean, yes, that's where we'd usually meet. Though not in Trumpington.'

'It was a treat, Freddie's birthday.'

Freddie closed his eyes; a thin young man, his face shrunk to an almost skull like appearance and pallor.

'Oh, I'm sorry,' I said.

'Lottie was very serious, passionate about the Poll Tax thing, wrote letters and stuff,' Tom said.

'I don't know why she did it,' Debs said. 'I don't remember her being unhappy or anything when she left us.'

'She left the pub before you?' I said.

'I don't honestly remember exactly,' Tom said. 'It's just like she went without us knowing. None of us saw that she'd gone.'

'It was often like that,' Debs said.

I didn't want to hear this, that nobody had seen her distress, no one came close enough to care that she was there or not, or suspected that she was so unhappy that she didn't want to live any more.

'What are you reading?' I said to Freddie. I thought to take the pressure away.

'Was,' he said, a hoarse whisper which broke to a cough. 'We've just sat our finals.'

'Of course.'

I looked at them all, tried to think kindly, not be the bleating mother wanting to shout and curse them for neglecting her daughter, weep and weep for her little one who should have been able to do that too, finish her education, obtained a degree. My clever child.

'My degree is in Classics,' Freddie said.

I could have asked about his intended career which would have been to continue the polite conversation I'd begun. I merely nodded.

'None of us were studying mathematics,' Debs said. 'We're all from different disciplines. I'm going on to journalism.'

I tried to look as if it mattered but wanted to say, 'I'm not interested in your future, not at all.' Instead I said; 'Were you all on bicycles that night? Did you all ride to the pub?'

'No,' Tom looked around at the others. 'Rick's got a car, we went with him, and Freddie came on his motorbike. And there were more of us but I don't know how they got there. It was just a crowd, the usual crowd.'

'Did you know that she was riding her pedal bike?' I said.

'That's what she always did,' Debs said. 'You know what she thought about petrol and the environment.'

'Didn't you offer to bring her on your pillion, Freddie?' Tom said.

'No,' Freddie shook his head, his pale face rising to a rash of red; I wondered if it was with embarrassment or he was forcing back tears. He'd drunk none of his beer.

'Did you know that Lottie wrote poetry?' I said.

They looked from one to the other and all shook their heads. There was a pause, an awkward silence, interrupted by an uproar of sparring dogs. Above the clamour, Tom said: 'Was it our fault?'

'No, you are not to blame in any way,' I said. 'Please don't think that.'

'Thank you,' he said and they all nodded an almost audible sound of their relief.

The pub garden was filling up, shrill voices of children, brash laughter; we sat awkwardly as if I was the grown up who needed to give them permission to leave.

'I don't know that there's anything else we can tell you, Mrs Salway,' Tom said. 'But we're pleased to have met you and to tell you how desperately sorry we are.' He was a bland young man with the grace and etiquette of the 'well born', assuming I was married. This incident would be forgotten, maybe remembered if some other tragedy should befall him in future. Or if his train were ever delayed.

We all stood, a fumbled farewell, everyone of them relieved that it was over, they could get on with their lives.

And Freddie. He walked away with them but then turned and came back. 'She didn't tell me she wrote poetry,' he said; 'I wish she had'.

'I wish that too,' I said

'That's, Lottie. Always unexpected.'

'Yes, she is, was,' feeling the pain of the altered tense.

He seemed stronger now that we were alone, more mature than the others, able to meet my gaze. 'It's hard to find words,' he said.

'It is, and the bits in between.'

'Yes. That's rather what Lottie once told me; that 'Waiting for Godot' was about the value of silence, what was happening in that space between.' His sharp features seemed to relax, the memory a balm. 'She liked to provoke a discussion; maybe she was serious.'

The air stirred around us; she had never mentioned him, this angular young man, shoulders sharp boned inside a thin tee shirt. I wanted to ask what else, what more. But I was afraid of frightening off this young colt. The sun cut square shadows of trellis fencing on the table in front of us, flies already finding the half finished drinks. It was as if we were waiting for a director's instruction, to break the pause, move on, to cut. A woman nudged past us trying to ease into the seats we'd vacated.

'I am pleased to have met you all,' I said. 'I hope I haven't upset you.' That's all I could hope for.

'Oh no!' he said. 'It was dreadful when I found out; meeting you has helped.' He engaged my eyes fully behind his round wired framed glasses . 'She was so proud of you, Ms Salway, but you will know that. And if it doesn't sound presumptuous, I knew she was a loved child.'

'Really?' For a moment it stung, a shock; had he said 'love child'?

'She was always certain, certain of what she wanted,' he carried on; 'a remarkable young woman. I am desperately sad, always will be. I am so sorry.'

'Thank you, Freddie.' All my strict censure on emotion shattered; there was a tight pain crushing my ribs, a welling in my throat. I swallowed hard; 'I hope we meet again some time.'

'Me too,' he said and leant forward to give me an awkward hug. He waited while I picked up my bag and we walked back to the car park without another word. There was his sleek black motorbike, helmet, gloves and jacket stowed on the back.

I turned to go but heard him call to me; 'I'm gay, you know.'

1990

The Funeral

'She was everything to us,' Joy said. 'That's what we'll say.'

I was preparing to speak at Lottie's funeral.

'Think of some stories to tell,' I said to Joy.

This was therapy.

For the two months before the inquest, Joy and I continually, bleakly, trawled through what we knew, looking for clues; why had it come to this? Our part in Lottie's suicide; what had we done or not done to cause her to take her life? Never in front of Jim and never overtly to each other but we knew that a reason needed to be found for the inexplicable. We nudged at things said, done; times, places and actions. Thankfully, Joy never referred to Lottie's unknown father though I was sure she harboured a belief that it contributed in some way. I didn't tell her what Freddie had said; speculation on why he'd told me that he was gay seemed irrelevant. Whatever I might imagine or try to reason of their friendship made no difference; she was gone.

Her funeral though, the body released in June, must be a celebration of her life, of that we were sure.

'Well, you've got the one about the peas in her knickers,' Joy said. Jim brightened, retold the story as if we'd not been there at the time.

'And what about when she caught her leg on barbed wire trying to rescue a pony,' I said. That was the scar on her knee, still there when everything else was crushed, not that I could tell them. 'Do you remember, she phoned me accusing you of trying to kill her with a poultice.' I'd wanted to make them smile.

'That was when she'd crawled under the fence to feed the horses,' Jim said, 'when I'd told her not to.' His face clouded, stricken with the memory of telling her not do something, and then being cross that she did.

'We weren't paragons and nor was she,' I said.

I got up and went to them, side by side on the sofa. 'You were and are the best, for her and for me. You will never think anything other than that, will you, please?' I leant over them, kissed each on the cheek, caught by the closeness of the two of them and the separateness of me.

Lottie wasn't a hugger, she was a slippery child escaping hands and holding. 'No slobby kisses, please.' She was a chatterer; words came easily with the stream of thoughts and questions. But she would sit, quiet and close to watch the pictures and words in books. Looking up at our lips and down at the page; 'Again,' she'd say. Which is why when they talked of her difficulty with reading at the age of eight we were mystified.

She studied what she wanted to study, avidly. 'She's rather an intense child, isn't she?' was a remark made by a Sunday School teacher; a criticism rather than praise.

'Do you remember Lottie's arguments at Sunday School?' I said.

'About the Holy Ghost?' Jim nodded. 'She said; "That lady told me that there was a ghost with holes in. And I know she's wrong because you've told me, there aren't such things as ghosts."'

Joy managed to smile; 'Lottie'd never keep these things to herself. She said to me; "I told Mrs Whatshername that it wasn't true, just like that silly bit about three people all in one. "I've never seen anyone with three heads, six arms and six legs, have you, Grandma?" is what she said.'

'I'm not sure I can tell that one in church, Joy.'

"Course you can!"

Memories kept us going.

When Lottie was eleven she often came to London for weekends and holidays. I was with Max, struggling between wanting more and less. To have my daughter with me was a kind of bulwark against making the decision to end the affair. And she was fun. Not in a frivolous, let's-go-shopping, funfairs, Top of the Pops, kind of fun. She was seriously interested in the way the world worked. She wanted to look around the bits of London that were less known; Highgate Cemetery, the Old Bailey, all the museums. I was pleased but Joy said; 'Isn't it a little macabre? Take her to a nice musical, Greta.' At the time I put it down to jealousy that made Joy think like that. I was pleased that my intense child viewed everything as an important project.

Was I wrong?

Lottie had been the sole focus of attention, for the three of us, the only child we had to love. No one suggested she needed a sibling, that I should have another child, despite Joy hinting at marriage from time to time. 'That policeman? It must be difficult to have time together with his job.' Of Colin; 'He must be going up in the world.' She never met either of them nor Max. 'This theatre man; do you want to bring him home?' And when Paul forced himself upon us she said; 'Paul's a bit fly-by-night, isn't he?' We always laughed, Jim and I. At the age of ten Lottie said; 'I think

Grandpa's the only man we'll ever love.' It was another of those chances when I could have said something, or could I? How do you explain the vagaries of your own love life to anyone else, let alone your child?

Douglas wanted to speak at the funeral. I was pleased. He asked me if there was anything special he'd like me to say that he and Audrey wouldn't have thought of.

'No, Douglas,' I said. 'You were very important to Lottie. She once said; "It's like playing ping pong with Douglas. Whenever I bat an idea or an argument to him, he always pings it back. Most annoying!"'

'I like that,' he said. 'But it was in fact the other way round. I frequently found that I'd no way of returning the ball.'

I went to see Lottie in her coffin at the undertakers a few days before the funeral. They had somehow 'dressed' her in a huge tee shirt I'd found with the slogan 'Ban the Bomb' which she would have liked. Her childhood counterpane covered the rest of her blitzed body. I stroked her arm, the one not chewed up by the train. It was like cool wax but she was still my daughter. I smoothed her hair, no longer the colour of a summer harvest. I thought of what she would have been wearing the evening she went to that pub. Jeans as she was riding her bike, and her rainbow striped leggings which she loved; a tee shirt and the leather jacket I'd bought for her nineteenth birthday, a treasured possession. They were rescued with her, the fragments, merely as evidence.

This will be a celebration we kept saying. We'd put a notice in The Cambridge Evening News with the date of her death and funeral. I couldn't think who would see it and know Lottie; her 'friends' at university would all have gone down. The service would be in the Waterbeach Parish Church, conducted on as humanist lines as possible. Joy and Jim were still believers in their practical sociable way and as Joy said; 'A funeral is as much for the living as for the dead.' It cost her a lot to say that. We chose their favourite hymns, and John Lennon's 'Imagine' that, I felt, was written for Lottie. As we walked into the church that song was played, and then again at the end of the service as we followed her out.

Her coffin was topped with a bunch of flowers from the garden, aquilegia, purple geranium, the first rose buds and even cow parsley. 'These are what she would have wanted,' Jim said. Cut in the morning, kept in a bucket of water until the last moment, they amazingly lasted until they went down with her into a hole in the ground.

How could we bear it? I knew I must stay strong for Lottie, and for Jim and Joy who sat through the service for, to stand would have been to fall. Heart stopping grief, anguish washing in to fill and overwhelm, had to be blocked out.

And then, as sometimes miraculously happens, sorrow was lifted out to bring a moment of elation. As the coffin was born up, to be processed down to the open door, the music filling and floating above us, a shaft of rainbow light, stained by the west window, washed over the aisle. And as I turned, shepherding Joy and Jim, there they were, all of them, a crowd of people who'd cared to come and say farewell. The church full, for Lottie. And amongst them I thought I saw Freddie.

What came after on that day I've buried along with her. The journey to the cemetery and letting her go, the wake at our house in Waterbeach, Joy would have seen to that. But what lived with me, for a long time after, was the disquiet of not knowing whether it was him or not that I'd seen, the young man who'd told me he was gay. And why it mattered.

Back in London I stared at the walls of my flat, opened and closed the fridge, leant on the lintel of her bedroom but could not go in; I walked out along pavements, on and round and back, saw nobody, nothing. Was there sound, did people speak, was the sun shining? I knew none of it. I wanted none of it. My body numb, the hurt in my head and heart a slab of unrelenting ache, a sickening void. Loss, a falling away of all that was good, that I should have held on to. That I'd let go, failed, felled me; I should have been there to tell her 'no', don't, to lift her up away from that rail. Lottie, Lottie, let me make it better.

Leo said; 'I'm not asking for a book, I just want to see you.'

'I'm okay,' I'd say, each time he phoned. 'Give me time and I'll be at it again.'

'No, not 'at it', with us. No writing, there's no need for writing, it's you I want, your presence.'

'I'm busy,' I'd say.

'Not too busy to see your old renegade, who's wilting away without the warmth of your presence.'

'Soon,' I'd say.

I'd had to go, go and shield myself. The leather hide, the brute armour I'd adopted all these months was frayed, battered; I was blistered and raw. Joy and Jim would have to look after each other. Paul had moved out while I was in Waterbeach. I wanted no one. I was alone, as utterly alone as I'd been all those years ago when I first knew of the little floating creature who'd come to invade my womb and there'd been no one else to tell. The void gaped, sucked and spat. Dreams flew in nightmare garb; I was always running, chasing, screaming. Lottie called, came and retreated, a fleeting evanescence. I picked up my pen, and wrote. And it was a sort of poetry that came to explain, to explore who or what or where I was, to try for the balm of words.

> I sit on the edge of the grave laying out
> my bones, the runes of a previous existence
> soundless witness to marvel
> at the symmetry of their construction.

I drove up to Wells-Next-the Sea. The sky as wide and high as I remembered, the depth of blue sky, the puffs of white cloud that might have tricked me; but no, happy times were gone. I wanted grey, blasting rain and wind, the sea to churn and boil deep oil green. If I'd had courage I would have tried those tides, the swelling roll of solid weighty water, the run in, urgent, fast and flat, a relentless force to pull me in, drag me out. I sat on the sea wall as dusk drew the owls to circle and swoop, their cries as eerie as the silent scurry of creatures in the grasses below. What did I know of them, or they of me?

> I see rose red petals fall, unopened buds droop, wither
> their shrivelled flesh turning and churning
> to sweeten the black compost, reaching
> into other roots and serving other seeds.

Lottie's grave was a mound of earth, grass would come later. I knew that Joy and Jim would be taking flowers every week, if not daily. Jim told me when I phoned one evening; 'I took her some strawberries from the garden today. Her favourites.' Joy came after him; 'She'd be pleased to share them with the birds and rabbits, wouldn't she?' They were coping better than me.

> *I lift out my head and shake free all thoughts to hustle*
> *into rough heaps and moulder down. My epitaph*
> *I wipe clean to a clarity as crisp as the crescent cut*
> *moon that stares from a star banked sky.*

> *I leave only a faint shadow on other memories.*

Leo came to my door. 'The mountain coming to Mohammed,' he said. He'd never visited my flat. 'I knew that man wasn't here any more, so thought I'd venture forth.'

'You never liked Paul, did you?' I said.

'I don't have opinions on your men, Greta. Well, not that I express until you've done the best thing possible, shown them the door.' Lightly said, but he was looking at me carefully, eyeing up the state of the flat. We were neat and tidy. It was the inside of my head and heart tearing me to shreds.

I said; 'I'm lost, Leo. I don't believe in salvation, that anything is meant to be, all done for a purpose, some good will come from it, all that rubbish. Being brave doesn't come into it; you scream and tear clothes, or stay still, breathing in and out as gently as possible.'

'Yes,' he said.

'I'll come back soon.'

'Of course,' he said. 'And old Brendan sends his love and says hold on.'

> *I watch fate bristle along the pathways searching*
> *me out but I have cut the strings and the soles*
> *of my feet rest easy in the square cut hole*
> *six by six, that I have dug in the ground.*

I drove down to walk with Audrey and Douglas on the Downs. Winding through single lane roads, villages, hamlets, sheep and horses, the perfect backdrop; cottages that were the English idyll, thatched, gabled, red roses round the door; I knew that this wasn't the place for me and perhaps that's what I'd passed on to Lottie; the need for something grittier, the disbelief in a romantic ending. That I wrote novels about crime had been Angus' idea but perhaps he saw I was suited to a world that was darker, seamier. I loved poetry but would choose Sassoon and Owen over Brooke, and I saw here in front of me as I drove what Goldsmith wrote of in the eighteenth century; 'The Deserted Village'. Who did own these cosy cottages, these swathes of land?

I drove on and on as far as the coast, bitter and desolate, a grey sky folding in the land and sea, the horizon blurred. I phoned Douglas and Audrey to say I'd been delayed and would come another day.

> Breathless I shout through the slit window far
> above my mind, 'I am in control; no more
> dancing to confusion, no more buffers or boundaries
> to tend. I have called time.'

Dora phoned me each week after the funeral; 'Are you up for a glass, love?'

'Not yet,' I'd say.

She didn't ask why.

> Then a wind comes to snaffle up the endless words
> that have gone before and between, whirling them
> about my ears. Senseless I feel the celandines stir
> effortlessly below as the worms wind trails reworking.

Leo said; 'I'm cooking supper; me with chopping board and skillet. You have to come.'

And he was right; I had to go. Leo was incapable of producing food that required sharp knives, hot fat. I didn't think he possessed a chopping board, except perhaps when slicing lemon for gin and tonic, and I was sure he'd never seen a skillet. I had to go.

I am caught on the promise that I must come back.

1994

Beached boats

Jim was like a beached boat; water gone, the flood and flow lost to him but still upright, a proud vessel with rigging stowed, a sharp outline against the sky, all visible, standing on his keel waiting for the freedom of water. I watched that tide going out, pulling the sandy mud, dragged and drawn ripples, scallops gouged and ruffled. Bereft. Lottie had been the tide coming in.

He and Joy shared the bleak landscape of loss, consoling without specifying, a routine redefined. Gardening was a comfort, memories of vegetables nurtured and culled with Lottie, flowers to garland her grave. That he lived on ten years after her death, at ninety-two dying one night without fuss or explanation, was his own miracle. It was January 6th, 2000; he'd seen in the new millennium. He hadn't needed to tell us that he was tired out.

After he died, Joy and I stopped searching for reasons for Lottie's death. At last we accepted that what we had done, or not done, didn't ease the sorrow.

Joy and I bore Jim's death with fortitude; his expression. Each birthday after his eightieth he'd say; 'Luck's on my side if I last another year, with a few prayers, of course, and the love of my women.'

Joy tutted about 'my women' but any small banter kept them going. Kept me from tears too.

He ran the whole of life's course, no need for an inquest, witness statements, an open verdict. Nothing to leave unproven.

Lottie's death was so different; too young, too soon, beyond reason. Her case came up at the coroner's court in the September after her death. No clear evidence of intention to commit suicide could be found, nothing explicit; health, mental anguish, a note. The question would hang over the rest of our lives, but would a certainty have helped? Murder or accident would have been harder to bear, I'm sure of that; Lottie's choice, though still carrying a freight of guilt for us, was preferable to someone else's deed.

The statements from her friends at University were exactly what I expected. Freddie slept at the pub as he was too drunk to drive home, witnessed by the landlady. The others left after the time of Lottie's death. They all said that there was nothing wrong with her that evening, no sign she was unhappy. They agreed that Lottie wasn't that sort of person; she was always in control of herself, never appeared to need or ever asked for anything. No one had seen her leave the pub. She didn't say 'goodbye'.

However she was seen cycling along the road to Foxton Station by the passengers of a car parked in a layby. The woman said; 'Her light came wavering along the road; it was eerie, we wondered what it could be. She was all over the place. I said to my boyfriend that she looked like she'd have an accident, fall off her bike.' He'd said; 'We didn't think or know that we should stop her, how could we, I mean you can't interfere and by the time we'd have caught up, I don't know what we'd have done? Nobody came along the road after her.'

The poems of love might not have existed. The girl, Maeve, hadn't mentioned them in her statement. There was no proof that they'd been written. Until I spoke to Freddie many years later.

Autumn ended on a slow burn, the last orange-gold leaves on the birches across from my flat, blown free to leave their parent stark and cold. I watched them day after day, talking to Lottie. I said; 'I will understand that for you it was the right decision and will bear it.' As much as is possible to believe, I heard her reply. 'Yup, get on with it, Mumma. It's what I wanted.'

All this was behind and before me in 1994. I was forty-four when I met Michael, with eleven books published, and had begun work on 'The Cat's Cradle Chronicle'. The research was complete, a plot sketched, my study awash with notes pinned to a corkboard on my study wall, notebooks full. I had to go on, no choice. I wanted no one else in my life, thought I never would. I didn't want the triviality, as I saw it. Assessing my previous lovers, passing fancies as I saw them, I didn't want the trouble of men's whims or deceit; nothing, no one would touch my heart ever again. So four years later why him, I wonder? Stop gap? An antidote? That I include him here, an incidental, is because he was a man of boats, coping with the tides of grief. And at that time, the unremitting dreams of Lottie, there and not there, coming to me and never able to stay, always out of reach, became less relentless; my grief eased, became a part of me. And I found another train track, a disused line, to walk with Lottie, imagined a child, and wrote a short story which was magical and real, written for a lost daughter.

Michael was grieving when I met him at a party for my publisher's birthday; Larry was sixty, the firm twenty-five. 'A quarter of a century, Greta, that's not bad,' Larry said, 'even if we're going to have to amalgamate with the big bastards before the year's out. They want my stars, you being one of them.'

Michael was a friend from their days in the Royal Navy. 'It's the Queen Larry and I served, not some tinpot shipping company. The white ensign was the only flag we sailed under.' He was bleary with drink and sorrow and I was one of the few prepared to listen; to talk is prescribed as the best therapy, even though I was adverse to indulging myself, closed inside an indestructible shell. His pomposity amused, though I must admit to watching the clock, drinking more than usual and regretting it in the morning.

'Maggie was a live wire, into everything; take on any battle to win. We thought she'd beat the bastard cancer, did all the treatments, positive, proactive; it was wrong that she lost. Cervical, it's the worst. Comes at you before you know it's there. She was only fifty-three, no age to die.'

We were hedged into a corner of the hotel salon, which is how Larry had described it. 'The management call it a Function Room, but my secretary's hired those poof people who tart a place up; it'll look lush.' And it did. The scent of lilies drenched the air so that I feared for anyone suffering with allergies. The chairs were velvety green, plump and low, an elegant trap for those who dared to sit down, which, of course, we did.

My original intention had been to arrive at the party when most guests would be in place, tour the room discreetly and leave after an hour. I needed an early night; 'Shall I Wake You, Baby?' had come back from the printer for checking; I needed to get it to Leo before the end of the week. It was Tuesday, November 5th, Guy Fawkes and his mates roaming the streets, fireworks causing mayhem.

Michael said; 'I used to have a lovely lab, as sturdy a dog as you'll ever see, came out on the boat with me, no fear of the water, welcomed strangers, a bit soppy really, but fireworks set her off. Couldn't control the shakes, sad to see her like that. Which is why I hate tonight and what it represents, whatever your politics, and I'm not political. Whatever government you've got, well, if you've been in the Services, Maggie used to say, you have to be above all that.'

As if from another island, in the centre of the room, a rousing, 'For he's a jolly good fellow,' broke out followed by someone shouting 'Hurrah' and 'Here's to you, Larry. Everyone raise your glasses!' Grasping the non-existent arms of our seats, swivelling and heaving ourselves out, Michael and I struggled to a swaying standing stance to join in the toast as requested. Solemnly we lifted our glasses to find no wine but down his elegant white tuxedo and shirt bloomed blossoms of a shade between pink and maroon.

'Oh my God,' Michael burst into great guffaws of laughter, 'what a waste!'

'Oh no,' I said, 'Was that me?'

'You and me, both I think, a joint effort.'

'I'm so sorry,' but I had to laugh, laughter that we couldn't stop.

'So you should be, that was a half decent Beaujolais,' his voice a strangled squeak.

Doubled over like a pair of kids, giggling hysterically so that we could hardly draw breath, we turned our backs on the rest of the crowd. 'Where's a waiter?' Michael cried, 'where's a top up when you most need it? A chap may have had an untimely accident at a lady's hand but ...' and he flung his hand up as if to call a cab.

After that, when we'd recovered our decorum he said; 'Where do you hail from?' which set us off laughing again.

We didn't leave together although he tried to persuade me that being out alone on 'a night like this with idiots brandishing fireworks as lethal weapons' was not advisable. He wondered if I'd like him to walk me anywhere, which I declined. I took a taxi to placate him, though thinking that a crisp dark night with a few ghouls and the smell of cordite on the air might be an antidote to the contrasting moods of the evening.

When I dropped the printer's copy with Leo later that week he said; 'That was some tête à tête, darling. Such charity listening to that man. You'll have jumped a few places in St Peter's queue at the Pearly Gates, I'd say. He'll let you through right away.'

'You mean at Larry's party, Michael whatever his name?'

'Michael Fitzherbert Smith, Greta. Minor aristocracy, though a runt in the family's opinion, I've heard.'

'How do you know all this stuff, Leo?'

'Ear to everyone's door, sweetie, and mixing with the best, always. If you're not one of them, a full-blooded heterosexual, you have to know it all. Be astride the horse before they've put their jodhpurs on.'

I laughed at the idea of Leo facing up to a horse, let alone mounting it, but it was also one of the few times I heard him express bitterness; sarcasm and playful innuendo were normal, this was different.

'Is he someone to avoid, Leo?'

'Darling, me give you advice about men?' he twirled a circle in his swivel chair stopping elegantly to lean across his desk and say; 'He's no worse than the rest of them. In fact, I've an inkling this Maggie woman did wonders for him, smoothed the scratchy edges, plumped up his ego and left him a pile of dosh.'

'Larry told me he writes children's novels. Any good?'

'Oh dear, that's a whole other story. Think Enid Blyton crossed with Arthur Ransome. For a while he was quite popular, bought for nostalgia, the Granny market, Christmas trade. There were a series of six, I think. Larry wasn't his publisher, of course, even though they're friends. Ask him sometime.'

'Am I interested?' I said.

I was for a while. After that first encounter he proved to be an amusing companion, easy going, undemanding, with a boat in the Solent where he'd take me to sail. I've sometimes wondered whether the fifteen year gap in our ages was a pull; a throwback to my romance with Gerald. So different though, for he admired the popularity that my writing brought, was pleased to lurk on the edges of any publicity parties, being jolly though never proprietorial. Perhaps we both knew that we were stop gaps; me for Maggie, and he for someone I thought I'd never meet, never wanted to meet.

'Why choose this place?' I asked him.

'It's quiet, not too uppity.'

This was the village of Langstone on the south coast, with a previous reputation for smuggling, once upon a time. Michael was a 'once upon a time' man.

'I'd thought you'd need somewhere with more water for the yacht,' I said. It was June of that first year together.

'The big boat's gone, too much for me to handle on my own,' he said. 'Yachts are for youngsters.' Which relieved me of any thought that I might have to share the sea for company. 'The cottage with dinghy is going to suit me fine. I can be up and on the water before you can hang the seaweed out.'

'But you used to go off to France and Cowes, all those kind of jaunts,' I said. 'Won't you be frustrated with such a limited horizon?' We were sitting outside a pub surveying the mudflats, the tide having gone out leaving a minimal channel of water.

'It'll do me fine. There's the flat in London when I'm bored. I'll be like royalty, the winter palace and summer residence.' Wearing baggy Aertex, shabby shorts, his bronzed arms and thighs so hairy you wanted to stroke, he was the image of sweet content.

As we looked out a layer of shell pink cloud deepened to hot orange, the blue retreating to dissolve through to a purple black. The accidental magic of clouds reflecting the setting sun was the perfect aphrodisiac. We became lovers that night; a comfortable bed with duvet, no frills. He was as experienced as me; it was not hard to find mutual satisfaction.

Over a hearty breakfast next day he said; 'And I'm well away from them here.'

'Who?'

'Relatives; got the same taste for the rolling waves and a decent horse's neck but otherwise nothing; a snotty crowd. Want to avoid them if I can.'

'But ...'

'Maggie's death brought them up from the bilges, ignored us before. Sympathy of the wrong sort's a killer.'

I was intrigued but knew what he meant. If he was the 'black sheep' of the family as Leo intimated, the others sounded rotten. He was a thoroughly decent man; 'decent' was a word he used frequently of other people, other things, and he was generous though never flaunting the rumoured wealth.

Ours was an easy friendship; sleepovers, never living together, fancy meals out. 'You can't beat good nosh,' he'd say. Theatre would have to be a straight play, music of the 60's and I learnt to sail though he knew that I preferred dry land. His was an unwavering fatherly support. When Jim died he neither fussed nor belittled my loss.

Joy was pleased that I'd taken on a 'bereaved soul' as she put it, though Michael rarely indulged in reminiscences of Maggie, or his marriage. It was years later, soon after Jim died, when they actually met at a book launch and I found them, he and Joy, huddled in a corner, as we had been that first evening. 'You've done a good job there, lovey.'

'In what way?' I said.

'Oh, just that he was able to talk like he still loved her, didn't need to hide it. Nothing worse than having it all bottled inside you.'

'No,' I said, 'nothing worse.'

'And I'm the lucky one too, all my friends from church to talk to, all of them knowing Jim, all those years. All those years, we were the lucky ones.'

The words were poison, a seeping sickening which I knew I ought not to feel. Poor little me was only part of it. 'All those years' were pure loss for me. Worse, though, was to realise that I'd never wanted, been able, to share Lottie, had guarded her from all of those men; didn't think that I'd ever wish to allow anyone near my remembrance of her.

My visits to his 'summer residence' began intermittently; work and Waterbeach took precedence. At first the sailing was a challenge and I liked the Grace Kelly image, dark glasses and wind in my hair. Michael assured me the sea was constantly changing; 'Alters on a whim, never the same,' but I rarely saw difference. His horizon was further out, pitting his craft against the elements, even when becalmed; mine was to the shore. I wanted to walk along the coast, beach-comb stones and shells, smell the seaweed, see how far I could go in either direction; taking paths inland, discovering other places. Those places as a writer I adopt; visual anchors,

I think. A landscape is my usual starting point; Larry once grumbled about this obsession. That disused railway line which once took holidaymakers from the mainland to an island, is where I walked most often. There, I found escape and comfort.

LOST

A pair of gloves left on a bench along a path open to the public, were not an unusual sight. Except that they appeared to be brand new. The woman picked one up; they were similar to her own, though the leather was softer, the stitching finer, large enough to belong to a man. A fine pair of gloves. Placing them back exactly as she'd found them, she hoped that whoever owned the gloves would realise where they'd been left and come to retrieve them. When they'd disappeared the next time she came that way, she thought nothing of it.

She often walked this trail, always alone. The old railway track was disused and reinvented to a wide gritted path. It started at the top, where once the level-crossing gates were in place and the rails curved to join the mainline, ending at the mudflats, the tidal channel bereft of a rail bridge, broken piles poking stark from the water, useless props describing the loss.

Loss she knew too well, worked with it, fended it off, wore a false face as armour to guard against pity or guilt. Here, as she walked, she was free to wallow, confront the hurt, count and court the memories.

In the summer when she'd first found the path there had been a profusion of grasses and flowers; cow parsley, speedwell, bird's foot trefoil and pussy willow, the names she remembered from her childhood. Their beauty, with the birds, bees and butterflies, company enough. But soon there were droves of walkers, with and without dogs, jovial greetings, comments on the weather; cyclists jangling their bells and hardly waiting for her to jump out of their way. She wasn't a recluse, her work required constant accommodation of other people, their desires, their needs. Here was timeout for a few hours, the solitude to leave the smile, allow the tears, so she began to come later and later until the evening, the twilight hour, was all her own, the fag end of the day.

Winter set in, dank, cold and drear, fallen leaves lying dark and shrivelled. The woman wore her thick coat, woolly hat, scarf, and leather gloves. The sun shone frail, never reaching the top of the sky, no warmth in it on the day when she saw and admired the gloves. And there was no mistaking that it was soon after they were taken, that the child came, a face peeping from behind a tree, a glimpse, drawing back and gone. Was it an illusion, the woman wondered, a trick of the light, fissures on the bark creating an image?

The following day when she saw a movement from the same tree, a peek and retreat, she called out; 'I've seen you!' so there could be no escape. The child crept round to lean against the tree trunk, eyes black beads. 'Who are you?' the woman said. The child shook her head. Judging the child's sex was guesswork based only on long uncombed curls; the coat and boots signifying neglect. 'Where are your parents?' the woman said for surely it was too late and the light too low for someone so small to be here alone, but the child turned and ran.

Frost came to crisp the grass, grip the ground tight from dawn to dusk when the woman walked again and there she found the child sitting on the bench.

'You been a long time.'

'What did you say?' the woman looked carefully to see that it was the same child. 'You spoke to me?'

'I been waiting for you. You taken them gloves.'

'What gloves?' though, of course, the woman remembered the ones that had lain there a few days back.

'Those you got on. You stole 'em.'

The woman held out her hands to show her own gloves. 'These are mine. I would never steal.'

'But I saw you pick 'em up from just here,' the child put her hand on the bench where the other gloves had been left.

'That's silly, I was merely looking; they were taken by someone else, the person who owned them, I imagine.'

'No, it were you, you with your red coat, and look, see, those are them gloves.'

'Them gloves, as you call them, belonged to a man, were much bigger than mine. And they were more expensive, I'm sure.'

The child jumped off the bench, stood tall, proud and pleased. 'Yes, they were special, very special. They were for him.'

'Who?'

'My Auntie made them for him.'

'Where is your auntie?' for, as before, the woman was worried to see this girl out so late and alone when it was almost dark.

The child stared but didn't answer.

'You shouldn't be here on your own,' the woman said but the child looked past her, blank and still. Annoyed the woman walked on, not only was her quiet hour disturbed, but also her mind. There was enough to worry about, enough to regret without adding strange neglected children. Her own child had never been neglected, never been out so late accosting strangers, never known anything except love, but she was lost. That was enough to cope with.

The woman avoided the trail for several weeks; tried to think of the incident as a childish game and yet, when going back to the old railway line, she was aghast to see the girl there, come as from nowhere, to stand blocking her way.

'Why are you here again?' the woman said. 'Did you find those gloves?

'No,' the child said. 'You got to give 'em back. They're a secret.'

The child's distress was obvious; those coal dark eyes were watery, causing the woman to feel pity, remembering her own child's tears, her inability to make her better.

'Little girl,' she said, 'I don't understand what you mean. Go home, it's too cold out here, too dark. Won't they wonder where you are at this time of day?'

'I'm not little. And I'm waiting for my Dada. He's on the train and it's coming soon.'

'At the station?' the woman said. 'So you'll need to go back that way.' She pointed up the line, circled round the child and strode on. It troubled her, though; the girl didn't seem normal and yet was as real as any other person she met on the trail.

It was a relief to find no one else there when the woman walked the next day. She'd argued with herself that the silly provocation of this child shouldn't upset her routine. Whatever prank the child was playing it needn't concern her.

Weeks went by, the length of the days increased, and there were a few more late walkers like the woman. Strangely, she began to be pleased with their occasional presence, passing her with a nod or a smile.

Celandines were wresting through the dead leaves, offering their metallic yellow flowers to the sun, when the child again appeared.

'My Auntie is crying like me,' the child greeted her at the top of the trail, close by the present train station. 'She says I done it and I won't be able to work at the factory. I want to make some pennies now my Dada's gone.'

'Your father? Where is he? Didn't he come on the train?' the woman said.

'No, you got that wrong. He's dead.'

The woman stared hard at the child. What could she say? Should she ask when it happened? The child wasn't unlike her own daughter at that age, eight or nine perhaps? But her child had been fair and smiling, this one dark and so shabby.

'He was the one what stoked the coal,' the child was saying, no longer upset. 'Showed me once, took me on the train, all the way down to the sea. Told me to mind the tracks, listen for the whistle.'

What on earth was the child talking about? Steam trains, with stokers, hadn't run on the mainline since the middle of the last century, let alone on this one; had she mistaken what the child had said?

'What do you mean? I don't understand. Trains aren't ...' but she stopped and asked instead; 'Where does your Auntie work?'

'Where they makes gloves. You see I know how to turn 'em, the gloves; Auntie brings them back from work for me to help her. She gets extra pennies for doing it, gives me some. It's not hard, I can do it easy.'

The woman knew of no such factory in the area; weren't most garments made in other countries by cheap labour nowadays; possibly by children of this child's age? She wished that someone else would come down the trail, someone to ask, but no one had ever come past when she was talking to the child.

'Why were the gloves lying on the bench?' she said. 'Did you put them there?'

'It was a present for him, like Auntie said.'

'Who's 'him'?' The woman decided it was better to hear it all, find out as much as she could. 'Your auntie's husband?'

'No, he's a soldier, and he loves her and he'll marry her too, after the war.'

The woman was about to ask which war, but surely the child wouldn't know and so said; 'This is a very strange story, and I'm sure you think it's true but it's late. Go home and I'll think about where the gloves have gone.'

The child screwed up her face, cocked her head on one side, the ratty pigtails she wore this day, lopsided. 'You'll give 'em back?'

'No, I haven't got those gloves but I'll make enquiries.'

'What's that mean? You're not to tell or I'll get in trouble. Don't tell!'

A streetlight lit up an orange glow out on the road running beside the trail, showing clearly terror in the child's eyes.

'No, of course not,' the woman said. 'I promise.'

A flicker of what might have been a smile lit the child's face. 'You promise,' she said and backed away.

The woman stood watching where the child was going but it was as if she'd merged into the thick hedge. Slowly the woman walked down to where she'd disappeared but there seemed to be no breaks in the bushes, no holes where she could have crawled through to the road on the other side.

Was there a home for disturbed children nearby? Ought she to have taken the girl to the police? Even made enquiries at the railway station?

That evening the woman visited one of the town pubs. It would be the best place for any gossip, information on local oddities. She'd been there for a meal once; the landlord might be willing to chat. In fact it was his wife, the barmaid, who was pleased with the company, priding herself on knowledge of the 'goings on' as she put it. 'There was a factory here that made gloves, famous too, customers were royalty; it was when posh women always wore gloves, whatever the weather. It closed back in the sixties, like most places down here. Shame; it was good work for women, a jolly place my Gran said. She worked there, was proud of what she did.' The woman didn't tell her about the child or about her ridiculous tale, and the landlord's wife knew nothing of 'homes for naughty children'. ' It's all this looking after your own now,' she said, 'no help from doctors or the social these days. Out in the community, well, that's a laugh!' There was more of that outburst but nothing to shed light on where the child might have come from.

The rain came, weeks of high wind and rain, trees torn up, twigs and branches strewn everywhere, no opportunity for a walk. The woman thought of the child, worried for her, surely she wouldn't be waiting on the trail? So she was relieved when at last a day came that was dry, although large puddles covered much of the ground. On each side of the trail, two streams ran helter-skelter; one flowed wide and clear, the other, though a dry ditch in summer, tripped and gurgled water on its way to the sea. Everything was alive amongst the skeletal trees, roots reaching down, shoots prising through, the remnants of last year shouldered aside, buds fattening up.

Above the noise the woman heard; 'You told! You didn't keep your promise, like you said.' The child was standing on stepping stones, water gushing around and on.

'No!' the woman said, though she felt uncomfortable remembering her discussion with the barmaid. 'Why would you think I did?'

The child scrambled up the bank onto the track. Her coat was soaked round the hem, her boots sodden and it was light enough for the woman to see her face, red swelling on her cheeks, one eye bruised and blackened.

'What's happened? Who did that to you?' She bent to examine the child; it was the closest she'd been and smelled a fusty though not unpleasant odour; the scent of old wood, fermenting apples. But the child drew back, her hands covering her face.

'She didn't mean to; said she was sorry. It's bad for her, him dying.'

'Who? Your father?'

The child screwed up her face in confusion or was it with grief? Tears swelled in her eyes, crept down her cheeks. 'It's her soldier man dying. He was nice, I saw them holding hands, walking, here,' she pointed to the ground, 'I knew the gloves was for him.'

'I'm sorry. How did he die?'

'The war, I told you.'

The light was sharply fading, the sound of the streams insistent. The child's desperation was tangible.

'What can I do?' the woman said.

'Give me them gloves.'

'I haven't got the gloves, I told you.' The woman put her hands in the pockets of her coat. 'The soldier must have taken them, that's what you wanted.'

'Yes,' it was a whisper. 'For him to have. I thought that's what Auntie'd want. I didn't know she'd took 'em and she'd be in trouble.' The child was shaking; was it the cold and damp of her clothes or the fear of what she'd done?

'You must go home, child. You're cold, you'll catch a chill. You said your auntie was sorry.'

The child looked startled, all tears gone.

'I'm sorry,' the woman said. 'You're too young to be burdened with such sadness.' What else could she say? What else could she do? 'Would you like me to see you home? All the light's gone.'

The child shook her head, drew back and back further down the trail.

That evening the woman tried to remember all that the child had told her, tried to make coherent what appeared to be nonsense. As she'd done so many times after her own child died, she gathered together what was believable, what was not. Here again nothing was comprehensible but she couldn't ignore the child. No longer was she angry at the intrusion, or worried that she was being tricked. The child's fear was genuine. Should she go to the police as she'd first *thought, thinking now of child abuse? But wouldn't that betray her promise?*

The next day she walked down the trail to the sea and then halfway back to sit on the bench. The noise of water was incessant but there was no sign of the child. This she repeated everyday for a week, at the weekend and then for two weeks after that. Feeling anxious and sad, the same feelings that had brought her to need her solitary walk, she went to the local police station. Standing outside she assembled the statement she would make, what she would ask them to do. Of course, it was crazy; there was nothing of substance to say, no evidence of any malpractice, apart from the apparent physical abuse of a child that she would find hard to describe and impossible to tell where it lived.

Later that evening the woman revisited the trail and the bench to find the child waiting for her.

'Thank goodness, you're here,' the woman said. 'Where have you been?'

The child shrugged.

'I thought I should give you these,' and the woman handed her own leather gloves to the child. 'Do you want them? I don't know how else to help you; will these do?'

The child nodded and took the gloves without a word and left, fading into the dark.

The woman sat alone for a long time, a moon rising up to blink through the tangle of trees, cool bright silver. How stupid and futile her action had been, she thought, and at the same time she wanted to laugh and to cry. Nothing was resolved and there was no one to tell. She would never tell. Whoever, whatever the child was, a promise was given not to be broken. Warmth and peace seeped through her as she sat alone that night.

The woman continued to walk the trail acknowledging those who passed her with a smile or comment, one way or the other. Each time she came to the bench she looked to see that it was empty. And it was a full six months later, when her story had begun to fade, that she saw them lying as the others had lain nearly a year before. Hesitantly she approached, looked carefully around to see if she was being watched and then picked one up. Turning it over and inside out there was no mistaking it was her glove, ordinary leather, not the finest skin, the stitching hidden, not proudly shown. She stood and remembered, wondered whether she should take them back. The track was silent, hushed as if holding its breath. The woman peeled off the woollen ones she'd bought as a replacement and put on her own leather gloves.

'Thank you,' she called to the child who was no longer there, the child who would never come again. 'Thank you.'

The story was never sent for publication. My own piece of therapy, remembering the essence of a place, a time, and the handsome gloves that lay forlorn on a bench and then were gone.

2002

Turmoil ensued

Which brings me back to the beginning in 2002 when meeting Gerald at the crime writers' social gathering in Cambridge appeared to trigger this whole catastrophe. Not to when it all went wrong, the worst calamity, for how can Lottie's death be right in any state of being? That was the greatest horror; my raison d'être was encapsulated in her life. Isn't that how all children become to their parents? Their loss a milestone which you can never skirt around, or want to. Their life and death colouring our blood, singing music through our souls, giving life meaning. I cannot think of it in any other way. As I continuously think and talk of her.

But that she had come and gone between when I had last seen him in 1969 and this unexpected encounter, was shocking. All the anguish of keeping secret his involvement in my pregnancy; I still shy away from admitting that he was her father. All those years of finding and abandoning other men, never finding love. All those years since her death of concentrating on honouring the life I'd been given by purposefully continuing the career I'd always craved. In one year from this point in time, turmoil ensued.

June

The University Arms

Leo said; 'I need food, Greta, real food.'

I must have raised my eyebrows because he went on to insist that 'soggy canapés and bits on sticks,' weren't enough to soak up all the 'dishwater wine'.

'You were the one who wanted to keep going for this extra,' I checked my watch, 'hour. It's 9 o'clock.' I was ready for an early night. What Leo calls schmoozing I refer to as prostitution. 'No, no, that's too brutal, darling,' he's told me; 'a social evil which is regarded as trade.'

Boring though it was, I'd stayed upright, ignored several catty remarks born out of jealousy, bitten back to the most objectionable, and suffered that weird exchange with Gerald. I was exhausted.

But Leo pleaded; 'I need a juicy steak or even a mess of creamy chicken. Body and soul, Greta, body and soul.'

So it was after 11.00 p.m. when we swung through The University Arms doors to collect our keys at reception in a merry mood after 'a commendable bottle of claret,' and if it hadn't been for Leo fussing with the man behind the desk about whether his room faced on to Parker's Piece or 'the bowels of your hotel's internal workings,' he wouldn't have found us.

'Greta, and Leo, isn't it?'

Gerald stood, empty glass in hand, beaming down at us. He does have the advantage of height.

'Are you staying here?' Leo's question sounded like an accusation.

'Yes, last minute change of plan. The place they'd booked me into was too pokey.' He smiled at me, that shamefaced, poor-little-me expression I remember so well. It went with the extravagant phrases of needy lover; 'You're the one I want to run away with, climb moor and mountain, lie beneath larch trees, the sky a dazzling lapis lazuli,' or something similar. It was self indulgent to be fooled back then but it had fuelled the silly daydreams I'd allowed myself. 'What about the Isle of Skye?' he'd say and answer himself with, 'No, no, too cold, too forlorn. Dubrovnik, Bologna, Padua? Renaissance Italy, that's where we'll go, Greta. We're Renaissance people.' On and on the apologetic swoony voice fading as the kisses stopped my mouth and our bodies moved together on that grubby sofa.

'The bar's closed I'm afraid,' he now said, 'but what about a drink in my room? I'm sure there's a mini-bar.' The last comment directed at the receptionist who nodded a 'yes, sir.'

'Gerald, it is Gerald, isn't it?' Leo said. 'Too late for me, I fear, eaten and drunk enough for tonight.'

I wished he'd said 'us' but he's far too egalitarian.

'I'd have joined you,' Gerald said as if he'd refused our invitation.

'Too bad.' Leo sounded positively hostile.

How had he found us, I wondered. Then I remembered Leo's throwaway line about meeting later and mentioning the name of the hotel; now Gerald wasn't to be put off.

'Had to settle for a ghastly pizza,' he was saying. 'Funds aren't what they used to be.' He was always good at the suffering martyr.

I wanted to say; 'Really, Gerald,' as I don't remember any extravagant dining back in 1969. Had we ever eaten together apart from the college canteen?

'Greta, you'll come and join me in a nightcap won't you? So much to catch up on.'

'No' should have been my immediate answer. I'd cast off his spell as well as poetry back in 1976 with Angus, dear Angus.

'Come on, just one.' His mouth, I saw, hadn't changed, the full lips, their tendency to smile even when pathos was the mood he wanted to evoke.

'A cup of tea?' I said.

His room certainly wasn't overlooking the park; a tiny single which if the curtains had been open and it hadn't been dark, would have revealed the well below accommodating the refuse bins.

As he opened the door to usher me through, I thought of Bluebeard. Would he lock me in? How many other rooms contained his ex-student lovers? What idiotic pride, curiosity or weakness had brought me here, I didn't know.

'Take the chair, Greta.' He beamed, as at a trophy he wanted to cherish. 'Sorry it's a bit meagre. Laura's very tight with money these days. Pathetic really.' His wife was the one with wealth; I always knew that. Only once had I visited his home where he did live an elegant lifestyle, if the furnishings were anything to go by.

'You're not serious about the cup of tea, are you?'

'Yes, thank you.'

'Oh, I thought that was a cover for that Leo man.'

'Leo is my valued agent,' I said, 'but he dictates nothing in my life except to encourage the best price for my work.'

'Oh, God, I didn't mean …' but he was crouching in front of the mini-bar, his attention entirely focused on the alcohol content. 'Look,' he sprang up with an agility I had to admire, 'two tiny bottles of whisky. Come on, perfect night caps.'

He grinned as at an accomplice. 'You know I was always keen on a wee Scotch at the end of a hard day.'

'That isn't something I remember, Gerald. But if that's easier than tea, I'll accept.'

'Sweet girl,' and he positively pounced on the two glasses which were more suitable for soaking false teeth overnight, unscrewed the bottle tops and poured our drinks. 'To the past, Greta, happy times.'

'Cheers, Gerald.' Easier to respond neutrally.

He perched on the bed, the glass cradled in both hands, head bent forward. What was I doing in here? I knew I oughtn't to be there; his entry into and exit from my life having left a resounding trumpet post which I'd repudiated long ago. But the crushing weight of first love is another thing. The first is the worst is a saying, I believe, and if isn't it should be. And although here he was, the chancer, trying to churn up those silty waters I was convinced that I was immune.

'So much to talk about, Greta,' he said, not looking up. 'I missed you, didn't know how to contact you, whether I should. Were you all right?' The look was piteous. 'I think it broke my heart.'

Your heart, I wanted to shriek! Mad, deluded, self-absorbed man, how can you? I didn't say that but my expression must have recorded some of it.

'Gerald, don't be so melodramatic. I was merely another of your students who went farther than my admiration should have allowed. And I'm not a 'sweet girl,' and never was.'

'You're wrong there,' his shoulders slumped, toes turned in, a pathetic pose. 'There was something truly special between us. You occupy many of my dreams. I wrote poetry for you.' He looked up, fixing his tawny eyes on mine; was he going to try and hypnotise me?

'None published, I hope.'

'A few. I did achieve some fame in America with a couple of anthologies. I would have sent you one if I'd had your address.'

'Well, I'm glad it wasn't as unproductive out there as you implied. What brought you to this particular gathering?'

'I was going to ask that of you, but Leo tells me that you're somewhat celebrated in the crime writing world.'

'Yes, and you?' I said, but his eyes were glazing over; was it the drink or the pretence of servile swain? I looked away, took in the open suitcase, clothes already strewn on the bed.

'Oh, my old college, my alma mater,' as if he'd suddenly remembered the script; 'I often get invites to their little soirees.'

'Crime isn't of any interest to you then?'

'Greta, where's the cosy chat; why the third degree? If anyone needs interrogating it's you.' He leant further towards me, took a swig at his whisky. He was waiting for my reaction. 'I am thrilled to find you again.'

'Thirty plus years, Gerald; you certainly were the last person I expected to meet.' Aftershave, expensive, wafted on the air conditioning; it was another of his trademarks, smelling good. I thought, he's put that on since the party.

'Are you married, Greta?'

'Yes, to my work. And I'm pretty sure that's something you taught we students. Be wedded to your writing, 'that's all you should care about.'

He was meant to laugh, or at least smile. Instead he shook his head as if the weight of those words wounded him personally. 'Did you really think that?'

'It seemed pretty profound at the time.'

He hung his head and I think his eyes were closed. I took another sip of my whisky, wanting to leave but was trapped into wondering where this was going. 'I never wanted you to suffer,' he whispered.

'I didn't, Gerald. I certainly didn't. Life's been good, on the whole, lots of fun.' Whenever I say this, the quick reply to so many standard questions, I inwardly cringe. That glib response masks the terrible scar, crater of horror and sorrow, I want no one else to come near.

He looked up, a wan smile. 'I wish that I could say the same for me.' He gazed into my eyes, imploring some sort of response. 'I've struggled to understand the profound effect those few months with you have made on me.'

I laughed. 'Gerald, that's ridiculous. Out of sight, out of mind, that's you.'

'Greta, that's cruel.'

'Honest.'

He gulped back the last of his whisky. 'Another?'

'No, I must be going.'

'Oh, please, don't leave me.' He was up on his feet. 'I'll even make you a cup of tea.' He stood over me, expectant, as if waiting for me to rise up into his arms. 'I'll put the kettle on. I need to go to the bathroom.' Which is what he did and as the ensuite door opened a rush of steam escaped into the bedroom.

I am a woman who works with clues, setting them up for my readers; that Gerald had showered since arriving at the hotel and re-dressed for our arrival was hilarious and tragic. Was he expecting me to be the next dish on the menu after his poor pizza? I heard the flush of the toilet and gush of water into a basin. He came out wiping his hands on a towel.

This should have been my moment to escape and I have no justification for why I stayed, apart from that foolish curiosity. Or perhaps it was the pleasure of closure, the true closure I was sure that this occasion would give me.

'I'm fifty two, Gerald,' I said. 'How old are you?'

'What makes you ask?' He fiddled with a tea bag, poured the already boiled water on top and struggled to open a milk carton. As if to prolong the time before he had to face my answer, he squatted in front of the mini bar again. 'That's a bleak outlook,' he said, referring to the lack of any more whisky. 'Do you think it'll matter if I have a brandy?'

'Your call, Gerald.'

He ignored the remark, handed me the tea and settled back to unscrew and top up his glass. 'They're tiny slurps,' and he smiled, more the little boy entering into his own joke.

'Do you believe in soul mates, Greta?'

'Don't think so,' I said. 'And I seem to remember you rubbishing a poem written by one of our cohort on that subject due to the content as much as the skill in the writing.'

'Oh, that's good, you do remember our time together.'

'Of course.'

'Really? But you wrote no more poetry?'

'They weren't good, Gerald, unpublishable. You might say that I peaked too early.'

'Who was the judge?'

'Me. And, as I mentioned previously, my tame police inspector.'

'How the hell was an officer of the law allowed to pass comment? Did you send them out? I mean you had such flair; first published within six months of starting your degree.'

'Money, Gerald. Angus wasn't making a critique, he never read them, but he did say, quite rightly, that I was unlikely to make money that way.'

'Mammon!'

'Yes, keeping body and soul together, as Leo would say; and it's fun.'

'How sad!'

'Gerald, that's enough.' I finished the tea and stood up. 'Some poetry's good, some bad, most mediocre. I'm sure that's what you once said.'

I put the cup on the fridge and picked up my coat and bag. Facing him I said; 'Go well, Gerald. It was extraordinary meeting you again after all these years.' I held out my hand to shake his but he was already on his feet coming close, closer than was necessary. His aftershave came between us, labelled 'aphrodisiac', I thought.

'Please, Greta, you can't go, not without a kiss. We were good at that weren't we?' He had both arms around me. 'For old times sake. I know this is a pokey room, and I'm sure yours is far more swanky, but the bed's comfy …'

But I'd pulled away. 'Not appropriate, Gerald. As, if we're honest, it wasn't all those years ago.'

He stood head bent, arms limp at his side, the perfect picture of dejection. 'Don't say that, please, don't say that. It was beautiful.'

I was at the door. It wasn't locked and I slipped out.

I was shaking when I got back to my room. I sat on my bed unable to fathom why. Outrage, shame, regret? Or perhaps the whisky was one glass too far? It was gone midnight; our train back to London was leaving just after 9.00am, I needed to sleep. Why wasn't I laughing at his ridiculous manner, his extraordinary suggestion? I decided a bath was a good idea not a shower.

Fifty two, I'd said, as if that affirmed my maturity, precluded me from sex. So untrue, and, of course, he'd not told me his age. And he'd not asked about the child I was carrying all those years ago. What did I expect? What a relief, except it wasn't. I set my alarm for 7.30, fell into broken sleep, skipped breakfast to be outside for the taxi promptly next morning.

Leo said; 'My God, Greta, you look remarkably fresh. You obviously didn't have to endure that man for long.'

'No.'

'I did feel a bit guilty after I'd left you, but knowing your finesse with old bores ...' he wanted me to laugh.

It was a God-given morning. Sun aching to burn through a mist so thick the fields were lost as the train sped back to town. I remembered a poem I'd written and had shown to Angus.

> This is the time of day
> when the mist keeps
> the hedge within bounds.
>
> Skeletal hemlock, stark
> against the white
> softens with the sun.
>
> Swifts skating the sky
> dive from a high wire
> to finish on a helter-skelter.
>
> Clustered under eaves
> the stage is cleared
> for a next act.
>
> A blackbird drives straight on
> his performance
> catching the wind.

He'd said; 'Not bad, Greta. At least it's not one of those pompous ditties about a lovelorn lass or laddie.'

June

A brief encounter

'Why can't they have their bloody incidents on someone else's bloody line? When was the last? Two weeks ago, that's all.' The woman wanted to be heard.

'No thought for us poor bastards hanging around on some God forsaken platform, homes to go to. And the bloody police blocking it all off; what's there to sort?'

She carried a briefcase, wore three-inch heels, black suit and impeccably white shirt; her companion was bunched into a beige raincoat, a suitcase on wheels by her side.

'It's their choice, the ones that jump, mashed up on the line they may be but it's us that suffer, stuck here with our lives busted because of them.' She pulled out her mobile phone, flicked and clicked it into life. 'Christ, no reply!' her anger directed at whoever wasn't there at the end of her line, her phone held like a plate in the palm of her hand. 'And the poor bloody train driver; he's not going to be able to sleep or eat his supper tonight.'

Her companion shushed her, looking round to see if anyone was taking any notice which started the woman off again.

'Bloody hell! If I can't say what I want out here where I've got a valid ticket which is bloody useless right now, what do you suggest? A polite word to the fucking station master? Can't even bloody smoke ...'

The other woman replied as if to her own boots. Shaking her head as if ridding herself of an annoying insect, she pulled her suitcase to and fro, gazed away at the adverts on the other platform, a platform that seemed like another country, across a chasm of forbidden rails.

'Christ, no! Hear that, half-hour delay, and that won't be the end of it,' the woman was off again. 'The kids, what am I going to do about the kids? Bloody railways; charge a fortune and can't even shift a bloody body.'

The beige woman suggested they hire a taxi. The cost between the two of them, might be worth it?

'For fucksake, why should I fork out because some basket case can't get their life together.'

'Excuse me,' a man stood over her, six foot to her five foot six with heels. 'Yes, you have every right to express your opinion but it might be kinder to keep your voice down.'

'Huh! And who are you to tell me what's appropriate?'

'We don't know that it's a suicide.'

'Look, Mr whoever you are, when I'm mad I'm mad, every right to be, and this is a public space. Are you one of those religious nutters?'

'No one's trying to deny your anger, but it's just unfortunate for other people to hear it.'

'Then don't bloody listen.'

I watched them, St George against a fire-breathing dragon. I ought to have been sickened by the woman's diatribe, ought to have said something myself, except I've heard it all before, learned to grow a carapace on such occasions. It's enough that she's dead.

The platform was busier than I'd expected and my pleasure from the good lunch that had ended earlier than I'd expected, evaporated when the announcement came that the train was delayed. I should have sat down, patiently taken my place on one of the benches, or even used the waiting room. Instead, like everyone

157

else, I stood out there watching and willing a train to come down the track. The minutes ticked by with constant updates of further delays until they finally said, the words I dread hearing; 'Due to an incident on the line….' I wasn't there for Lottie; I wasn't going to think who it was out there now.

I'd been booked to speak at a literary lunch in Guildford on that Friday which my publicist had assured me would finish by 3.00pm so that I could be back in London in good time to change and get the train to Waterbeach. I kept my car up there as it wasn't much use to me in London, and I knew that Joy would take it out for a spin from time to time. I was planning to go on some outings with her, make it a long weekend. At eighty-seven, though still sprightly, she deserved a bit more of my time.

'Thank you,' I said, making sure that I was heard by St George and the women.

The man looked at me, gave a brief smile. No one else acknowledged the altercation. We all stood as before, gazing out at the line, tense, despondent. Had it been as silent as this before the woman spoke? The woman whose sullen stare was focused on her phone, chuntering quiet obscenities to whoever was on the end of her line.

Only yesterday I'd been on the journey out of Cambridge. A Thursday in June, Leo and I taking the train back to London; a glorious morning that turned to a radiant afternoon. All my irrational confusion over the evening before with Gerald melting away with the mist; the sadness, anger and pity dispelled by Leo's commentary on 'men who come back for more', which is the way he put it. I didn't know what Leo imagined of my evening with Gerald; I'd said nothing.

'Greta, you would not believe the tiresome turds who've turned up on my door decades after our dalliance was over. And it was only after the flings. Never the ones I loved.' He was interrupted several times by his mobile phone which, 'I can't ignore. I'm a martyr to my clients,' he'd say apologetically.

I'd switched my phone off. Joy would not expect a call so early. She hadn't known that I was in Cambridge mid-week and that I might have popped up the road to visit her. Since Jim died two years before I was astounded by her bravery, her lack of pity for herself, a stoicism which ruled her. 'Life is to live, Greta,' she had told me when I was old enough to understand what life meant. 'The bit between when you're born and when you're dead and buried?' I'd said. 'Yes,' Jim had cut in quickly, 'that's right; right until your ticker stops ticking.' He'd wanted me to laugh, which I did. It was a mantra that served us all well, even Lottie. 'Yes,' I remember her saying; '365 days in the year for three years, and then 366 in the fourth, all of them to the best. How many days have you lived, Grandpa?' And Jim had told her. 'Live it to the full,' had always been Joy's belief. 'There's just this one life, God given, so make it good.' Had Lottie?

'Did I ever introduce you to Johnnie, Greta?' Leo was back to interrupt my reverie.

I nodded; 'The red headed boy that I called the vixen?'

'So right, darling; sharp he was with bitey teeth. Still comes back from time to time, dragging his pathetic tail to beg forgiveness, that I might take him on again.' Leo paused and lowered his voice. 'Positively mangy he was the last time he fell on my door. Like that Gerald man, age hadn't done him any favours.'

The train sped on and I called Joy to say I'd be with her early on Friday evening. I didn't mention Cambridge.

'Would you like a cup of coffee or anything?' the man on the platform said. I'd forgotten he was there. 'It's just that ...'

'A good idea. Yes, ' I said. 'There's no point in standing here.'

He insisted on paying because it had been his idea. I told him that if I'd known I'd have ordered something stronger which made him smile; my flippant remark which didn't deserve any attention, still eased a tension which I realised was not entirely mine.

'The incident is just outside Clapham so they won't be able to take us round on another route,' he said.

'Do you work for the railways?'

'Lord, no! I just use them a lot. And this is not an unusual occurrence.'

I looked at him more closely; he didn't look like a train spotter, or any sort of obsessive. Boasting his knowledge though. 'No,' I agreed.

'I do sympathise with people who've deadlines to meet, family, like that woman, except ...'

'You've no need to explain. She was thoughtless, and it is extraordinary that people in a crowd discount those around them as anonymous. I'm a writer and find their scraps of conversation most useful.'

'I guess you won't be using that.'

I shrugged.

An inaudible loudspeaker announcement mingled with the hiss of the espresso machine. We both raised our eyebrows. 'I'll go and find out,' he said. And I sat there to contemplate the satchel bag and mobile phone that he'd left; I was obviously a person he could trust.

'They're hoping for twenty minutes,' he said, when he came back.

'Good. And I'm impressed that you left your worldly possessions with me. I'm glad to think I have an honest face.'

He smiled; 'You do.' Extending a hand he said; 'The name's Roger Harlow.'

'Greta Salway,' I replied.

Despite my annoyance at being organised, dislike of his authoritative manner, we stayed together until the train eventually arrived, and all the way to Waterloo. He chatted companionably, admitting that he rarely talked to people on trains, and that he didn't want to stop me working. That pleased me; a man offering the possibility that a woman worked, and even on a train. Although he didn't ask questions directly, he ventured openings such as; 'Is this a line you use regularly?', and 'Do you travel much?', he accepted my non-committal answers. And it was on that journey when he told me about his mother.

'Harlow was my mother's maiden name, she never married, so in old fashioned terms I'm a bastard.' We were sitting side-by-side, intimate, for despite or because of the buzz of the crowded train, we could have been alone.

'That's not a term used these days,' I said.

'No, more difficult then, I believe.'

I offered neither agreement or otherwise. I hadn't suffered.

I decided he was gay; a collarless jacket, open necked pastel shirt and spectacles with the latest trend of square, slim dark frames, which also described him; plus the satchel briefcase.

'She committed suicide, hence my reaction to that woman,' he said.

My intake of breath would have been enough, but I expressed sorrow, what else?

'I think it's an incredibly brave act,' he continued, 'despite the horror it leaves for those who have to face the aftermath. Can you understand that?'

It felt like a blow to the sola plexus; did I understand? I don't know how I looked but he immediately said; 'I'm sorry, I shouldn't have …'

'No,' I cut in. 'I'd never thought like that. But you're right, it is.' I knew I mustn't consider Lottie's 'bravery' at that moment. This was his confession not mine.

'I was safely at university,' he went on, 'and she must have felt she'd done her job and all that had plagued her came up like a groundswell. There was a black angel on her back which she'd fought for years.'

'I'm so sorry,' I said, again, those inadequate words, the only ones worth saying and worth being heard. Outside the sky was blurring to a lilac haze, a deep orange glow where the sun was setting. It would be dark by the time I reached Joy. Would I tell her of this encounter?

'I've never heard that expression before, 'black angel',' I said. 'Black dog was Churchill's.'

'Yes,' he said. 'My mother was unique and never hid her problem from me. "If I'm tired and grumpy," she'd say, "it's the black angel come to stay for a bit, but because it's got wings it'll fly away soon." I could cope with that.'

'It must have been hard.'

'I've survived pretty well,' he said, 'and forgive me for burdening you. But not only do you have an honest face,' and he was smiling broadly, 'you invite confidences; an expert listener.'

'Good,' I said, and I was pleased.

I began to like this man I didn't expect to meet again.

And that was it; all the little stations raced past as we talked trivia. I didn't volunteer anything of my private life and he didn't ask. I mentioned the lunch, that crime was my forte, 'though not the practice of it,' I said. We shook hands on Waterloo Station and dashed off in different directions. I hadn't asked where he was going, what he might be late for; that was it.

He didn't tell me that he was a writer too.

It was dark when I reached our home in Waterbeach; I was making a huge effort to think of it in that way. Joy never asked me to spend more time with her, or that the house needed any of my attention; nothing should be a burden to me. That it was a valuable achievement for her and Jim, and that it had provided a safe nest for me and Lottie was unspoken. They'd bought it in 1980 after Mrs Thatcher promoted the Right to Buy scheme. Lottie was ten.

'You look like a ghost, Greta,' was Joy's greeting as I stood under the new security light.

'Those things turn everyone into a zombie,' I said glancing up and hugged her hard. She'd not lost her pigeon plumpness; her tongue was not always soft but her body enclosed me in cushioned comfort.

'Leo rang,' she said. 'He's a prankster, isn't he? Always makes me laugh.'

'What did he want? Do I need to ring him back?' I wondered why he hadn't rung my mobile.

'He thought you'd be here already. He wanted to know if you were all right. Are you?'

'Yes, just a difficult journey, the delay.' I didn't say why.

'No, it must be more than that. Leo doesn't phone here, except Christmas and birthdays, and after Lottie.'

Here she was, back on track. She'd lost none of her verve for dredging out undercurrents. As my mother, the person who cared for me above all others, she had to know what might be troubling me. I still feared that I might tell her about Gerald one day, which would have been beyond shocking after all these years.

'Oh, he's possibly fussing about the lunch today,' I said. 'He can't believe that my publicist is capable of taking care of such an event. Which of course is ridiculous because that's her job; she needs to sell my books more than I do. And she did.'

Joy puffed up; I felt bad to have provoked her mother's pride in her daughter's achievement in order to divert the conversation. I was able to wander off into anecdotes of the people there, what we'd eaten, what I'd said. I hadn't the strength for an inquisition.

The photographs of Jim and Lottie, with us or on their own, surrounded the room. I never believed that it was just us and nor did she. As soon as it was possible to slip past the latest bits of our lives, we tracked back to reminiscences of when we were all together.

'Do you know what Jim said to me the day before he died?'

'No,' I said not bothering to think whether I did or didn't. She needed to say it, fresh.

'Lottie never needed a father, did she? We got that wrong, is what he said.'

Joy and I 'tackled' the garden that weekend; her expression, as in the past Jim quietly kept it up and running without noticeable effort. I'd tried to persuade her to employ a gardener but she greeted the suggestion as an insult. The previous summer I'd cleared the vegetable patch, was allowed to plant two fruit trees and put down turf around them. Not particularly clever as she wanted to keep the grass mown, under control; meadows are a new fangled garden concept it seems. Strange how fads come and go, and despite the rambling roses, old fashioned lavender and marigolds which make up her garden, letting the grass grow long with poppies and wildflowers wasn't to be considered.

Wearing scruffy old shorts and vest, the sun on my back, I laboured, ridding myself of any angst from the previous two days. I didn't return Leo's call but I contemplated his remarks about Gerald, what he'd construed. Perceptive should be Leo's middle name; that he hadn't mentioned some of my other strange fly-by-nights surprised me. Paul 'the snapper' was his expression, had not been a favourite. Little Max he'd loved, but then Max had loved every one of his worshippers. I hadn't chosen my men wisely, or in fact chosen them at all. 'You always let them fall in your lap, Greta darling. I know that I'm not one to talk but we have to learn. We both need a lovely man to lean on.' And although I knew little about his Finlay, this is what I was contemplating as I dug the garden on that particular day in June after my first encounter with Roger.

Coincidence, chance or fate? That I met Roger the day after that brief encounter with Gerald, I might consider all of those. Except I dislike the idea that anything is preordained. I have control of my life is what I've always wanted to believe; that I make good or bad decisions happen, that I neglect or fail to notice what other people want of me, I'm ready to accept. But that some hocus-pocus, other world power is influencing my life, I want to deny. However that he came then, and came again with all his strange baggage is extra ordinary, I will admit.

July

Letters from Gerald

Swept up by the overwhelming impulse of first love? From this distance, with the horror, the mayhem of what has happened since, it's extraordinary to remember that fact, the emotion. With what a lethal arrow Eros wounds! The devastation of a life lost or a heart hardened, encrusted with the cynicism of experience and hurt. Is that me?

I'd dismissed the evening in Cambridge when Leo and I were accosted by Gerald and I'd stupidly endured that bit of nonsense in his room, as a bit of middle aged vanity. Falling out of love, realising the object of that passion was a fraud, had happened to me so long ago. But it had still been mortifying to see that, unlike chutney, age had not improved his flavour. However I had hoped his intelligence was still intact.

So the first letter caught me off guard; the handwriting, tiny and precise, like Lottie's, gave me a heart-stopping jolt. Michael was in the kitchen of my flat cooking his usual breakfast fry up. Irritation at the smell of bacon, the smoky fat at that time in the morning, had never left me. Our loose relationship of eight years was unravelling; neither of us had ever claimed love.

Dear Greta
To meet you again last night was the utmost thrill and I apologise profusely if I became a bit overpowering.

It was, of course, a fortnight since we'd met; the delay due to his problem in persuading my agency to give him a home address; they had eventually agreed to post the letter on. Leo told me later; 'That was my credulous secretary, darling. Being away as I was in the sunny uplands, or are they lowlands, of Provence, fortifying the inner me, I was not able to give my permission. It should not have gone out of my office; straight in the bin was its due, pleading telephone call or not. No, better I'd set it on fire, ashes to the wind. The man's a charlatan.' He didn't ask if that's what I'd done, burnt it. Discreet is my beloved Leo; his advice comes at a slant.

It was hard to believe that all those years had passed; you were as lovely as I remembered. You, my perfect student, the sweetest woman that I ever encountered, have not aged one iota. Verily you have become more real and beautiful. For me it was as if time had been eclipsed, memories of those years together flooding back and I was young again.

I don't know why I carried on reading. The spit of fat and scraping of spatula on frying pan disguised my exclamations and swearing. For 'those years' were ten months of one year or less. And if he 'was young again' it was not apparent.

To make up for our time apart I propose that we meet soon, very soon. I am up in London frequently; please telephone me so that we can arrange to go out on the town. Or more appropriately a delicious supper, which is only what you deserve.
Your faithful poet
Gerald

Later that day, having reread with a mixture of awe and disgust I put it through the shredder.

I took Joy to Paris a month later, my first visit since Lottie died. Eurostar was so easy and different; memories of flying back with Paul after I'd heard the
167

terrible news weren't going to spoil the trip. Joy had never visited another country. 'Jim wasn't fussed,' she said, 'not that he didn't like foreigners or 'abroad' as he called it.' Money was the reason and neither of them had itchy feet.

Joy and I were the tourists that Lottie and I had been and it was comforting, not sad, to remember how she'd reacted when I'd brought her here, to see what she'd seen. Joy's curiosity and unflagging interest in all we did was quite remarkable. On one afternoon while she rested; I went up to the cemetery at Montmartre. The sky was an incredible deep rolling blue. The sun spiralled through the trees, tracing patterns on the paths and tombs, lighting up the stone. Lottie was right, peace and grace lay over that place.

I returned from Paris revived, renewed, only to find another letter on my doormat.

Dearest Greta

I was fearful that the girl in Leo's office wouldn't deliver my first letter to you. It must be so difficult to find good staff these days; she was charming but seemed a bit flighty.

So I'm feeling bereft.

Fortunately the people at your publishers appeared more reliable so I feel confident that this will reach you; though I still don't understand why they wouldn't give me your address. I did emphasise that you were a student of mine and would wish to hear from me.

I will say again what I said in my previous letter; it was such a joy to meet you last month, and am certain we are destined to spend more time together in whatever capacity you feel appropriate. I gathered from our brief moment that evening that you are unattached; I did ask your publisher if you were married but they couldn't say. All this modern secrecy is ridiculous, data protection gone mad.

Suffice to say, I am eager to take you to dinner as soon as possible and look forward to hearing from you earliest. My mobile number is: 07923345561. My address at the top of this letter will find me, but not as quickly as a phonecall.
Yours ever
Gerald

Reading it through I felt sick. True, it was late as I'd taken Joy back to Waterbeach, briefly stayed with her while she unpacked and settled in, and then taken the last train out of Cambridge. I shouldn't have opened it then but the handwriting again threw me. 'Damn the man!' I shouted at the empty flat.

Larry was no longer my publisher; he'd sold out to the 'big boys' as he called them. It made little difference to me; Leo was my bulwark when it came to finances, negotiating contracts, making sure they gave me the best publicist. She, this new publicist, was unapologetic; 'He was very polite and I did check his credentials, the fact that he was at UCN at the same time as you.' Her smile was innocent of any irony. 'I'll make sure it won't happen again if he comes back.'

I didn't mean to tell Leo but a few days later he asked how I was finding 'young Caroline.'

'Early days,' I said, 'though I'm glad it's you who haggles for me, looking after my best interests.'

'Haggle, darling?' he rolled his eyes. 'You make me sound like some old market crone. Negotiate, promote, exercise your rights.'

'Yes, yes, Leo, and I love you too!

'Better. And you're happy?'

'Well, yes, and no. She did redirect a letter to me from Gerald, sent it on like your secretary. Said she'd checked him out first.'

'Oh, damnation! Can't think what's the matter with these young things. They've no comprehension of privacy.'

I burnt this one; Leo had been right; I didn't want to leave any trace in my shredder.

A week later Audrey telephoned to say that Douglas had died. 'I wanted you to be one of the first to know, Greta. He didn't suffer,' she said, 'and I know that I mustn't too.' Such brave words and I wondered whether I ought go to her immediately but she told me that a niece was with her and 'countless local friends'. The funeral was a fortnight later; Leo and I drove down together.

'What a man, Greta! I hope the eulogies are fitting or I might have to get up there myself,' Leo said. 'A true gentleman of the old guard and yet with such a principled and unbiased outlook; he accepted me as I am.' I often forget the stigma that Leo has fought all his life; I remembered Freddie's confession; 'I'm gay.'

We went straight to the crematorium so I didn't recognise him at first, the man sitting in a pew two rows from the front, the man Audrey acknowledged by briefly taking his hand on her way down the aisle behind the coffin. After the service as mourners gathered in the cloisters, rain fell in an outburst of fury. 'So appropriate for Douglas,' Leo said. 'He'll be calling the shots up there; I always imagined him as sidekick to Thor at the very least.' I was struggling with tears that welled and trickled, my handkerchief splodged with mascara. I knew that Lottie would have been crying too; 'I know he isn't my father,' she'd said, 'but he's someone I'd choose if I could.'

Back to their house, a wake laid on by local caterers, Audrey was in her role of hostess. I knew it was an act so familiar, a front easily assumed to cover the terrible loss she was enduring. Nieces, nephews and godchildren who I'd never met, were in abundance as were her friends, and I was introduced to each of them as if we were doing the rounds at a cocktail party. To talk of how we'd known Douglas, to share our memories was a pleasure, but I was sinking deep into my own loss. This was the first funeral since Jim died, but it was Lottie who haunted me. So much of the time I am happy, know it would be an affront to those I care for to sink into gloom, to carry my hurt as a breastplate. It wouldn't bring her back. But the past lurks, a mound of ash, cherished, never forgotten, and then there are these moments when it flares, hot rage, a blaze of misery; she should be here. I think about what she would have been doing, what she would have achieved, how much I want her to be with me. The pain burns as harsh as it ever was.

I moved away to look out of the wide windows to the spread of garden as if studying the neatly cut lawn, the trimmed edges around the beds of shrubs, the rain sparkling on the grass, diamonds set in the sun's rays. But I wanted none of it.

'Excuse me,' the man was behind me, 'I think we might have met.'

Reluctant, I turned to know immediately who he was. Roger, the man on the platform, who'd objected to the way a woman was talking about the cause of a delayed train, an incident on the line. It had been two months before.

'I am right aren't I?' he was saying but on seeing my smudged face added; 'I didn't mean to disturb you but I, well, …'

'Yes,' I said, 'of course, it's good to meet you again.'

'It's not easy is it?' he half turned to the crowded room. 'Audrey is putting on such an incredible performance, and I know Douglas would have been wishing us to celebrate.'

'Yes, that's so true,' I said. 'Just, you know, reminders of other occasions like this, well, the memories that are still hard to bear. Can't always be brave, can we?'

'No, we can't.' He looked out the window. 'I've never been here in daylight but the garden's as I would have expected. Trim and green and peaceful.'

'How did you come to know Audrey and Douglas?' I said.

'From some time ago and then recently. I'm an economist, was freelancing; wrote an article on Greenpeace, which was taken up by a publication that Douglas read. He took the trouble to get in touch, invited me for dinner, January I think it was. I just know it was dark when I arrived. Then I met him at a conference in March.'

'That's interesting. And Audrey; she knew you?'

'Yes, in true Soames' fashion the dinner was here and then I was invited to one of their poetry evenings.'

'Oh, yes, Douglas and poetry, synonymous.'

'And their amazing skill in finding out who you are, your interests; I'd forgotten I liked poetry but somehow they dug it out.'

'My daughter used to argue with Douglas about the value of poetry. He always took her seriously.' And I immediately wondered why I'd said it; I never talk about Lottie to strangers, not wanting false sympathy or misunderstanding.

Then Leo was there to ask if we should leave.

Book festivals are a boon and a bane. They're necessary publicity, wind in the sails of what I write. Travelling I enjoy, meeting other writers, people who like what I write; Prague, Warsaw and the States were already scheduled as well as book signings in this country.   But they take time and energy which I seemed to be losing in equal quantities.

This was September in Warwick; it was a last minute arrangement as another author had dropped out and they begged me to fill in. I wasn't anxious to go; true, 'The Whispering Walker' had just come out in paperback, 'All Hail Brave Beauties' was hot off the press.   Caroline was persuasive, promised I could be there and back in a day, first class.   Leo shrugged; 'Accept, Greta, darling. Their gratitude will be eternal.' I didn't bother to look at the rest of the programme, who else might be there; I didn't intend to do the rounds.

'Greta, how marvellous! You've come!'

I couldn't avoid him. There he was on the platform as I got off the train, Gerald with programme in hand, bulging holdall slung from his shoulder. For one brief moment I thought he'd become a festival gopher and had been sent to meet me.

'I was distraught not having heard from you, my letters not getting through. But this is terrific; you've come to hear me speak.'

'Gerald, I …'

'No, not another word, my dear; coffee, we've just time and then we can get a taxi.'

'I didn't know you'd be here, Gerald. I can't stop.'

'Oh, but I'm not on until 2.00.' He took my elbow. 'Such a lovely surprise.'

'No,' I drew back from him, 'I can't,' I said. 'I'm here as a speaker and I'm booked for 12.00. I have to get a taxi right now.'

He paused, a look of mystification and annoyance; 'Oh, well, yes, let's find you that taxi.'   Thrusting forward, he regained control, an aged knight leading his troops; if he'd had a sword, or even an umbrella, it would have been held high, charging forth to the fray. I followed.

The first taxi he tried after a disagreement with another passenger, was already taken; it was the second which was available and whose door I'd opened and climbed into before Gerald realised and had to hurry to jump in too.

'This is so good,' he said, spreading his arms across the back of the seat. 'I'm here to talk on the lesser poets of the Romantic period. It's something I used to do a lot, especially when I was in America.'

I said nothing.

'A friend of mine's helping to run the Festival here this year, got me a slot. Feels good to be back on the circuit.'

I said nothing. This predicament would be sorted out as soon as I arrived and was whisked off to my appointed event by someone whose name I'd noted in my diary. I ought to have let them come to meet me at the station.

'You obviously didn't get my letters,' he was saying. 'I have tried hard to get back in touch; your agent and publishers aren't reliable you know.'

'In what way?' I said.

'Not forwarding letters. Surely that's their role.'

I'm not a deceitful person in most of my life. The one big secret, yes, but otherwise I'm uncomfortable with pretence. White lies told not to hurt feelings are more often a false claim. I had to say; 'I did receive your letters, Gerald, they were sent on to me.'

'Oh!' He finally looked at me, the expression of a wounded dog.

'Gerald, I couldn't see any point in renewing our relationship, as you called it. Years have passed, years and years, and my life is more than full, as yours must be.'

'Oh.' There was no upward beat of surprise but he still looked at me, frowning disbelief, defenceless.

'I'm here unexpectedly,' I said, 'joining a panel of two other crime writers, our subject; "Why the rise in popularity of crime fiction?".'

'Ah.' He hadn't moved; his arms still abandoned along the back of our seat, his gaze troubled but focused on me.

'I have to leave after my session and catch the 3 o'clock train back to London.'

There was nothing more to say; he appeared as if stunned and I felt that nasty worm of guilt and pity. But we were there, at the entrance to the venue. I opened my door and paid the driver, waited for the receipt.

'I hope you have a good audience,' I said, unnecessarily adding, 'I'm sorry that I won't be able to hear your talk.'

'So am I, Greta. Such a disappointment.' My resolve to walk away immediately diminished as the seconds passed. Was it charity or curiosity?

He stood on the steps as if rooted to the stones. 'I will come to hear you, Greta, but I have a problem which I'd hoped to talk through with you. I feel you're the only person who will understand. I'm desperate.'

'What?' I couldn't leave him standing there, bleak, shrunken and looking incredibly grey. 'Why me after all this time?'

'It's come as a bit of a shock and I just need somebody and after meeting you in June and then this thing coming up right afterwards, it seemed obvious that it had to be you.'

I needed to go, find my fellow authors, work out the angle we were going to take, together and individually. 'I don't know how I can help but here's my phone number,' I delved in my bag and handed him a card with my email address and mobile phone number.

'Thank you,' he took my card and my hand, which he bent to kiss and continued to hold. 'You see, I found out recently that I fathered a child some years ago without knowing and I can't think what I should do.'

October

A lunch with Gerald

Fate following me, a smirk on its face, to jump ahead, lay the trap and watch me fall; that's how I saw it that day. For thirty years I'd hidden Gerald's identity from my parents and Lottie; I'd expended anguish in not telling as well as worry as to whether I should, and finally I'd written that letter to Lottie which she would never receive; to be found out now was too cruel.

Terror at his revelation flooded every pore of my skin; I was a hedgehog in reverse, the spines sticking into me. Did he notice the bristle as I pulled my hand away, the fright on my face? I ran up the steps into the venue in Warwick wanting to be swallowed up, to disappear into the crowd and then hide in a pile of dead leaves.

Was I ashen, visibly shaking, wide eyed with panic as I walked in to join the panel? Whatever I was feeling, nobody appeared to notice; I was a crime writer of some note, my latest books piled on a table for me to sign. I needed to perform; whatever was to come would come. And of course it did, an email the next day.

'Greta dear,' I read; *'I am so grateful that you've allowed me to contact you. To be brief, please can we meet as soon as possible? I live in the New Forest but can travel to London in time for luncheon. I await your reply fervently. Gerald.'*

Bad news has a habit of following on; that same evening I heard that Audrey Soames had died, two months after Douglas. I didn't want to hear or repeat those hackneyed phrases, a happy release, to be expected at her age, trotted out by the person who telephoned;

Audrey was a special friend. Joy, who had to be told, was equally upset; 'There aren't many as good as them in this world, her and Douglas. I don't like it.' I needed to go up to see her in Waterbeach at the weekend and, although the email and its consequences also required a decision, I put it off. Despite a constant niggle of dread which, as a child I'd imagined as a stone lodged between ribs and tummy, I thought he could wait. But, of course, he couldn't. He telephoned; 'Hello Greta,' his voice too loud, 'did you get my email?' I shouldn't have answered but didn't recognise the number. 'Can you hear?' Joy, who was sitting beside me, raised her eyebrows. It was after nine o'clock on Sunday evening. 'When can we meet?' I got up carefully, scared that she'd see my dismay. Cheerfully, falsely, I answered him, giving him a date that week. I went to get a glass of water before coming back to sit with Joy, thinking is this when I have to tell her? A child is supposed to share her worst fears with her mother, but, of course, our roles were reversed and on this subject I certainly couldn't look for comfort, solace. 'Just someone who wants to write an article on crime novels,' I lied, and felt far worse.

'Greta! Thank you for coming.' Gerald looked better; the mole brown cords teamed with checked shirt and green sweater, a short wool coat, were typical dressed-down poet, and his hair was neatly trimmed; curls sprang from his head, a tawny cap. 'I hope you don't mind, I booked a table at one of my favourite Italian restaurants not far from here.'

We'd met at Charing Cross station, the last overnight stop of Queen Eleanor of Castile's body on its way to rest in Westminster Abbey. Briefly I mourned a woman who'd survived sixteen pregnancies and kept her husband faithful and devoted for thirty-six years. Why this came to mind as I approached the porticos of the station I have no idea, but it is a fixed memory of that moment; perhaps it was a distraction from the trepidation I felt for what I was about to hear.

Gerald did not try to take my arm but pointed the way down Villiers Street. He looked slimmer, more sprightly, as we made our way between the traffic of people. The last day of October, a cold wind funnelled through the passageway and I was pleased to have worn my winter coat, red, with black boots, bag and scarf. He and I didn't blend.

'What is it you need to talk to me about?' I asked as soon as we sat down. I kept my coat over the back of my chair despite the waiter's plea to hang it up. I might have to make a quick getaway.

'A drink first, please, Greta. White or red?'

I wanted to decline, for this was no mutual assignation, no celebration, but I succumbed to the offer of a glass of white wine. After a silly preamble, Gerald showing off his knowledge of various vineyards, the waiter went off and came back with the order. The tablecloth was pristine white, sharp against the dark interior of the restaurant. I stared at the vase of red pinks between us; at least we were a match.

I waited for the attack to fracture, splinter and crush me. I'd prepared nothing, no declaration, no defence, explanation or excuse. This was his call.

Gerald raised his glass; 'Here's to you, Greta, and your success.'

'Thank you,' I had to say, surprised at this new version of Gerald, polite and appreciating someone else.

I realised that I ought to ask how his poetry talk had been received in Warwick but he was already saying; 'Quite out of the blue this letter arrives for me from a man – I won't tell you his name in case he'd prefer privacy – telling me that I was a student with his mother at university and that she'd named me as his father on the birth certificate.'

I stared at him, a rip tide of relief ran through me, a surge of gratitude; it wasn't me, it wasn't Lottie. We were free. I hoped that the glow which suffused my body, flushing my cheeks, wasn't obvious in the low light. I was glad of the wine but drank too quickly and choked. I had to ask the waiter for water which gave me time to recover.

'Why do you want my advice?' I said.

'Well, how do I know it's true? Why would I want to meet someone who may dislike me for neglect, or even demand money?'

This wasn't what I was expecting and although my life wasn't going to be turned upside down, I was shocked by his questions. Suspicion of the man who claimed to be his child was his first thought, his concerns all seemed to be somehow obscene. I sipped more wine unable to form a neutral reply.

'I mean why has he taken so long to get in touch?' he said.

'How old is he?'

'Oh, I don't know exactly; forty something I suppose.'

The waiter came for our order but I had no appetite and thought of leaving. Dislike for Gerald was at its height. Self-absorbed, inadequate, intellectually stale, cruel; if our association hadn't produced my beloved child, he might have been a pinprick in my life story, a first affair probably forgotten. But I was sufficiently curious and I was taught and agree that bad temper and rows are a pointless waste of emotional effort.

I ordered spaghetti carbonara and he did the same.

'Should I meet him, Greta?'

'I don't know. What does your wife say?'

I expected him to wince, hang his head in sorrow, the indication that his marriage was not easy. I'd seen it so often before, been taken in by it so often before. 'I can't tell her; I think she'd kill me,' he said.

'A love affair before you were married? I presume that's what you're talking about?' I didn't say this is ridiculous but he must have understood from my intonation.

'It's not as easy as that.' He stared at me, troubled hazel eyes, lowering eyebrows, tufts growing in all directions. I thought of those terrier dogs, Irish I think, but dismissed the likeness as unflattering to the animal. He said; 'You see, I know it sounds odd but I told her, when we met, that I was a virgin.'

There was no way to stop it; my outburst of laughter caused the other diners to turn in our direction. I took more than a sip of my wine to stem the laughter, which had the reverse effect. I became uncontrollable causing the wine to fill my nose and once again I was coughing and sneezing. The waiter brought our food at that moment, placing it warily in front of me. I looked up at him happily, laughing and choking, wanting to bring him, and the rest of the restaurant, in on the joke.

Gerald was looking at his plate, unwrapping his napkin slowly, waiting for the fuss to die down, pretending that it had nothing to do with him. At last he said; 'Greta, she's a Catholic. It just seemed easier.'

That was not funny. 'You deceitful bastard!'

'Have you never told a white lie, Greta?'

We looked at each other. Disgust is what I felt and he would have read that into my expression but he was blank, a barrier raised, and I was flipped back to those moments when I'd been over eager, asking for more than he wanted to give in that long gone relationship.

Yes, that was exactly it, the shutters closed. How were we going to eat together, how or what could I give an opinion on, how advise? Why should I?

The spaghetti, giving off an appetising aroma, was there to be eaten; I wasn't going to be the one to leave. He was nothing to me, even if at that semi-triumphant moment I recognised the awful truth of a tag he'd attached to me, one that I'd never be rid of; he was my daughter's father. I picked up my fork, twisted the pasta around several times, ate the mouthful and said; 'Delicious!'

'I wasn't asking for sympathy, Greta,' he said.

'No. So what have you done?'

'Nothing.'

'Well, I suppose that's how you can leave it, do nothing. I don't expect the man will pursue it unless he's a charlatan, and then you could charge him with harassment.'

'I can see you know your stuff, always thinking with the criminal's mind.'

I should have reached across the table and poked my fork through his eye. I wanted to strangle him and my scarf was the perfect weapon, but I knew I didn't have the strength for that manoeuvre. And the waiters might step in.

We continued to eat in silence until a waiter came to ask if he'd like another glass of wine.

'Would you, Greta?' he said. The hangdog look was back, the diminished man.

'No, thank you, I need to keep a clear head,' I said.

'I don't,' and he accepted the waiter's offer. When we were alone again he said; 'Do you think I ought to meet him?'

I'd eaten enough and put down my fork, finished my wine. 'Write and ask for more details first, perhaps? Did you recognise the mother's name?'

We parted politely. He had paid the bill and I didn't demur. There was even a sense of appreciation on his part and, I thought, a realisation that I was no longer worth pursuing. He thanked me for listening; 'It's obviously something I need to sort out, and I believe you're right. I need to know more before I meet him and then we'll take it from there.' This declaration pleased him. 'Can I just give you a hug, Greta. It seems to be the modern thing.' So we did and then turned and went our separate ways.

I was going to Warsaw two days later. I went back to my flat and wept.

November

Another brief encounter

It makes little sense that I let Roger into my life at a time when I was incandescent with rage at Gerald, and determined that I would live my life without lovers. Such bitterness sounds juvenile but perhaps my teenage persona was revisiting, the one which should have blamed the man, fought him, exposed him then and there. In calmer moods I remembered my reason was to protect Lottie, and in light of what I'd now learned, I was vindicated. Nevertheless I was setting out my future where men would only be friends and, as a friend, Roger crept in under my barbed wire fence.

He was there at Audrey Soames' funeral, two months after we'd given thanks for the life of Douglas. This was before what I thought was a final meeting with Gerald, when I was thinking that was the end of it. I was in control.

When Roger greeted me at Audrey's wake; 'You're Greta Salway, the crime writer', he seemed taller than before; a dark suit, the jacket open to show a blue shirt checked with pink and darker blue tie, somehow extending his frame.

'How do you know that?' I said.

'Audrey, of course, she filled me in at Douglas' wake when I asked who you were. I should have realised when we met that first time on the station.

'You knew of me?'

'Well, I do sometimes read the bestseller lists.'

You've read my books?' I didn't know why I was pursuing this line, a teasing challenge.

'To be honest, no. Mostly I read factual stuff, and am keen on some American authors …'

'Literary fiction; not how my novels are described by my ex employer.'

'Ex employer?'

I gave him a brief outline of how I came to be published, why the crime. 'I've often wondered whether it's a form of laziness, sticking to the same formula.'

'Why? Success of the sort you've achieved doesn't seem lazy to me.'

We were distracted by other people at this point and it wasn't until I was about to leave that he found me again.

'Douglas and Audrey, Romeo and Juliet?' he said and must have noticed the wince, my intake of breath for he added; 'Sorry is that crude?'

'No,' we were standing again at the picture window, the lawn as clean cut, as green. 'It's so right, just what my daughter once said of them; she would have expected Audrey to be unable to live without his love, or vice versa.'

'There can't be many marriages so compatible with neither partner crushed,' he said.

'I agree, though my parents achieved that sort of bliss,' I was pleased to say. 'At the same time my mother is managing her widowhood; Jim gave her permission, in fact ordered her to 'look on the bright side' or some such motto.' I explained that Jim had died two years before and, without meaning to, that they'd already borne a huge loss together. 'Perhaps that prepared them, that there could be no other grief more terrible.'

He didn't ask what I meant, which I appreciated, and we both looked out to the garden where sparrows were fluttering in and out of one of the bushes, fierce tweeting, an eruption of enmity

'House or tree, do you think?' he said.

'I honestly don't know,' I said. 'But aren't they supposed to be in decline?'

'In which case it's great to see them, in whatever mood.'

I liked the way that he picked up on my focus, didn't pursue my personal outburst.   A tactful man.   I remembered what he'd told me of his mother.

As we were leaving he said; 'I don't know whether you would consider meeting again? Losing Audrey and Douglas from my life will leave a big hole despite our very short acquaintance; perhaps we might share memories.'

I said, 'Yes,' though regretted it as we exchanged cards. I was trying to distance myself, no more picking up odd men. Then seeing his hand as he took mine, the long fingers, clean cut nails, I thought, as I had before; fine, this man's gay.

Two months later without a word from Roger, having suffered Gerald's bombshell, I flew out to Warsaw with no thought of fate following me, though, in retrospect, it's easy to see it that way. Was it purely coincidental that we kept bumping into each other? Roger couldn't have set it up, known I was there. In fact he could have accused me. He was the one at a conference; I was the one who'd stayed on for the weekend after my author events there in Poland.

Mine was a spur of the moment idea. Two days on my own was what I needed.

Gerald's little fantasy had been exhausting. Having initially rejoiced, I kept revisiting the scene; that he'd embroiled some other woman, turned another two lives upside down, shocked me. And yet why? Wasn't it just as I suspected, would have expected? I knew I wasn't unique, was one of many students he'd picked up and flattered. I didn't want to think about her, yet couldn't help wondering why she, like me, hadn't told Gerald at the time, made him responsible. What was her motive in keeping him away from her child? I couldn't ask her. I wanted to forget Gerald's flagrant lack of decency. Worse obscenities I shouted at my empty flat; wished there was someone else to tell. Secrets, I've learned, harm the hoarder, no one else.

Michael was expecting me back at his 'sailing cottage' but I had to ease myself away from that affair. I didn't want to admit that I was bored but it was true. I was convinced that being a couple wasn't for me. Sex was overrated; my pool of love for my child was the most precious, so much more than anything else I could experience and would always be. Sacrosanct.

The Marriott Hotel's breakfast cannot be missed; a spread that will last a whole sightseeing day. A five star treat. I sat at a table by the window, my tourist guide open, juice, coffee, bacon and scrambled eggs waiting, with croissant and yogurt on the side. My newly acquired reading glasses blurred the rest of the room; I turned away from the world.

'Hello, Greta! What an extraordinary coincidence meeting you here.'

I immediately recognised his voice.

'Roger Harlow! Fancy seeing you,' I said taking off my specs, self-conscious that I needed to wear them.

'I can't believe this,' he said, 'I've been trying to pluck up the courage to phone you, to see if you had time to meet.'

I didn't say, 'why would you need courage', but instead; 'How come you're here? Holiday, stag weekend?'

'Conference. Sorry, that's rather boring, work at weekends, but needs must.'

'Not boring, I'm sure. I've been working here too and decided to stay on for a few days.'

He stood and I sat. I could have asked him to join me, or he could have said anything to fill the gap. He was the one to find me.

'Perhaps we can meet later,' he said at last. 'May I call your mobile?'

I had to say 'yes' though alone is what I wanted to be, should have written it across my forehead. My thoughts spun; a frantic spider, constructing a web, not to catch a victim but to fend one off.

After he'd left, I focused on the view out of the window. The Palace of Culture and Science, the iconic Stalinesque building, dominated the skyline. I'd marvelled at the pride and courtesy of those I'd met, the Polish people who'd suffered at the hands of cruel, alien regimes. They hadn't pulled down the ridiculous structure which was a hideous reminder of that brutality, they'd pragmatically left it and rebuilt what ever else had been destroyed. It's fatuous to say those thoughts inspired me to pull myself together, but I do remember a definite decision to stop wallowing, to get out there and see what I'd come to see.

The call came as I was wandering in the Old Town looking for a restaurant that had been recommended; it was 7 o'clock. My sense of direction is poor; I'd been circling the same streets becoming increasingly ratty, the old self-pity in danger of taking over.

'Greta, am I too late?'

'Who is it?' I was foolishly pretending that I hadn't recognised his voice.

'It's Roger Harlow. I wondered whether we might eat together. I know it's late, you're probably already booked.'

'No.' I said when it should have been 'yes'.

'Good! Where are you? Can I join you?'

I had to laugh, even though the old grump demon was close to taking over. 'You're welcome if you know where I am, because I don't.'

And he did. I found an unpronounceable street name, spelled it out to him and somehow he joined me twenty minutes later as I sat in a square close by, which he'd told me how to find. I was impressed.

He navigated us to the restaurant that was, as I'd been told, authentic Polish, with a menu of dishes which needed translation. This should have broken the ice, melted my animosity; I knew I ought to be grateful that he'd rescued me but at the same time was cross that I'd needed his assistance. I couldn't shake it off and was awkward and unresponsive, and he was reserved and monosyllabic which I couldn't understand; it was his idea after all. At last having drunk far too much, I embarrassed us both by saying; 'I'm trying to avoid men at the moment, but then I thought you were safe being gay.'

The silence was thick, a vast pause which I wasn't going to fill and wanted no one to do it for me. All around us the tables were full of celebration, noisy people, laughter, cheers, and I was defiant and ashamed. I watched Roger like a child who's poked a snake with a stick and waits for a reaction. I wanted him to spit back; for all the men who'd let me down, this vengeful Eve was on the attack.

He laid down his knife and fork, neatly side by side, refilled my glass and his, emptying the bottle. He turned to attract the waiter's attention and then back to me.

'I'm sorry, Greta, both that I'm a man and sadly, not gay. Shall I get the bill?'

'Touché,' I said. I raised my glass to him. 'And yes. I know I'm bad company tonight, and I don't know why you asked to join me.'

He began to laugh, the corners of his mouth twitching at first, followed by a mild giggle turning to a sustained chuckle. 'Yes, me too.'

'Why?' I said.

'Why what? That I'm not gay?'

'No, of course, not. You're making me feel a fool which I know that I am, but I don't need it accentuating. Water, maybe it's water I need.'

The waiter was at his side, water ordered with the bill. And Roger said to me; 'I don't need to know why you want to shun men but I really am sorry that I'm not better company myself this evening.' He took off his glasses and rubbed his eyes. 'A dreadful day, exhausting arguments none of which I could agree with.'

'What was the subject?' Why hadn't I asked this before?

'The environmental impact of Poland's reliance on coal.'

'Is that any of our business?'

'Exactly what the Poles say and who can blame them. But, I didn't want to talk about that. I shouldn't have asked to join you. Please forgive me.'

'No, no! It's me and please, I'm paying,' as at that moment the waiter placed the bill in front of Roger.

He put his glasses back on again and picked up the bill. Looking at me sternly he began to tear it in half. 'Why not go Dutch? That's the expression I believe.'

'Yes, let's,' and I watched as he took out a pen to calculate the division. I waited unable to decide whether I was mollified or annoyed that he was being so reasonable.

He passed it across to me: 'Do you agree?'

We both paid with cash, the waiter bowed us out of the door with English salutations and the freezing night air dragged the breath from my lungs. The street lamps laid ponds of light on the pavement and the silhouettes of the restored buildings against a starry sky might have been a backcloth for a romantic opera. I remember looking furtively at Roger, wanting to say something poetic and appreciative but decided I'd made an idiot of myself already and there was no need to compound it. We found and shared a taxi back to the hotel in almost complete silence. Though I do know it was comfortable, no feeling of animosity, and as we said goodnight formally in the hotel lobby, I wished there was some way of making amends.

The next morning I woke up with an appalling headache; daylight cringed around the edges of the heavy drapes forcing me to face up to a morning as a tourist. Breakfast was an impossibility; I showered, left the hotel for a chemist and having dosed myself with Paracetamol and coffee, took a couple of trams to the Vistula River, crossing over to a park where I saw red squirrels scampering among the trees. I walked back and into the Old Town again, came across the restaurant where we'd eaten the night before and peering through the window wondered why I'd not appreciated the Rococo splendour or complimented anyone on the food. Back at the hotel I paid my bill at reception and was given a note.

Thank you, Greta, for your 'bad company'. I apologise for being a dull man and not gay. Perhaps one day we will do better. Yours, Roger Harlow.

'Is the gentleman still in the hotel?' I said to the receptionist.

'His name?'

I told her and she searched her computer, asked a colleague and came back to me shaking her head. 'There is no one of that name has registered with us, madam. A man came this morning to leave it for to give you.'

I flew back to London with a head full of contradictions. I admired his note but wanted no more complications. No more men was a mantra I wanted to adopt, but why? Apart from Gerald, whom could I blame; Angus, never; Colin, a mere crumb I discarded; Max, a pocket sized challenge, Paul, a clumsy puppy, and Michael, the safe rebound man, they'd served me, not I them. My censure needed revision.

I was a kinder person when we landed, ready to ease my way out of Michael's life, resolving soon to phone Roger and apologise. It was, though, Freddie who came next.

December

Freddie Falkirk

'Ms Salway; I don't expect you'll remember me. Freddie Falkirk?'

The man leant forward offering his copy of 'Rebels, Saints and Mammon', the first in a trilogy with Jack MacArthur, the black detective I'd raised from the slums of Glasgow.

'We met in Grantchester; it was after Lottie died, I'm afraid.'

I looked up at him, the dim light of the book shop, the queue of ardent fans were obliterated by the image of a sleek, black machine and a fragile youth outlined against a bright grim day saying, 'I'm gay.'

'I'm sorry, I've shocked you,' he was saying, 'but hearing that …'

'No, no,' I said. 'I'm pleased to see you, Freddie. You came to her funeral, didn't you?' For twelve years I'd wanted to be certain that was true, hoped even that I might meet him again.

'I did,' he said, 'and I wish that I'd spoken to you then.' He was no longer fragile; the man in front of me, who would be in his mid thirties, had an air of the patrician about him. A classical scholar, of course, it fitted. 'Would it be possible to meet,' he was saying, 'later after you've finished here.' He looked back at the patient followers piled up behind him. 'If you've time.'

'Yes,' I said, knowing I'd have to cancel dinner with Michael. 'But it'll probably be a couple of hours before I'm free. Do you have a mobile phone?'

He gave me a number, I signed his book and we agreed to meet in a café on King's Parade.

'I'd like that very much,' I repeated. Such an understatement, such a mundane reply for the surge of gratitude I felt to the forces of nature, the conscious world that brought him to me. I'd be able to talk about Lottie, to bring her back with someone who knew her, differently; perhaps to even make sense of what I'd once imagined.

It was the beginning of December, the end of term, so few undergraduates to take over the streets and a mere sprinkling of tourists. As I walked up Trinity Street to meet him, a sharp winter sun turned to gold the stonework on the Senate House. This was the first time I'd been to a book signing here, in Cambridge, and more than a month since that lunch with Gerald.

Freddie was there, at a table outside the café. He got up and offered me his hand, holding mine as if in some sort of tryst. 'I have read all your books, you know. I bought this one for my partner,' he said, flourishing his copy with the other hand. 'Is it too cold or do you think we could sit outside?'

'A good idea,' I said. 'And I need a sandwich. Can I get you one?'

'Oh, no, I'll do that. My pleasure. I'm no longer the poor undergraduate.' He let go of my hand. 'It's the least I can do to welcome you to my home town.'

'Good,' I said. 'I'll be interested to hear more.' I wasn't going to say that I'd lived close by far longer than he and considered it my city too. I said; 'And thank you.'

I sat across from the magnificence of King's College chapel that never ceases to fill me with awe; all that technical artistry creating symmetry and elegance, built with the crudest of tools. Lottie once said as we'd sat right here having tea when she was still at school; 'Being inside there for the Carol Service makes even me think about rising up to a heaven. Clever weren't they?'

What was I going to ask this man, Freddie Falkirk, the surname which I'd also learned from the statements given to the coroner? Older and slightly stooped as if he needed to come down to our level, his height a burden rather than an achievement, the gaunt pale boy was a professor of classics, an appointment of which he was clearly proud. 'I live in Trumpington quite close to that pub. I've never stopped thinking about Lottie, wishing that, well, I don't know what I'm entitled to wish,' he said before disappearing into the café to buy my lunch.

Twelve years on nothing had changed, except the raw heartache was overlaid with layers of love and regret, kindness, memories and the need to carry on, strata to soften and soothe. Occasionally that earth was dug into, shovelled up, like molehills erupting pain; her birthday, the anniversary of her death, thoughts of where she'd be now, if only.

'You were very kind to us that day,' he said, laying the tray with teapot, sandwiches and flapjack in front of me. 'I've never forgotten your decency; you were well within your rights to tell us we were selfish, useless friends to Lottie.'

'I wasn't there for that.'

'No, and that isn't why I've come to you now. It's because of what I realised later.'

I poured the tea, a cup for each of us, the sandwiches no longer appetising. 'I was pleased to see you at the funeral,' I said not sure whether I wanted to hear what he had to say. 'So many people there, it made a difference.'

'I'm glad about that, and as I said, I should have stopped to speak but, well, I didn't know what else to say at the time or whether my presence might disturb you.'

'Tell me about Lottie,' I said. 'I never want to share her with strangers, but I constantly want to remember her, talk about her, and I was thinking that I'd like to know more of what you all did together, what you knew of her.' I lifted his cup off the tray and put it in front of him. He looked down on it, bewildered.

'Yes, that's what I hoped you'd say. But can I start by telling you what I've been doing all these years to bring me back here?'

'I'd like that. And I can eat my sandwiches,' again I saw him as a singular young man that I needed to protect.

He told me how he left for Yale that summer after Lottie's death for a post graduate degree returning to Cambridge for his PhD and was now a professor in the classics department, living with his partner, an American psychologist, Robin.

'Life's good,' he said, 'but sometimes when I think of Lottie I feel guilty that I'm so happy.'

'That's ridiculous,' I said.

'I know, that's just what she would have said, what Robin tells me.'

A woman leant over us asking if she can take the spare seat from our table to hers. Freddie immediately got up and carried it across for her, a button on his jacket catching in the lattice back as he set it down. There is laughter from her other guests as he extricated himself.

'Typically clumsy,' he says as he comes back to join me. 'Lottie told me that I was the only person who could spill an empty bottle of beer. She told me to go to an optician.'

'Oh dear, she could be brutally frank sometimes.'

'Yes, and she was right. My specs are correctly calibrated now, but I can still make a fool of myself. It's a good act for my students though; living up to an old expectation.'

I laughed and offered him the other flapjack; the distraction had taken us back to where I wanted to be.

'When did you first get to know Lottie?'

'I don't know exactly,' he said. 'The poll tax thing was when we were particularly drawn together. Her views were always precise, passionate. I can't say I was as committed as she was. "You're too dreamy, Fred," she'd say. I liked her a lot, you could trust her, that's why I told her I was gay.'

'That was on the night of your birthday?'

'Yes.' He looked at me, fiercely, as if he'd practiced the unfaltering gaze in a mirror, his eyes enlarged by the lenses in his glasses. 'I never thought, never realised, and I don't know if I'm right, whether that made any difference.'

The air was just warm enough; he wore a jacket of grey mix tweed with a muffling scarf and I was grateful for my thick coat. I was aware of other voices rising and fading around us but I was glad that we were out in the open.

'You can imagine her fury at Clause 28,' he said. 'I knew that she'd be the one to sympathise, the one person I could come out to. And it was because of the way she reacted, tearing into the terrible damage Thatcher had done, I never thought that she might - well, let me show you her card.'

The envelope he handed to me was white, torn at the edge where it had been roughly opened.

As I held the card he'd given me, smoothing its surface between my finger and thumb on the way back to London, the light still bright on the shorn trees, their structure bereft of leaves, a different beauty, I knew it was an answer to the question I would be asking for the rest of my life; why did she do it?

'You see, she'd arrived after the others,' he said. 'By then I'd drunk quite a lot. She gave me the card and I hugged her, tore it open and looking at the picture, well, you'll see, it was what I needed her to say, which is why later, we'd been talking about Greenham and how people labelled all the women as lesbians as if a derogatory term, that I wanted to tell her that I'm gay.'

I pulled out the card. Shiny white embossed in large red letters, FREE. I drew in a deep breath. To have in my hand another piece of her, something she'd chosen, touched and given, shook and soothed me. All those plaguing nightmares of her coming and retreating were confounded. This thing was real as if she were speaking.

'So Lottie,' I said as if to myself. 'Everything was black and white to her, or red and white in this case.'

'But I didn't look inside at that moment,' he was saying. 'Debs had brought a cake with candles and there was mayhem while they were lit, blown out and we'd all had a slice.'

I looked down at the card. 'Can I open it?'

'Yes, but can I tell you first when I saw what she'd written?'

I nodded; I was in no hurry.

'I'm afraid it got put aside with all the others, later gathered up and put in my motor bike box. Which I'm ashamed to say wasn't opened again until I came back from Yale, two years later.'

The transcripts of Freddie's statement had told me that he'd slept at the pub that night, offered a sofa by the landlady who saw that he wasn't in a fit state to ride his motorbike back to Cambridge. I was surprised that he'd remembered to take the cards with him; perhaps she'd noticed and had given them to him when clearing up the bar. I should be grateful to her as well.

'My bike had been in a friend's garage and when I decided to sell it on returning from America, I found the cards. I was pleased; a memory of a happy evening for me, especially having spoken to Lottie, involving her in my secret. Even if its end was so dreadful.'

'They go together I find; good and bad, which is obvious really.' I looked down at the unopened card. 'But Lottie had a secret too, didn't she?'

'You knew?'

'I speculated after I was told about the poems stuck on the wall of her room. A girl who lived next door told me that Lottie had written them, all about love, but they'd gone by the time I went there; the girl, Maeve, was her name I think, said that she thought Lottie took them down the day she died.'

Freddie shook his head slowly; 'I had no idea, but I should have done. If only I'd known.'

'But if what we're both thinking is true, what was there to be done?'

'I shouldn't have challenged her.'

'What?'

'It was a running joke with us that she hated poetry and I loved it. When she knew what I was studying she told me I was beginning to look careworn and desiccated; "Unravelling all that ancient abstruse stuff, it's not good for your health," she said; "You need the purity of numbers." I remember it so well. I told her she ought to try writing poetry, that it was good for the soul; it was a sort of dare.'

'I love poetry, have found it exhilarating and …' I looked down at the envelope in my hand, 'at one time I thought her antipathy was a child's rebellion. You know, having to be different from their parent.'

'Open it,' he said, 'look inside, see what she wrote.'

Many times since I've taken it out and read again and again and the same sense of joy and sorrow seizes me. Her neat, meticulous handwriting covers both inside pages. And I physically hear her, can feel her breath on my cheek, see the slightly cocked head, a bright little bird, the smug smile of, ' See, I can do it too.'

I promised you a poem

Rock cracked wide by glaciers shouldering
through to gouge a gorge of water,
sluicing a rush of foam and spray to tell the story
of the inside out of love.

Willows wiping a river with lazy leaves
meandering through meadows wet with
buttercups shining gold for fools and lovers to tell
the inside out of love.

Skylarks singing on a thread of blue air high
above a hill where harebells ring a riff as clear
as the water that pools on paving stones reflecting
back the inside out of love.

Lady slipper, rosemary, meadowsweet, forget-
me-nots, violets and the darling buds of May speak
the botany of poets' language which I foolishly
adopt for the inside out of love.

To Freddie, my love, on your umpteenth birthday from
Lottie Salway

We sat, Freddie and I, staring down at the card for I don't know how long. I felt him near and yet far, far away for I was back to the place she'd described, swept up by the overwhelming impulse of first love.

'She was good, wasn't she?' I heard him say. 'I wish I'd been able to tell her.'

I couldn't disguise the tears, didn't want to, but I could smile for he was right. 'Yes, she was good, but she'd have denied it. Can't you hear her; "It's just a bit of fancy fluff," I think she'd have said, don't you'?

2003

One after another

Twelve years after I lost her, they came, one after the other, three men to disturb my grief.

First Gerald's incursion although thankfully having nothing to do with Lottie, felt like a raid. Freddie coming to give me Lottie's birthday card with her poem of love, brought her back stirring up the 'what ifs'. Although to talk of my clever daughter who was valued and loved, even though not as she would have wished, was a gift. And now there was Roger.

Before that moment I'd dealt with the dinner I'd postponed with Michael; a farewell meal with none of the misery of lovers parting; he was aware that I, and he, needed to move on.

'Tea at Claridges, Greta,' he'd suggested.

'Why not?' I'd said.

When I told Leo he was waspish; 'Like two old crones eating wispy sandwiches and fiddly fancies at some exorbitant price.'

'You're jealous, Leo,' I said. 'I promise I'll treat you with my next batch of royalties.' I noticed the white hairs beginning to distinguish the shorter cut he'd recently acquired. The ageing process for Leo would be discreet, chic.

His eyes flashed. 'You're a good woman, Greta. And happy to be free, I hope? Fitzherbert Smith was too old, too safe for you. You deserve someone with more intellect and grace. One day, one day.'

I didn't bother to tell him I'd closed that proverbial door.

Christmas came and went. Joy and I tried to be festive; she gave me a hot water bottle and bedsocks, so appropriate. I came back to London on January 2nd relaxed and planning to gather all my author friends together for a celebration. My intended celibacy was a secret I wanted to inaugurate, not publicise; friends were what I needed to cultivate in this new year.

I'd phoned Roger after Poland to apologise, arranged a date to meet; lunch when I'd promised to be a lovelier person. I could have left it but that would have been cowardly, I thought. And his note had been amusing. But he was busy until February, he said; I asked if we could put a date in our diaries. I couldn't believe how persuasive I was being and afterwards worried that I'd overdone my eagerness.

So here we were, Roger and I, meeting for a late lunch at a Thai restaurant in Soho, arriving at the same time, he walking from one direction, I from the other, both under umbrellas. Sullen clouds hung heavy that day but the fine rain danced like diamanté in the lamplight, the pavement shone black silk; if I had been thinking romantically it was a good enough setting.

And it was easy to begin; he knew as much about Thai food as me, very little; white wine was ordered. There was a single white gardenia floating in a bowl between us, branches of pussy willow upstaging the bar. I told him about my Christmas, the repairs that needed to be done on the house in Waterbeach, why the next novel was hard to get started, a new detective to create as I'd killed off a predecessor. Douglas and Audrey were the link we were here to discuss though and I warmed to the tales I could tell, he proving to be a good listener, and then reliving his experience of them. 'I thought what super parents they'd make,' he said, and I remembered what Lottie had said about Douglas.

Roger told me why he'd been busy; 'As a freelance economics journalist I choose who I work for which is a bit of a tightrope financially, but it keeps my conscience clear. Now that sounds sanctimonious,' he said, 'but it came with my upbringing; my mother would never buy goods not ethically sourced, constantly sent letters of complaint to various organisations including her MP, stood on picket lines.'

He sounded apologetic so I said; 'My daughter would have approved.'

And that's when he said; 'I know, I met her.'

I thought I must have misheard and asked again what he'd said.

He repeated; 'I met your daughter, Lottie.'

This ought to have allowed me to say, 'Oh, did you?' with an expectant smile, curiosity leaning in to this perfectly respectable man with his impeccable manners, who I was beginning to think might be added to my list of friends; and who looked more troubled than triumphant at having offered this piece of information, his claim on Lottie. Yes, that was it, his claim on Lottie, is what disturbed me.

'How?' I said.

The day had shifted, he and I, strangers; why were we here? I stared at him, a man who I'd met on a station, bumped into, become acquainted with, the reason not this. The pendant light hanging over our table made him look ghostly, far off, a snared rabbit; or perhaps that was me?

'I'm sorry,' he was saying; 'Perhaps I shouldn't have told you.'

He was staring at me, scrutinising my reaction, or was that what I was doing to him? Take hold, Greta, a voice from inside caught me; calm and cool, you know how to do this.

'I wanted to tell you before,' he spoke urgently, as if he thought I was about to walk out. 'As soon as Audrey told me about you, and then Lottie, I realised. She thought you'd want to know, but I think I've misjudged it, a comparative stranger coming from nowhere professing an acquaintance that isn't appropriate for you.'

I shook my head; 'Appropriate? I'm not sure what you mean by that. When was this?' I said. 'How did you meet her?'

'Cambridge. March 1990.'

We left the restaurant. It was I not he who'd paled, ashen faced, shrunk, brittle. He apologised again; thought I needed fresh air and although we hadn't finished the meal he called the waiter and paid. I think I did remonstrate that it wasn't necessary, but dark spaces around us seemed to close in; a miasma of pungent odours which had seemed so tasty a matter of minutes before, swelled sickly in my throat. Perhaps it was all too reminiscent of that other lunch with Gerald, even though the flowers had changed, the food of another country, another man.

Roger suggested Soho Square a few streets away. The rain stopped, the trees dripped and the seats were wet but we didn't need to sit. Roger bought us a takeaway coffee and by the time we were circling the paths and grass of this little park which I will never forget, I was ready for truth or fraud.

'The Poll Tax, you remember?' Roger said. 'I was researching public reaction, especially student protest.

Young people tend to be discounted, hot-headed anarchistic attitudes is the common view, but they're the votes of tomorrow. As you'll know Lottie was involved, and when I met the group outside the council offices she was determined to be the spokesperson.'

Whether it was the warmth of the coffee, the caffeine, or seeing the first snowdrop needles poking through the grass, I was bolstered and receptive, hanging on to what he had to tell me. He wore a woolly beanie hat, discreet charcoal black, which he'd pulled from his pocket, and good leather gloves; we must have looked a sombre pair. Not unlike the couple of sleek crows, ancient dowagers flaunting widow's weeds, who strutted around us in search of leftover snacks, disdainful of our presence.

'Lottie knew all the arguments,' he said, 'was vehement in her condemnation of the government, insisted that I send her a copy of the article prior to publication.'

I smiled; this would be true. 'What did she say?' I said.

'I don't remember exactly but something like not wishing to be misquoted; the argument was too important.'

'Did you send her that copy?'

'Yes, and it came back by return of post with several corrections in red.'

We were both smiling and stopped to enjoy the moment. But then we knew what had to come next. 'I'm so sorry,' he said. 'I didn't know what had happened to her. I'd hoped that she might get in touch when the article was published, but that was too late. Audrey explained.'

I nodded. And we stood looking at one another and he didn't look away, he had the courage to keep on looking at me; I liked him for that.

206

'It was terrible, is terrible,' I said, 'but I imagine you'll know that.'

He nodded and kept looking, unwavering as if absorbing the wave of grief, the moment when a tide finds the crack in the seawall, defences breached. I didn't want to look away; he was another pilgrim on Lottie's journey. I'd no reason to disbelieve.

We didn't need to elaborate that day; he didn't ask me how or why she died. Our coffee finished, the rain resumed and under umbrellas we parted. He said; 'Please can we meet again. I've wanted to share that with you, selfishly perhaps, my sadness needing to be expressed.'

I nodded and I was the one to move forward for a hug, my head resting briefly on his chest, the wool of his jacket already absorbing the rain. I said; 'You'll smell like wet sheep shortly. Give me a call when you're dry,' and left.

I phoned Joy that evening. 'With whom do you talk to about Lottie?' I said. An unfair question, maybe, but she wasn't fazed.

'God, and you, lovey, that's all.'

I talk to no one else. Dora knows the bare details but was aware soon after Lottie's death that I didn't want to discuss it; she'd never met her. Dora's kids, her man, growing up, getting older, keeping fit, 'maintaining the glamour', her expression, keep us laughing; light-hearted, it's enough for an evening. Leo is my guardian angel, his tact legendary and his occasional oblique pep talks are all I've needed. Paul, a child-man, is long since gone and Michael, like all the other men in my life, had never known her. Friends who've come since have been kept in ignorance; that part of my life private. I've never told them about my daughter, even though I know they would be receptive and sympathetic. They would be surprised at my secrecy, though never condemnatory. But I didn't want to talk to anyone else, until Freddie.

The reasons are easy to fathom. I can list them.

It isn't fair to burden other people; grief diminishes their own lives, brings on feelings of guilt that they are happy, and have escaped. Or have they? It trips that certainty of 'it could never happen to me'; their own escape is called into question. Why would I want to take friends and acquaintances down that path?

The list includes my fear of exposure. To tell about how she did it, the brutal nature of what she chose, is shocking. Suicide, the taking of life so full of promise, is impossible to envisage, let alone understand. In the past victims were feared; buried at crossroads like common criminals with the thought that if they rose from the dead they would find it hard to find their way back to haunt those left living. And it was only in 1961 that the law criminalising suicide was revoked. How could I talk to anyone of my lovely daughter making this terrible choice, and why?

The secrecy of how she came into the world, from where, from whom, has added to my decision for privacy. My most loved and precious gift is not to be torn apart by other people's curiosity. She was mine, is mine; the sign 'keep out' has aged with the years, become rock hard, more substantial. Why disturb that tender soil of acceptance with double digging? She didn't understand 'the inside out of love' so why would they?

Roger came back quite soon with; 'I have tickets for a concert at the Royal Festival Hall; one of those populist programmes where you can just wallow in works you already know.' He had no idea whether I knew any music at all but made the assumption that I did. The date was a week ahead so I'd easily be able to make an excuse, to say I couldn't go. Treading the shifting sands of commitment, my fear of being sucked in.

He sensibly didn't suggest a meal beforehand; I thought he'd never wish to share food with me ever again. A drink in the bar was enough to take us in and he was right, it was gloriously easy listening, magical. Sitting beside him was equally unfussy; he reminded me of Angus in that way, totally absorbed and then the lit up face at the end of each piece. He even surprised me by shouting; 'Bravo' when we applauded the solo violinist. I, on the other hand, was distracted by niggling curiosity. Who is this man? What else ought I to know about him? And Lottie, I wanted all he could tell me about Lottie. Was he waiting for me to bring up the subject again? I guessed so.

As we left I suggested a quick bite at a restaurant on The Cut. 'I promise good behaviour. I would like to talk about Lottie.'

I was as good as my word. I told him how Lottie died, even how I saw her shredded body in the mortuary, the funeral, the flowers, her grave with Jim tending the earth, the inquest. He listened as caught up in what I was saying as he had been in the music; that's how it felt to me. 'Of course, you will know something of this yourself,' I said.

He nodded, pausing before saying; 'To lose my mother, yes, terrible, but she'd waited for me to be independent. I have to be grateful for that, though I miss her constantly, wish she was here to know the good and bad bits of my life.' He shook his head; 'But to lose your child ...' and as before he held my gaze.

I said; 'Thank you,' and I didn't feel as if I'd betrayed Lottie even as I said; 'I haven't told anyone else before now; no, not all of it even to my own parents.'

He took off his glasses and rubbed his eyes. 'It's hard putting into words something so intimate, precious and mind-blowingly awful; it can sound prosaic.' Without replacing his glasses he looked at me again as if absorbing the pain. 'Strange, when I met you that first time I told you, someone I'd never met before, about my mother and I've rarely talked about what happened to her.'

'You did and I was grateful; it was appropriate after what we'd had to listen to.'

There must have been other diners around us for I know a crowd followed us in as we arrived, but I only remember sitting by a window looking across to the Young Vic. And an audience coming out of a show, something popular and fun from the laughter, shouts of farewell and calls for taxis.

'The world goes on,' I said.

'Yes, which is a scourge and an inspiration.' He'd still left his glasses on the table, which I learned later meant that he couldn't see me clearly. His eyes, though, were not diminished by the lack of magnification; green grey with lashes as dark as his eyebrows. His frown, his expression of sorrow genuine, I was sure of that. And I think it was then, inappropriately, that I thought again he was too perfectly tailored not to be gay.

I said; 'I think that's enough gloom for one night. The concert was fantastic; I still feel the uplift, perhaps that's why I could talk about Lottie.'

He said; '"After silence, that which comes nearest to expressing the inexpressible is music." I can't remember who I'm quoting, I'll have to look it up.'

'Aldous Huxley,' I raised an eyebrow, smiling. 'I've always thought that's one of the best.'

March rolled into April when I invited him to a press night at The National with tickets I'd been given for 'Jerry Springer the Opera'. He was pushed for time so we only had a few minutes for a drink beforehand and then, at the interval, talked about the show.

I said; 'It lives up to one of the reviews I read; "a foul mouthed fiesta."

He said; 'That's a bit harsh. We've only seen the first half.'

'You mean it could get worse?'

'I expect nothing less. And I'm enjoying it, something different.'

'I'm sorry, I thought ...' but he interrupted; "Never make a defence or apology before you be accused."

'Who said that?'

'Charles I. That was before he had his head chopped off, of course.'

I knew that I liked him and there was the thread of shared experience, shared narrative between us. To some extent I'd exposed myself by telling what I'd told no one else, but it wasn't something to worry about any more. We parted easily outside the theatre to go our separate ways. It was only later that I wished that I knew more about him. Was he in a relationship, gay or not? Where did he live? Vague references to 'Hackney way,' and for me 'on the Central Line' had seemed enough. That should have been enough; I was far too busy and, obviously so was he.

May

The constant writing of plots

'I'm not doing a Sherlock Holmes, there's no bringing him back to life; Jack MacArthur died, he's dead and buried,' I said.

She wasn't happy, my editor; 'Loyalty, brand loyalty, you know readers want the connection, the continuity. There must be a way for you to ...'

'Dig him up, pretend another body was buried?'

'Well, it's been known.'

'Exactly! Which is why I won't.'

Harsh words; others pointed out it was commercial suicide. To be honest my anger was particularly vehement as I was without inspiration. That 'form of laziness, sticking to the same formula' I'd boasted of to Roger was a myth. I was as dead as dear old Jack. I needed reassurance.

'I've done it before, Leo, haven't I? Lisa Battle took over from Morag Maclachlan. They move on, out or up, or in this case, down.'

Leo wasn't arguing, wasn't persuading or putting forward any theories of what I ought or ought not to be doing. He was the sounding board.

'Brand loyalty, is what she said. I sound like a washing up liquid!'

'No, champagne, darling, that's your 'brand'.' He signed the quotation marks.

We were having that tea at Claridges, as promised, and seeing Leo so sleek and trim across the table, his sharp dressing befitting each occasion, I thought of Roger. He was floating in and out of my mind far too much; probably because I constantly wanted diversion. Anything to fill the blank page.

'Perhaps this is the end of the line, Leo,' I said, 'the muse has flown.'

Leo's raised eyebrow is a work of art which he uses to full effect. 'The muse or lack of, like writer's block is baloney; you know that, Greta. I've always thought a better analogy is the collecting of a series of ingredients and seeing how they cook up together; patience and hard work creating the best recipe, the best dish.'

I laughed; 'You know nothing about cooking as I've remarked before.'

'Exactly; it's why I'm not a writer, merely their confidante and negotiator.'

Confidante, Roger. I'd allowed him to be my confidante.

To work; Leo was right. Looking back at collected scraps of information, cases from the news, old newspapers, trawling through characters I'd cooked up and discarded in the past, perhaps this one would be gay. And so John Aynsley Howden was born, straight out of university on to the beat and then dropping out; the homophobia was too much to take. 'Private detective with more intelligence than the entire Met put together,' was how he described himself. I was back on track and the words flew from keyboard to page; Leo, as always, had given good advice.

At the same time I was rushing up to Waterbeach to tend the garden, make sure workmen had come to make good the house. One day it would be mine and it was the place I'd begun to consider home, more than when I was there growing up. It was where Lottie lived nearly all her life; it was her home.

I went into Cambridge one day, walked up Castle Hill to Shire Hall and imagined Lottie standing outside with placards protesting, found by Roger. I decided that I would contact him some time soon and ask him to tell me more. But before I could do that we met on King's Cross Station; me on my way back, he going up to Leeds.

'This is extraordinary,' I said, 'we seem to be masters of the unexpected.'

He laughed; 'Time for a cup of tea?'

'Yes, if you have.'

'A quick one,' and he pushed his way into a café while I guarded his case.' This is strange,' he said, 'another train station.'

We sat outside on the concourse. The hubbub around us masking an awkward shyness which I filled with babble about unpunctuality and cleanliness.

'Look,' he finally said, 'I really would like to meet again properly. You said once before about marking in a date rather than leaving it to chance. Next weekend I'm back and have nothing planned for Sunday. Could we go somewhere, do something different?' He picked up his cardboard cup of tea. 'Is that okay? I'll call when I'm in Leeds to make sure you agree.' And he was off. And he hadn't left me with the bill, just a smile on my face.

It was the first weekend in May so there would still be Monday free for me to be with Joy. That I continue to allot Monday to Friday as work days after all these years of being away from a normal job is perverse, except it isn't. Lottie, Joy and Jim managed their lives to that routine; and routine is what we cling to when life goes awry.

On this Sunday Roger suggested taking a boat up or down the Thames. Tate Britain and Tate Modern would both be open; the day dawned bright. I worried that a whole day, or even several hours, was going to be difficult to stretch with memories of my child and polite conversation. I reassured myself that this outing was for Lottie, and ignored the curiosity that itched and I needed to scratch. If he wasn't gay who was he with or was he? Where and how did he live? A new friend for a new year, that's all it was to be.

The water lapped luxuriously, sunlight on the Thames a taffeta sheen, this ancient river upstaging everything. I wore new khaki chinos, a flowery top, sensible jacket and trainers; my sunglasses were the type that reflect back, eyes masked, making me appear inscrutable. Why I remember these details is evidence of how nervous I felt; and which is the reason I complimented Roger on what he was wearing. The same shades - in American parlance - and, true to previous form, his long shorts, V necked teeshirt and dark denim jacket were fashionably appropriate for the occasion.

Later I commented; 'The only other man I know who dresses well is my agent, Leo, and he's gay. You understand my misconception.'

Roger laughed; 'I've been teased for fussy dressing in the past, but I like clothes, enjoy fashion, have the gene, or something. And it gives me confidence if I'm appropriately dressed.'

'Yes, I understand that. Lottie liked my glad rags, as she called them. "Are you wearing your being-an-author-person clothes?" she'd ask whenever I phoned.'

He looked at me then, hidden by dark glass, but as if acknowledging again that to talk of her was special. The tour guide butted in, loud in pointing out historic spots. Roger leant in close; 'I used to wear my school uniform most of the time to feel important.'

'I did the reverse, to be different!'

We'd boarded at Westminster and decided that Tate Modern was our destination. 'I've never looked around their collection,' Roger said. 'The Turbine Hall is as far as I've got.'

'What have you liked?' I said, hardly listening to his reply as I was framing the next question. I was the Spanish inquisition with one day to extract all I needed to know.

By the time we'd reached the Gallery, I'd told him as much about me as I'd found out about him. I'd extracted his artistic preferences, that he plays the piano and that he'd lived outside Manchester as a child, holidayed in the Lake District. 'Camping with my mother and friends.'

'You've no accent,' I said.

'Only the short 'a' as in fast, path, bath. That's stuck. My mother came from Woking, "deep south, true blue Conservative country," she'd sneer.'

I had to vouchsafe the council house with garden back and front, cosy East Anglia town and working class parents.

'Both cum up in't world, then,' he said, 'vying for the validity of our working class roots.' His raised eyebrows couldn't compete with Leo but his prim pouting lips made me giggle. 'No offence, of course,' he said, a perfect imitation of Julian Clary.

Later as we motored back by boat, I thought of the men in my life, who'd ranged from ordinary to scruffy, to way out, to out-dated. I'd never cared till now.

It was so different from visits to exhibitions with Paul who'd constantly want me to appreciate what he'd found and liked. I'd had to rebel. 'I'm not going to get lost,' I'd tell him, 'we'll meet at the exit.' Which, of course, meant that I could develop my own opinion. Roger and I, walked around the Poetry and Dream collection separately; having read the curator's blurb we drifted off naturally to find each other an hour later circling back.

'Coffee and a bun?' he said.

We sat by a window in the café looking out at the stands of silver birch which line the walks to and from the gallery and along to the new bridge over to St Pauls. The trees white papery bark, traced black trunks, remind me of Russia, of Chekov's heroines suffering their melancholy men.

'How would you describe yourself?' I said. 'Is your glass half full or half empty?'

'Heck,' he said, 'is this what authors always do? Bleed innocent bystanders of their character traits?'

He was laughing and I blushed. Without the specs it was impossible to hide my embarrassment. 'Only the interesting ones,' I said, 'the ones I believe might have criminal tendencies.'

And we sat grinning at one another for some time. I'd like you for a brother, I thought.

For the record he did admit to being half full, fearing the empty which is what had taken his mother. I said; 'I'm sorry, I shouldn't have asked.'

'No, I'm not sensitive like that.'

'We're lucky, then. I don't think it's acquired necessarily, or in our genes; hard to say and not to dwell on.'

Small details of his meetings with Lottie emerged, small but each was priceless. When he told me of taking her and the group for coffee at The Copper Kettle on Kings Parade, I realised he would have met Freddie. I told him about meeting Freddie before Christmas, and Lottie's card. 'I still wish I'd been able to see those other poems, if they existed.'

Roger said; 'I've still kept boxes of my mother's mementos; things she wrote, some sketches. All neatly packed for me to find; I believe she wanted me to have them,' he said.

'That's good.'

A week later I received a letter from Freddie. I couldn't think why he was writing, what else he could have to say. He'd phoned me the day after we'd met in December wanting to know that I was happy to keep Lottie's card and poem; he didn't want me to think that he was off-loading her; 'She'll always be a special person in my life.'

I said how much I'd enjoyed our lunch and what a relief it had been to find the poem. 'I often wonder about those poems. I'm so pleased that I've found one, whatever it's implications.'

'Part of her archive, as well as mine in a way.'

'Yes, I like that.'

'Good.'

'Where the other poems went I'd love to know, of course,' I said. 'The girl, Maeve, the one who'd shared her room, was quite certain there were many more. She talked about not barging in on Lottie; she said; "Lottie was always busy, you'd never see her fiddling with make up or anything; it was always reading or writing, serious stuff."'

'That's Lottie,' and I could hear his smile at the other end of the line.

I had to go on. 'The girl told me why she'd noticed the poems as they were on scraps of paper torn from a notepad; it pleased her to imagine Lottie writing them during lectures, making her seem normal. The girl said how she'd asked Lottie what they were and Lottie'd laughed and said; "A project, I think it's a project."'

'That's Lottie,' he repeated.

'So where are they then?' I said. 'Did she get rid of them before going to the pub? There was nothing in the waste paper basket.'

There was a silence at the other end of the phone and I apologised. 'I'm sorry, Freddie, I'm being too obsessive. Is it the detective in me, the crime writer, the constant writing of plots?'

'No, you're her mother,' he said, but that was all.

Reading the letter that was not all. Here was proof that I'd passed on my obsession.

Dear Ms Salway
Since we met and our conversation before Christmas I have been thinking so much about you and Lottie. After so many years, finding her card and being able to explain was both disturbing and a joy.

Disturbing and a joy, yes, Freddie, that is exactly how I felt too. I read on.

I was troubled to learn about the lost poems for, although other people's testimony isn't always reliable, her roommate is hardly likely to have invented the idea. And we have proof that there was at least one.

Lottie's vibrancy, her determination and friendship, will always be safe in my memory. So I don't think that Lottie would have destroyed her writing. She was imbued with the scholarly belief that drafts, workings, evidence, are part of the process. And when could she have done so, as you said?

I haven't asked you about her effects, particularly whether you were able to recover anything she was wearing at the time. I do realise that the nature of her death might have made this impossible and maybe I shouldn't even be asking you now. But my strongest memory is of the leather jacket, her beloved jacket. You will know how proud she was

219

of it, I'm sure, and it's 'secret pocket', the lining providing a place for the safe transport of leaflets, for instance. The card she gave me was produced from this space.

Please forgive me if I have been presumptuous or hurtful in bringing up the subject, raking over what is best left unsaid. But you mentioned being obsessed which I understand completely; it's the reason that I felt I had to write to you.
With my very best wishes
Freddie

It was eight o'clock in the evening, the light through the windows of the flat fading to leave shadows curling in the corners of the living room. The post, that letter, had been sitting in my letter box all day, the white A5 sheet folded inside a matching white envelope. I sat on the edge of the sofa, the familiar feeling of feathers filling my ribs and stomach. Should he have written, was he right? What would Lottie think? That leather jacket had protected her, the animal hide tougher than her tender body. It was torn, gouged but enough remained for them to retrieve, for me to be given. I sat on, a brittle statue, my breathing shallow, darkness wrapping round me, a streetlight glazing the glass of the uncurtained window. And the telephone rang.

It was Roger saying what a pleasant day it had been on that Sunday, wondering whether we could 'pencil in another outing. I'm away for a fortnight but the last week of this month, any evening, or day time, if better.'

It must have been the pause before I spoke or that my voice cracked when I did which made him ask; 'Are you okay? Is this a bad time?'

It was the best time he could have called. Of course I would have eventually got to my feet, shaken myself off, ratcheted my way through to the woman who can take it all in her stride, as they say, but being able to tell someone who already knew, that I'd talked to so recently about what had happened to Lottie, was relief on a grand scale. And I wasn't betraying her. As he said; 'You'll know whether to look at her jacket, what is best for you, won't you? There'll be a time when it's right or not.' I didn't resent his advice.

The jacket was in Waterbeach. Five years ago I'd moved her things back there. Joy kept her little room, not as a shrine, but as it was because there was no need to do anything else. There was no one else who wanted it. However I'd decided that her continued part-time occupation of a room in my flat was not necessary and I ought to make a more accommodating study for myself. I knew she'd be pleased to think I was there, with the window which 'spies on to other people's back gardens'. She'd said to me often; 'Come and see. This would be the best place for you, Mumma. All those dark secrets stored in their sheds, gangsters holed up behind trampolines, bodies buried, so many places to dump your victim.'

I knew that I would have to take apart those boxes, boxes bought from Ikea in sturdy card, which I'd so carefully packed with tissue paper, no plastic, thinking it all had to breathe. No rush, but soon.

June

Love and a leather jacket

Is it easier to tell a stranger? I've often thought, sitting opposite or beside an unknown person on train or bus, that innocent bystander whose demeanour appears untroubled, to tell what is bugging me. Success or failure needs to be shared, those times when the world, like a balloon, has taken in too much air and gone pop. But he wasn't a stranger any more. Roger was a friend through knowing Lottie. At the same time it seemed a paradox that after all these years of safeguarding my child's privacy, I was willing, even eager, to confide, take his advice.

I didn't need to wait to follow Freddie's lead. It was now, the first Sunday after his message, Joy was at church; I had an hour to myself. I didn't want to say what I was doing. She and Jim had never asked about what I'd seen of Lottie in the mortuary. It was as if they could go so far and no further in their grief; I didn't need to distress them any more. Our roles reversed; I wanted to hide the worst, and raking over reasons for Lottie's action ceased when Jim died. What I'd brought back of her possessions I'd placed in those boxes privately. Nor had I ever mentioned the hypothetical poems.

At Christmas I'd been on the point of telling Joy about Freddie and the card, when she launched into a long explanation of life taking on a different hue – yes, hue was exactly the word she used. 'I'm eighty-seven, lovey, and content. If I go tomorrow I'll be ready. We know how precious life is, given and lost. You'll be all right without me, I know that.'

'Please,' I began, but she interrupted.

'You will. We've shared enough.' Momentarily I was shocked, brutally cut off, but she was right; she'd given me more than I deserved.

The boxes were in the wardrobe; pale oak with a mirror on the inside of one of the doors, a kidney shaped dressing table and bedside cupboard to match. This had been my room as a child; I knew it by heart. The way dawn crept cold around the curtains, the door opposite left ajar until I'd drifted into sleep, a light left on in the lavatory to confound the witches and ghouls. A crack still shot a lightning streak from ceiling to skirting board beside that door. No amount of filler or paint kept it in check. It was a persistent reminder that bricks and mortar may be planted on foundations appropriately deep but the earth beneath shifts to its own will.

For a moment I sit on her bed to admire the curtains, am struck at their prettiness, the yellow blossoms enclosed in the squares of blue checked gingham. The yellow candlewick bedspread is as fresh as the day it was bought, the floorboards as bright, the three blue rugs on each side of the single bed, one at the foot, complete the picture. There is not a swirl or mote of dust in the air, all surfaces clean as clean. Joy will have been in here every day to hold on to the perfection. Even the east facing aspect of the room is banished by this sweet and loving attention.

I have an hour or so alone. Joy is to meet me at the pub for lunch. Once she would have grumbled at my profligacy, we oughtn't to be wasting money on meals out when we lived a hands throw down the road. Not now. Is she used to my extravagance or eased into not making the effort any more?

I open the wardrobe and am overwhelmed by the scent of sandalwood; a fragrance redolent of ancient woods, eastern lands, peace and devotion. I wait as the air seeps out into the whole room before pulling out the box which I know contains the clothes she wore that day. The lid lifted, the tissue paper pushed aside, they lie as I left them, bits of denim, blood and dirt moulded into the fabric, and the still gleaming black of her leather jacket. I take them out one at a time, determined not to think of their survival as against where she lies, what she has become. I am here to find her, what she left of her self.

An arm has been cut from the jacket, another part chewed by wheels and rails. The rest is stiff, scratched and almost whole. The lining is disintegrating and as I open it out there they are, my mystery solved, scraps of paper, sandwiched together, white paper turned sepia. I touch with my finger first, afraid they will fragment, wary of pulling and tearing. How many small sheets are there? A4 lined paper folded into quarters, sliced apart with a knife; this is Lottie, careful, nothing randomly torn. I lift them out, push myself up from kneeling on the floor and lay them on her bed. Sitting beside them I hesitate; is this what she would have wanted? 'I don't like secrets,' she told me when I was seeing Max at the start of our relationship and I hadn't told her. 'I can't see the point, not if you love someone, me, I mean. You know everything about me and I ought to know everything about you. Is he a bad secret?' I assured her that he wasn't, and never kept anything from her again. Except, of course, her origin.

She didn't tell me about Freddie.

I peel them apart; crisp and clean they ease away from each other. The writing so familiar, so loved, is faded but legible. I read the first;

Love shimmers in the sun breathes moisture into the air
ruffled by the wind, drying up if never refreshed

and yet

And another;

Love cries wolf in the night a melancholy howl
love creeps cancer along neurons to eat rational thought

And below;

An owl floats on love
I'll swear

When did she write these? They are jottings, bits that might lead somewhere, the scratches of a mind desperate to describe the indescribable. Love.

Purple pulls down the day ushers in the dusk
For you and for me.

Outside a robin is shouting for its territory not for a mate. I am stiff with hurt. I should have told her that love isn't kind, rarely mutual, suffers the vagaries of the human heart.

Love needs butterfly wings to tell its story
Ravishingly beautiful
Don't say it
Spoken it flies on the ear to be heard not seen
Careful with the written word
For no one else's eyes
Too much to say
Too much – love cruel and indifferent

Is this how I felt over Gerald? Is this what I've passed on? An impossible loving?

Every crowd full with you

Absence all around
Hope that between all these people
You will emerge to smile and say

First love as dangerous as a fire-breathing dragon. She would have laughed at that.

I stand shoulder to shoulder with you
courage raging to tell the outrage
     and as ragged and urgent the desire to sit thigh to thigh,
hand to hand - but is this all rubbish

But it wasn't, and you'd have got over it, Lottie, if only you'd waited.

If you think of love as puddles of rain falling filling madly softly
the water clear bright reflecting light transparent
an image of you.

I stop. There are more; no corrections, crossing out or word substitutes; Lottie's thoughts stream on to each separate sheet. They are written with a biro on lined paper, but for me they are as perfect as if on parchment inscribed with a feathered quill. And then I hear her again; 'Oh, Mumma, you're daft. Such a romantic.' I say out loud back to her; 'Yes, Lottie, if only.'

I sit, crisp as the paper I hold in my hands. Crying, for her loss is futile. She was a happy child, always sure of what she thought and what she could or had to do. And this is it; her grand opera of love leading to a tragic end.

I gather up and return what I've found to lay on top of her jacket. I feel the light of the spring sun on my back, the blue sky pouring through the window, a spotlight on both of us. None of this she'd wished to share, as I had never been able to tell her or my mother about that man I'd once loved, her father. Someone else once said and I don't know who; 'Life and love are what they are and you have to deal with it'. I put the lid back on the box and the cupboard door closes with a swoosh of scented wood.

This is another secret that I cannot share with my mother.

I wanted to tell Roger. I phoned when I was back in London. He answered his mobile abruptly; I was an intrusion and apologised. He was instantly contrite, asked if he could phone me later. And I cursed myself. Why this desire to share my experience and feelings? It was contrary to all the years of reticence, but it was urgent. Was it because he was the first person who had claimed to know and admire Lottie in her own right, apart from Freddie? Either that or it was my age.

I said to Leo; 'Does getting older make us more willing to bore people with our own deficiencies?'

I'd called at his office to offer the first chapters and synopsis of what was to become, 'Calling You, Foxy Baby', and I'd rambled on about the problems and success of finding my new detective.

Leo eyed me sideways, his eyebrows buckled in a fierce frown. 'You, a bore, Greta? Never! I'd liken you to a clam, or an equivalent crustacean, not a chatterbox. I've always thought you adopted your namesake's attitude, privacy paramount, the silent movie star.'

'That's good.'

'What's good, darling? Why the question?'

'An observation, Leo, merely an observation.'

'Well, at least you're not a barnacle, stuck to some ship's bottom.'

'And what's that meant to mean?'

'Just an observation!'

I laughed. 'I've stuck with you for all these years.'

'True, as I have with you. But then we're old timers, we go back, and back.'

'Not so much of the old; surely this conversation should have started with you denying that I was any age other than young.'

'Eternal youth is your gift, Greta.'

'A bit late but that'll do!'

Leo is the best of friends so why haven't I told him?

Roger rang back suggesting a new play; the tickets for 'Flesh Wound' came from a friend of his. It was the last day of May, a day that dawned with an eclipse of the sun; not that we could see it, too far south and too much cloud, but there it was shown on our morning television news. Was that an omen, I wondered? 'A reminder of the fragile floating nature of our existence,' I said as we waited for the performance to open at the Royal Court Theatre. 'That's most profound,' he peered over his specs. 'Is that you or a quote from another writer?' I ignored him. I enjoyed the tease but I was fretting that there wasn't going to be a right time to talk. This visceral and violent play wasn't what I would have chosen. I was fragile and piqued. Afterwards Roger said; 'The flimsy tie of family is torn to shreds if you're a member of a gang.' I raised my eyebrows; 'Is that you or a quote from an advert?'

He laughed; 'Programme notes, but I hope you're not going to have nightmares tonight. A cup of cocoa is what we need.'

He was right, I was mollified and I almost proposed that he came back to my flat but I wasn't going down that path; a path I'd drifted down too often. Not that I thought he or I were anything other than friends, but it just wasn't worth the risk. I wanted a platonic relationship; celibacy brought its own freedom, I'd decided.

We went down into the bar at the theatre, an under lit, cavernous space. The noise of an over excited audience, younger people who seemed intent on wanting everyone else to hear their opinion, jarred. As he elbowed his way to the bar, I stared at the posters of past plays, cross that I'd let him take the lead, reminded of previous occasions here with Max, him holding court, his acolytes hovering in silent awe. Was I back on the old game? Drawn to a man with questionable credentials and for a pitiful reason? I pushed my way through to Roger who was on the point of paying and said; 'I have to leave.' He couldn't have heard me for he smiled, nodded and turned back to accept his change. I didn't wait but shoved through the tide of those coming down the stairs and made my way up and out. Rain fell hard, I'd no umbrella, a passing bus splashed through the gutter, a girl yelled; 'Fuck off!', prancing and jigging her way to the tube station, sheltered under her man friend's jacket. Her shrill laughter trailed and echoed out of the entrance as they disappeared underground. What was I doing? How rude and stupid. What to do now? I wanted to curl up in a ball, woodlouse style, my defence. But there was Roger coming through the theatre doors and with great understanding, which is one of his most redeeming virtues, and is probably why I am caught in this trap. He said; 'This won't do, will it? But I can't think of anywhere cosy at this time of night.'

'Cosy?' I said.

'Yes, a place where we don't have to be critics or shout.'

I smiled, shrugged, placated.

'What about tomorrow? First day of June, coffee?'

'I'm sorry.'

'Okay, another day.'

'No, I meant rushing out like that.'

'Accepted.'

'I don't make a habit of doing that …'

'Except with me.'

'Please, not your fault.' I hesitated. Sundays were for Joy. 'Tomorrow, coffee would be good.'

'Or perhaps not?'

'Yes, that would be good,' I repeated and meant it.

'Where? Where's best for you?'

This is St James Park. My suggestion. I used to come here in my lunch break when working for Brendan. The surreal glimpse of those looming turrets and domes of the old Admiralty building, a piece of Ruritania squeezed on to the London streets, always causes me to catch my breath. If I'd thought of writing historical fiction or fantasy, this is the place I'd settle for inspiration. Maybe young John Aynsley Howden might come here to ruminate on his latest case.

Coffee at 11.00 o'clock in the open on an overcast day could not be more neutral. He is late, I am early. Perfect. I see him on the horizon coming down The Mall, not hurrying. I buy our coffee. The small café is rundown but I am pleased with the ordinary, the lack of glitz.

'What happened to those drinks last night?' I say.

'Oh, I went back and drank them both.'

I can tell he's joking; I'm beginning to read the runes of his face.

'The barman, I hope, drank them later,' he says. 'I didn't wait to offer an explanation.'

'Was there one?'

He takes a sachet of sugar, shakes, rips and empties it into his cappuccino.

'I didn't know you take sugar,' I say.

'Why should you?' He uses his specs to look down his nose at me.

I say; 'I make too many assumptions,' and leave it at that. We both look out over the lush green, a couple of joggers sweat their way round the lake. 'Are you a runner?' I do want to know more about him. I think it's a natural author's trait. Isn't that what he suggested to me once before?

He ignores the question; 'The poems. Were they in Lottie's jacket? Or would you rather not talk about it.'

The last is a statement not a question. I am safe, all antipathy gone, inhibitions dispelled in an instant; a child offered her comfort blanket. 'Yes,' I say and the sun sears through a cloud settling a swathe of sheen over the grass. We talk of Lottie, what she wrote, why she kept them with her, that poetry is the refuge of despair and hope. He admits to many attempts at 'writing it out' as he puts it, 'which all end in failure,' he says, 'but I think it's cathartic.' I agree.

He offers a second cup of coffee and I say that I must leave at 1.00. I explain about Joy, who is eighty-seven, that she's sprightly and of sound mind. 'I am lucky,' I say. The sound of police sirens or an ambulance cuts through, unfortunate. I change the subject. 'Where do you live?'

'Hackney.'

'I remember.'

'I moved in with my girlfriend, who's an artist, and then we bought the place when we got married.'

I am taken off guard. So much information without asking. I have an urge to say what is she doing while you're here, but resist. 'Would I know any of her work?'

'I doubt it. She rarely exhibits, puts anything on the market.'

I say nothing. The park is filling with families, people strolling with buggies, tourists clutching maps on course for Buckingham Palace. I'm drawn to busy spaces, the buzz of other people's lives. He's fiddling with his empty coffee cup, turning it round and round in the saucer; I wonder whether this is a good moment to say goodbye.

'We're not married any more,' he says. 'An acrimonious divorce five years ago, five years after we got together.'

'I'm sorry.'

'My mistake; I drifted into and continued a relationship because it was easier than getting out. As I found to my cost.'

'I've come across few happy marriages,' I say off the top of my head, aware of my own parents blissful union.

'I seem to think we talked about this before; Douglas and Audrey, and your parents you said?'

'Heck! You've got a good memory.'

'When I'm interested.'

'How old are you?' I say.

'Why?'

I shrug; 'Just interested.'

He looks pleased. 'Forty seven, and you are?'

'Fifty three. You obviously haven't looked at my website.'

'Of course, I have. I knew but thought it polite to ask in return; and to see whether you're a woman who doesn't mind about her age.'

'Hmm! My agent, Leo, won't allow me to be squeamish about getting older.' I tell him about Leo's reference to being old timers and that he doesn't consider I'm a barnacle.

'He's a good agent?'

'The best. And for someone who's the most flamboyant gossip, he is also remarkably discreet.'

'Have you ever considered marriage?' he says.

I'm not expecting this. There is no quick answer. I say; 'No, I don't think so.'

'Wedded to your work?'

'No,' I say. The sun has disappeared; the clouds roam sulkily. 'There was Lottie.' I need to clarify this. 'Her father was my lecturer at university, married. We had an affair, par for the course, no pun intended.'

He says nothing. I can't read his expression.

'He never knew,' I say.

July

An unreliable narrator

I am the unreliable narrator. It is inevitable. First person narration is of its very nature rarely reliable which is why it is so appealing to some readers. I too enjoy the superiority of distinguishing the flaws in the character's retelling of events and emotions. I sit in judgement. 'Catcher in the Rye' was my first encounter – I read it in two days when I was twelve, glued to Holden Caulfield's revelations, sympathising with and criticising his actions in equal measure, forgetting that this was in the author, Salinger's, gift. I was deceived.

In fiction there are varying degrees of deception with an allowance for point of view, bias, naivety or the need of the author to create a twist in the tale; the last most annoying. It can be an author's useful tool. Agatha Christie could not handle it satisfactorily in my view; my attempts in 'The Cat's Cradle Chronicle' caused me far more anguish in the writing than any of my other novels. But as I've stuck to the detective as main character, the plotting, solving the crime is of prime importance. Yes, I've allowed them emotions, back stories, quirks and foibles so that readers care whether they are successful or not; primarily it's about good overcoming evil.

None of that is of any import here where the reliability of what I convey is purely subjective; that is fact. What I have to say now, of a love story concerning two people, will rest solely on my thoughts, my assessment of what he felt, his intentions, the one sided nature of memory, my memory. That I think purely for myself to help make sense of, assess what this all means, evaluate what I should do, is of no consequence to anyone else. The side-by-side list of pros and cons is too personal, which is why I could never write an autobiography. Leo agrees with me.

'Insatiable, rabid dogs eating on the flesh of anyone with talent; leave them to their own foul middens. Ignore, Greta, your work is what you are.'

And how could I tell him of this love story gone wrong?

When I blurted out to Roger in St James' Park on that June day what I've kept tight hold of for thirty plus years, I was aware only of something falling away. It wasn't a feeling of being stripped bare, lowering myself in some way to ridicule. It was a relief; the secret no longer mattered. I'd dealt with Gerald who was unlikely to contact me again; Joy was letting go, making her peace with the world, and that letter for Lottie is redundant.

I left the park soon after my revelation to him. It'd brought closure; Roger made no comment and I changed the subject. Though he did ask; 'Can we meet again soon?' all serious, overcast as the day.

That isn't where it began, of course; it had been brewing from the day we met on a station platform when someone else had committed suicide. From then on it's been an accumulation of liking him, as simple as that, enjoying his company, wanting to talk, to tell and to know more about him. Gradually barnacles have attached to this ship's bottom. Is that an absurd way to describe the condition of love, a love that is painful and hard to remove, perhaps impossible?

Meeting was casual though the effort to do so should have put me off. Weekends were difficult; Joy never asked for my company, always expressed surprise and gratitude when I arrived on a Friday night or Saturday morning but she was shrinking, fading, almost ethereal. She insisted there was nothing wrong, wouldn't see a doctor, but she ate little, dozed a lot, as if dutifully bringing her life to an end. And the deadline for completing my latest, 'Calling You, Foxy Baby', was the end of July, which would mean the big redraft in August.

It was spur of the moment stuff, Roger and I. There were no long phone calls. We were like childhood pals; I'd get a message on my answerphone; 'Any time on Friday are you free?' Or I'd ring on the day to say where I was going to be and was he free. So easy come, easy go and at the same time I knew that I wanted this friendship to continue. When he was away in America for a fortnight I looked forward to his return. He slotted in around my other friends, the social life that's hard to keep up.

There were no outward expressions of love or affection. Once I had leant forward to rest my face on his chest in a small park in Soho, that time when he'd first surprised me, telling me he knew Lottie. That was all. We were the respectable friends, never a hand held, or a knee nudged. And I'm not a 'false kisser', Leo's expression. He has said; 'I can't bear all this French kissy-kissy stuff, the mwa-mwa people who insist on pecking at each cheek, utterly devoid of pleasure. Reminds me of pernickety hens. A hug or a discreet hand shake, infinitely preferable.' I agree. And we, Roger and I, kept it like that, even hugs we avoided.

Roger is intelligent, thoughtful and amusing, he makes me laugh, never takes himself or me too seriously. Except when it's work, that's important, which is how I feel; he fits in perfectly. He's a chum holding the ace card of acquaintance with my daughter and knowledge of her origin.

He is not pretty in the way Max caught your first breath; his eyebrows are bushy, dark and unrefined; his nose is too wide to be Roman, though his complexion suggests an Italian origin, not Viking stock. His full lips are possibly his best feature, his mouth always suggesting an easy smile. His hair, rich mahogany, is cut close to eliminate the curls which I begin to realise are prey to the barber's scissors; I thought I'd persuade him one day to let them flourish. He has said; 'Perhaps this need to be meticulously tidy is an affliction.'

And even here where I veer between past and present, he's still those things whatever else must be gone.

I try to remember the order of what we said and did and when. Scraps of conversation come back from the maze of easy chat. The evidence.

Following on from the park I tell him that Lottie never seemed troubled that she didn't know her father. I explain about the letter I wrote which she could never receive. He says; 'That's exactly what my mother did, left a letter with her will, plus my birth certificate. My father was named and she wrote of 'an insignificant love affair producing the most significant prize.'

It's a restaurant under the arches of Hungerford Bridge. He's come back from Paris on Eurostar; I'm on my way to join friends for a fundraising party at The Young Vic, so the time, 6 o'clock is convenient.

We are upstairs, alone, the noise of the bar downstairs funnelling up. It feels like a treehouse den, the dim lighting aiding my imagination. I tell Roger and add; 'One course and a glass of wine, that's me. Okay?'

He shrugs; 'Not quite what I'm used to, three leisurely courses I've been enjoying for the last week.'

'Liar,' I laugh. 'A hard pressed journalist is the line you've spun.'

'No spinning, true.' And we order the food and wine.

'I had a treehouse,' he says. 'There was a wood down the road from where we lived; me and my friends rigged it up from leftovers we found on a skip.'

'Wow! Proper little boy scout.' I like this. He'd have been the boy I'd have wanted to play with when I was a child.

'Did you miss having a father; did you ever ask about him?'

'No, and yes. Not often though as I sensed, in the way children do, that it wasn't a good question.'

'What did you miss?'

'You can't miss what you've never known, can you? Mostly it was the annoyance of other children's curiosity and taunting.'

'Lottie never mentioned that.' Another shadow of neglect rears up, the guilt of the absent mother; 'Did she keep that to herself?'

Roger says; 'I can't imagine Lottie keeping quiet if it troubled her.'

It was good to hear those words, another small act of understanding. I should liken them to feathers, not barnacles. Feathers to soften, stroke and soothe, adding up to a whole comforting cloak. But that is such delusional talk.

'Did you find him, your father,' I say, 'when you learnt his name?'

'No, definitely not. I was angry; why would I want a father – a man who'd either denied me or knew nothing of my existence?'

It is odd and reassuring to listen to what I'd believed would be Gerald's reaction to Lottie. Roger speaks cheerily as if the whole thing has been dismissed, though he's abandoned his knife and fork, taken off his glasses. I've noticed before, he does this when something is upsetting.

There is nothing I can say to help. I hold his gaze as he's done for me at other times, as if taking part of the pain.

He looks at his watch; 'Are you okay for time?'

'Fine,' I say, adding. 'You can't see without your specs, can you?' He smiles but doesn't replace them. 'Tell me then about what you were doing in Paris.'

He picks up his glasses, twirls them with a shrug, before putting them back on and leaning forward, as if delivering top secrets, to tell me briefly what he was researching. 'Essentially, Jacques Chirac; the effect of his right wing policies, the corruption scandal, his friendship with Putin and opposition to Bush's Iraq war.' I listen as he talks of his contacts and what he plans to write. We agree on the horror of what is happening in Iraq, and that it is one area where we wish that Chirac had succeeded. I chalk up the relief of political unanimity.

I talk of my friends who passionately opposed the war and marched against it in March. 'I should have gone too,' I say. 'Lottie would have.'

'Can't deny that,' he says.

I call for the bill and as always we scrupulously tot up and divide.

It is the 1st of July; his birthday. I gave him a choice; tea at Claridges or a picnic on deckchairs in Regent's Park.

'You chose.' I say as we put up umbrellas and pack away the food. A Tuesday, threatening skies, no one else was so foolish as to stop. It's a solitary celebration.

'It'll pass,' he says sticking out his palm to feel the weight of the rain. And, I think, such sweet optimism and a shadow of inexplicable fear shivers through me; that he might pass.

I say; 'Of course, boy scouts are proof against weather.'

'And Mancunians, though that's a myth, about the rain. It's only the soppy southerners who come up and complain.'

'Count me out. I've not been north of the Watford gap.'

'Greta Salway, that's a blatant lie. You told me about Sheffield last year. And didn't you mention Glasgow, or was it Edinburgh?'

I scowl and shrug. 'Mentally then.'

It's raining even harder but I'm not going to be the first to suggest we move.

'I'm still in love with the north,' he says, scrunched into the deckchair, his legs jack-knifed, his trainers absurdly large. 'I've a cottage just south of the Lake District, a place of incomparable beauty.'

'Landed gentry, eh?' I'm piqued that he's never told me. He's never questioned my allegiance and love of Cambridge and Norfolk, the flatlands but silly bits of jealousy and curiosity are rife.

'An uncle left it to me,' he says. 'Never married, a bit of a recluse, but he was kind, took me fishing, we caught butterflies.'

Perhaps it's my expression, I'm beginning to worry that he can read me too because he says; 'Is it disapproval of the hobbies or that I've so far not included this in my CV?'

He is joking and it's fun, but chastening.

'Too right,' I say. 'And you've not included your blood type or sock size.'

'Or why I spend my birthday with you rather than a girlfriend.'

'I assumed she's busy and you have an evening engagement.'

'Of course, that would be logical.' And he looks at me as if, what? Does he want me to ask if I'm right? I should but can't. To do so might imply that I want to be more than a friend.

It's an awkward moment. The air changes, still and hanging, or is it the rain, a temporary lull.

'To the bandstand,' I say, waving away my discomfort, struggling for an elegant exit from my deckchair.

I think afterwards what a sport he is. Angus wouldn't have considered a picnic, Paul preferred a dark room to fresh air, Max thought Glyndebourne the only place where people eat al fresco, and Michael, although revelling in the outdoors, wanted to escape London whenever possible.

It is a café in the crypt of St Martins in the Field. 'Central south,' Roger says. 'And whatever your beliefs, it does what Christianity says on the tin, works with the dispossessed.'

I don't challenge him. We are here for coffee, little time to spare, although he says we must come another time for a lunchtime concert. It is he not I who suggested we meet. It's 9 o'clock on a Friday morning and we order toast and jam. Outside the sun is ablaze, prisms of light caught in the fountain's fall. The brick fan vaulting lifts up and out and crowds us in. Many tables are free but he chooses one tucked in a corner; then comes the statement without preamble.

'My father has been in touch. I tracked him down last year and then regretted doing so.'

'Pardon?' I'm confused. 'I thought you hadn't, didn't want to. A few weeks ago, you said …'

'Yes, I did, but I was talking about when I first found out. And I didn't say anything more then as I thought he'd ignored me, which was fair enough. But then I had a letter yesterday, all these months later.'

'Why?'

'Which do you mean, my regret or why I wanted to find him or his delay?

'All of it.'

The toast is thick and brown. We spread butter and jam, separate but in unison.

'What happened to a friend started it.' He bites into his toast; this is seemingly not momentous. 'He'd found out that an ex girlfriend had had a child who he was sure was his. He tried to persuade her that he wanted proof through DNA testing. I couldn't understand how it would help; the woman didn't want him in her life or that of her child. I tried to advise him against but he was beyond reason.'

'How difficult.' Or was it? Someone else's life, I didn't want to think.

'He didn't know my story and I wasn't going to tell him. My mother's decision wasn't part of it, though I'm certain she was right; you can't manufacture a relationship; that she didn't think the man was suitable is good enough for me.'

Again Roger scores ten out of ten. I say nothing though I'm sure my expression tells him.

He's wearing a V necked teeshirt, his arms already brown. I note again that his skin appreciates the sun.

'And the regret?'

'That I'd become interested to know the man who fathered me, after all she'd written that he'd been 'insignificant'. Perhaps I was betraying her, so I was relieved when I didn't hear anything, no reply to my letter.'

'How odd, no reply, I mean.'

'Is it? He's probably got a wife, children; who'd want an unknown prospective child that you'd been told nothing about, forty plus years on.'

I did think of Gerald's reaction. His ridiculous fear of his wife; I almost tell Roger but I still cringe from the memory of that occasion. And we haven't finished the toast and this is his story, an important story.

'They were students at university,' he's saying. 'I've no idea about their commitment to each other; he could have been a one-night stand.'

I haven't asked how he tracked the man but college records, ex students often keep in touch. I never did, but then why would I?

Roger says; 'Last October I sent the letter and a reply came a week ago. Polite, apologetic for the delay, guarded. Now I don't know whether I want to meet him. Do I want anyone else in my life? I've disturbed the peace whatever I do.'

I was pleased he'd told me. I know nothing of his other friends; there've been odd references to seeing Jack or was it John, staying overnight with acquaintants in places he visits. I still don't know if there's a girlfriend. Does he keep in touch with his ex wife? Exactly where he lives in Hackney is a mystery; neither have I invited him home. Casual friends? That day I felt like a sister.

I say; 'I think I'd meet him. At least you'll have laid a ghost. Go, say hello and walk away.'

He smiles; 'You're a good friend, Greta,' and he took my hand. 'I don't suppose you'd like to come with me?'

I'm touched, not only by what he's asking me, but the hand. I didn't expect the warmth, the small spark, another damned feather in the cloak.

I say; 'Yes, if that'd help. What shall I be? You're agent? Your bodyguard.'

'I'll work that one out.'

I went to Paris a fortnight later, a kind of pilgrimage and for space to concentrate on the redraft. Working on Eurostar, booking into the hotel Lottie and I'd stayed in with the scary lift still there, retracing our footsteps. August in a city deserted; it was perfect. I needed space.

August

A gold plaque

I am sitting outside the Bistro Cyrano; 'Du café et un croissant, si'il vous plait.' The sun blinks off the gold plaque on a building opposite; I ought to get up, go closer, see what it says. My curiosity is not sufficient, my time too precious for me to find out why, on such a crumbling wall, pocked with bullet holes, a sign glowing with polished attention, might be here in a rundown street. A street divided by light and shade, water sluicing down one gutter, a dark rivulet at odds with the parched dust thrown up by cars changing gear to climb up and on to Montmartre. There is hardly enough space for customers to sit outside this off-beat place, tables spilling out over the pavement, umbrellas elbowing each other. I am grateful that the café is open, so much else 'Fermé en Août.'

I position my laptop on the table that's too small for the waiter to squeeze in my order. He looks to the next table, centimetres from mine, as if to place it there where a man, a 'Jack in the Beanstalk' giant, punches numbers punishingly into a calculator. 'S'il vous plait, monsieur?' the waiter tries tentatively, 'Est-il possible que vous avez fini?' I am entranced by this sympathy for my predicament, this wish to accommodate my work, but begin to remonstrate, hand gestures to show I can manage, when this potential ogre looks up, looks to the waiter, looks to me, and shrugs, 'Oui, oui, bien sûr!' beaming a golden smile, valuable fillings. I smile too and nod my gratitude; 'Merci, merci,' It is a benign morning.

Neither the arrival of workmen off-loading a pneumatic drill and the French equivalent of traffic cones to shut off part of the road, nor the pungent cigarette smoke drifting down from a couple in earnest argument occupying the only other table in this tiny area, disturb me. Even the pigeons that hobble and flutter around my feet, all are what I want, to be absorbed into the working life of Paris, away from tourists, to get on with what I have to do. I bring out my bound and mangled draft copy of 'Calling You, Foxy Baby.' Already copious notes clutter the margins; sticky-taped extra pages or scraps of paper bulge out of the dogeared edges; whole new sections already written up are ready to be inserted onto my computer copy. Queries needing to be investigated via the internet are listed on the back cover. It is 8.00 am. I prop this tome on my lap, enjoy my breakfast, change my sun specs for reading glasses and settle in.

Having managed for two hours to ignore the intermittent brain-boring sound of the men gouging out the road a few yards up, ordered and drunk another espresso with un verre d'eau, excluded disturbances due to the change of customers at adjacent tables, my mobile rings. I fumble to find it, instantly worried that Joy has a problem. She's the only person who knows where I am; she would not ring unless it is serious. In my panic I don't look to see who is calling.

'Hello, Greta, I just wondered … oh hang on, you're abroad. Sorry, the ringtone, I ought …'

'Bonjour, Roger, comment allez-vous?'

A mere intake of breath; 'Tres bien! Òu êtes-vous?'

'Paris, monsieur.'

'Pourquoi? Or should I have remembered?'

'No, you shouldn't.' The sun sidles round the umbrella, slides under, hot on my face. 'I came on a whim.'

'Oh. That doesn't sound like you.'

Was that an exclamation or a question?

'You'd be surprised,' which I immediately think is a foolish thing to say. 'I need quiet time to concentrate on the redraft.' I sound as if I am excusing myself.

'Ah, right, good plan.' Do I detect a note of disappointment? I hadn't told him. Why hadn't I told him? 'Then my question is redundant,' he is saying, 'you being free. I'll leave you in peace, but let me know when you're back in circulation.'

Roger notches up another bar in my estimation. Never intrusive, never too eager, never the faithful pet lapping up or wanting a nuzzle or stroke. Angus, also, didn't want either of these but he always kept something of himself hidden. I liked him a lot; the mystery, the challenge, but the distance prevented more than the beginning of love. Paul was slippery and needy, Max too up his own arse, and Michael, the standard substitute as I was for him. But who, what, is this?

'I will,' I say, 'I'm planning on being back for the weekend.'

There is a long pause. 'Paris, one of my favourite cities. Make sure you enjoy it as well as work. Good luck.' And he is gone. And the morning's glow, the mood of well-being evaporates; the noise, the heat bouncing off that wall opposite, the trail of tourists making their way up to the Sacré Coeur, are too much to bear. I pack up and leave.

I trundle up to La Cimetière de Montmartre, the cool of the trees, the greyed stonework keeping the heat at bay. Lottie had said; 'Whatever we are, dust to dust beginning from the Big Bang, we all have names, chosen and given. That's all that matters, isn't it, the name written somewhere to be remembered.' Too sensible, my child, and then that irrational supernova ending.

Later as I wander in the Tuileries Gardens I remember her saying; 'We'll never love anyone like Grandpa, will we?' when she was five. But then modifying this to; 'Grandpa will be a hard act to follow,' when she was here with me at the age of eighteen. 'There must be others like him that've floated down from some magic kingdom but I expect we'd need elfin powers to find them.' I almost laughed out loud at the memory, which I've obscured with time. Was Freddie such a one? I sit on a bench, the need to pause and contemplate. She is gone but so present, her unhoned wisdom, her raw assessment of love and life, are my comfort. And I don't think about what comfort there was for her. She would have rolled her eyes; 'Mumma, you're such a sentimentalist!' Behind my sunglasses my eyes betray nothing. I look out at this French formality; the planters, white boarded, topiary bushes pristine, the cut beds of flowers, orange through shades of red to pink, are flamboyant.

I think of Roger. It would be good to have had his company for supper tonight, or tomorrow. I should have apologised for not telling him that I was going away, but why? I wonder what he was doing that he rang me on a Monday morning. Would it have been nine or ten o'clock? And where was he?

What am I playing at, not needy but fascinated, liking and wanting to be liked, the good friend, or is it more? He's gay but not gay, younger only not that much younger, but neither of us wants anything other than this, I think. Too sensible, too cynical, too scared to go any further. I lean back settling the thoughts that are too ethereal; I need to take control, no more floating off into abstruse reveries. I close my eyes for even with dark glasses it's all too sharp, too glaring. I think of Leo saying at Audrey's funeral; 'Where did you find him, the Roger man? Nice one, Greta. If only he was one of us.' I didn't respond.

'Excuse me.' I open my eyes to a woman standing in front of me, 'I had to stop and say something. I am right aren't I, Greta Salway?'

I blink up at her; I can't deny it.

'I thought I recognised you.' Grey hair, plump chested, bright eyes; an English pigeon. 'I've been screwing up courage to come and say 'hello'. I hope it's all right. I didn't mean to disturb you. It's just that I'm such an admirer, have read all your books. And you so kindly signed two of them last year when you were in Cambridge. And what a coincidence to find you here.'

What do I say? She's not going to fly, feathers a-flutter. 'I'm pleased you enjoy my novels.'

'So much.' She turns quickly to beckon another couple of women who are hovering a few yards away. 'I was right,' she calls to them. 'It is her.' To me she says; 'We're part of a book club and all of us your fans. But they,' a bit of preening here, 'didn't manage to get their copies signed.' The two women scurry across, voluminous ladies in smock-like tops to rival the flowerbeds. 'This is Betty and this Diana.' They stand in front of me, blocking the light, staring down as if at a zoological specimen. 'Would you mind? Just a quick autograph?'

I have taken off my specs, smile briefly as they delve in overstuffed backpacks, the first woman regarding me possessively. There is a lot of 'Oh, I know it's here somewhere,' and 'Could I have left it at the hotel?' while I silently find my pen in my computer bag, alongside 'Foxy Baby.'

I am asked why I'm here in Paris to which I reverse the question. There is a long explanation which I listen to politely and then promptly forget. I can hear Leo; 'Your fans are the staff of life, Greta, mine too. It should be written on your heart, must never be forgotten.'

They go off happily, an ink scrawl, a brush with my celebrity and I'm fed up. This French sojourn tainted. I ring Roger. There is no reply, which is worse, but I leave a message. 'Contrarié à Paris - téléphone bientôt.' I go to find a café for another coffee, a croque-monsieur and decide my hotel room will be the best place to work. But it isn't, or at least I'm distressed by the stuffy air, dusty carpet, curtains, spray cleaner, a balcony door which opens on to a courtyard four storeys below, and I'm facing east. Why did I think coming away was a good idea? 'Five days,' I promised Leo. 'The rewrite will be with you on Saturday, midday.' I've always worked like this, setting a strict period, so many days, part challenge, part focus. Left over from when Lottie needed me and I needed the discipline to make time ordered. It is 3 o'clock and there are no more excuses. Computer open and plugged in, draft copy spread.

'Greta, qu'est-ce qui ne va pas? Roger.' The message blips in. I should ignore it but won't.

I phone and he picks up. 'Sorry, I'm being an idiot. I thought a French hideaway or whatever I pretend it is, was a good idea. Wanted to go native.'

'You seem to have succeeded,' he says. 'Most authentic.'

'No, it's childish. I should have realised that I can't disappear.'

'Oh, did you want to?' He's serious.

'I only thought fresh space, fresh view, fresh ideas. The redraft.'

'Ah,' he says.

'I will work, I always do but ...'

The ether between us hangs as if by a thread; I imagine a gossamer strand of silk strung across the sea.

'What about dinner tonight? Nothing fancy, glass of wine and two courses, perhaps one, or a crêpe or a crème glacée.'

'I'm in Paris,' I laugh, 'next week perhaps.'

'I could catch a train, Eurostar will have me with you by, what, 7.30 your time, maybe 8 o'clock?'

'Roger, that's crazy. A lovely offer but …'

'Can I come?'

That gossamer strand pulls taut, multiplies and plaits, and I don't want to let go.

'Please,' I say. 'I really would like to see you.'

'Good. Meet me at the Gare du Nord? I'll text you the time exactly.'

And he's hung up.

I sit opposite the station, a table outside the restaurant, Terminus Nord, fizzy water to hand; I need a clear head. I veer between embarrassment and childish excitement, severe incomprehension and pleasurable elation. I've completed a large chunk of the redraft, anticipation of the treat to come demanding extreme concentration. Yes, all the adjectives, the superlatives, are in operation tonight.

My draft copy is in front of me as I wait, affecting continued work, but the clock on the front of the station keeps my attention, and the statues standing aloft as part of the triumphal façade, stony eyes looking out disdainfully over my head, are unsettling. I think of Lottie ferreting in some guidebook to find out; 'why these weird toga clad men have anything to do with the railway?' She was triumphant on discovering that each sculpture represented the principal cities served by the company who originally ran this rail network, but said; 'Who in the nineteenth century wore Roman clothing? They look as though they've been caught coming out of the bath.'

'Am I interrupting?' Roger appears in front of me, genie and lamp style.

'No,' I press my hands on to the script, 'this is merely for show.' I look up at him awkward, off guard, and go to stand but he's already sitting on the seat beside me; our bobbing dance like a courtship ritual. 'This is mad,' I say, settling back on the edge of my seat. But he is all smiles, that mobile mouth seriously amused.

'Why not? I want to see you and I'm pleased that you want to see me. What could be simpler?' That clean herby, sun-scorched Lasithi Plateau scent that he must wash in or wear, momentarily overpowers the dust and diesel. He has a shoulder bag, the sort that can hold a computer or change of underwear and spongebag. 'Where do you want to eat? Here? It's excellent but très cher.' He's too breezy, nervous too, I think.

I stretch my arm across the table offering my hand, a gesture that is foreign and appropriate. He takes it and holds on and that shimmering thread is back, delicate, fragile, supercharged. 'I am so glad you came.'

'Let's go somewhere else,' he says, 'I don't plan on returning tonight.'

'Good,' genuine and terrified.

'Where are you staying?'

I explain. 'And you?' And a swoosh of relief drives the air in and out of my lungs as he replies without a second's thought; 'A mate living on a road off the Rue de Clichy, up towards Montmartre, near the cemetery.'

Hands released we set off for a restaurant I recommend. 'Good food, unwelcoming to tourists so we can only speak French.'

'A challenge,' he says, 'although maybe not for what we need to talk about.'

I'm pleased and uncomfortable; I know what we have to sort out and say; 'I value your friendship. Nothing must spoil that.'

'Yes,' he says and I know he experiences the fizz that runs between us.

Of course, we don't need to be natives and chat comfortably as we have always done. The redraft; I recount the plot and a point that's awkward to correct. 'I thought I'd made proof of the man's guilt watertight, the leads, the pieces of evidence, the alibi blown, except there's a crack, hairline, that any decent defence lawyer would find and prise open to rubbish the case.'

'Isn't that good?'

'Not if the baddie wins. My detective, new to me, new to my readers, John Aynsley Howden, has to solve the case, put a man behind bars.'

'Then isn't that better, the crack that he will fill at the last moment, and ride to victory, the triumphant stranger sweeping all before him, converting the whole town.'

'It's not a Western,' I say.

'No, just similes and all that. But tell me again, run through it, what's the problem?'

I do and, bless him, he is involved and 'in awe' as he says. And I, under the spotlight, see how I might resolve the case.

He tells me, after talking about the article he's researching, and the friend who lives in Paris, that he wrote back to the man traced as his father but has had no reply. 'After the last gap between letters I expect to hear sometime around Christmas. I wish I'd never started but like Pandora's box, you have to hang on to hope, or do I mean dread, as in can of worms?'

'Yes,' I say for anything else would sound prosaic.

The waiter arrives to ask if we'd like a coffee, maybe a little cognac. I decline, as does Roger. 'Maybe another glass of wine? I need …' he doesn't finish the sentence but I agree and the waiter leaves with our order.

I look around at the décor which is, as so often in French restaurants, a clutter of paintings, lavish lights and bric-a-brac which are more akin to the 19th century; dark shades the perfect back drop for the waiters' black and white uniform, upright and slick in shirts, waistcoats and aprons, a proud profession.

'Greta,' Roger has taken off his glasses, laid them carefully on the table. 'I have to say this without wishing to give offence or to make you uncomfortable.'

'What?' All the ease disappears; I want to put my hand over his mouth, stop him from ruining what we have. Or do I?

There is a pause and he attempts a smile that fades as he speaks. ' I have no wife, you know of that failure, and the last girlfriend left me out of boredom six months ago. She told me I was too preoccupied and it wasn't with work especially. She said; "There's something more that's captured you and I don't want to compete."'

'Was that a shock?' I have that odd sensation of shallow breaths, quick intake, hold, expel before grabbing another dose of oxygen.

'No, I knew it was you,' he speaks slowly, weighing the words, 'all my thoughts were of you. At the grand age of 48, I've fallen in love, I think for the first time.'

He looks so sombre, a child offering an explanation for something done that shouldn't be done, a tragic declaration. He is studying me, that holding gaze, as if fathoming what I am thinking. I close my eyes and open them as if to make sure that he's real. And the place is suddenly full of air, rich energising air. 'Thank you,' I'm nodding and smiling, shrugging and shaking my head; 'Thank you, and for saying it first.'

'What?'

I hold out both my hands across the table, across the starched white tablecloth, my bare arms, brown from the sun, silver bracelet glinting, fingers spread, as the waiter brings our wine. We ignore him. Roger meets me half way. 'This isn't what I planned,' I say, 'you're supposed to be gay, I keep telling you. You're far too special to be any old chap. And I'm older than you.'

He's trembling; his eyes, troubled, scan my face, eyebrows pucker and relax and he expels a deep sigh. 'That means?'

I shrug, the dizzy seventeen-year old girl I never was, light as air, shrug; 'Me too!' and I smile and smile. 'How did this happen? It was against all the odds.'

He raises my hands to his face, brushes them against his cheeks and kisses the fingertips. 'If someone somewhere was betting on us, they'll have made a fortune.'

We both laugh, shake our heads, call for the bill, and he says; 'Have you brought your calculator?'

As we dance out of the restaurant, waiters bowing a cheerful 'Bonsoir', we call back again and again, 'Bonsoir', 'Bonsoir', two giddy lovers holding hands, wondering where to go next.

We might have been clumsy, first time, past lovers hanging above us comparing every move, old habits encrusted, fear of failure. No. Lottie was right; there is a man like grandpa and I'd found those elfin powers. I took him to my hotel; 'Someone else's place is too inhibiting.' I was past caring; free, nothing to lose, or, perhaps, at the last chance saloon. But there was no frantic scuffle to rip each other's clothes, scrabbling in the lift to raise the game, bring the race to a climax; I knew we were already there. We had a whole night to explore, to trace the contours of each other's bodies, draw in the smells, the sweat, the chosen scents; to adore.

It was new. And it always was new. Unsure and certain: the exquisite touch, the slow stroking, each replicating the other; the thrill, the joy. Dying and living with ecstasy, utterly lost and found in the pleasure of each other's giving.

I will always remember that gold plaque, what should have been written there; Roger Harlow and Greta Salway, ordinary names, no dates, it happened here.

September

Too idyllic

The perfect chord, that's what I thought I'd found in Paris. Roger and me.

That momentous change to what I might expect in the future, should have tripped me into idleness, an inability to stay there and finish 'Calling You, Foxy Baby'. But we were both old enough, not flighty fools. He went back to London the next day and I remained to return on Saturday as planned. We'd found something unexpected and intense and I was going to hold on. No need to rush.

I emailed Leo the time of my return and to ask whether to take the script to his home or office. I received no reply but found him there, at Waterloo, to meet my train. He drew me into a bear hug before telling me that Joy was unwell. 'Pure chance I rang her,' Leo said.

'Why didn't you tell me?' I pleaded as I sat by her bedside.

'There was no need, lovey,' the words a hoarse whisper. 'I knew you'd be back, I'd hold on.' There was an oxygen cylinder by her bed, a mask hanging which she refused. 'My time to go,' she said.

'No not yet, Joy.' I held her hand, stroked the filmy skin, ran my fingers along the blue veins. I had to keep the blood flowing.

For as long as I could remember I'd never wanted to talk about the men in my life with her; a subconscious knowledge that they didn't match up to the standard I expected her to want for me. What barriers we erect to please or supersede our parents! And here I was at her life's end with that all gone. All gone, I realised, in one evening: I wanted to tell her, I was a child desperate to share my new toy. But he wasn't a toy, he felt like a coming home. I needed Roger to meet her and more urgently wanted her to meet him.

'I have someone I want to show you,' I said as she slipped into sleep. 'Stay with me.'

The curtains in her room were open as dark drew down; streetlights popping on, taking up the daylight. Drizzle wept down the window panes. Someone had already brought her flowers, stuck in a discoloured cut glass vase, a bunch of sunflowers. How kind but how wrong was all I could think. Joy was tough, a woman who'd worked above and beyond, but she was never gaudy. I think of buttercups and daisies, harebells and ladyslippers as her flowers, tough, wild and gentle.

Leo had found and booked this hospice, transported her here all within a day. 'I caught her, gasping for breath; there was no disguising her distress. A good actress, your mother, Greta, but she wasn't fooling me, even on the end of a telephone line.'

'Why didn't I realise?'

'Ah, well, she knew when you'd call; I was a surprise. My mission in life, Greta, always to be a surprise.'

I phoned Roger as I was driven here in the taxi Leo had ordered, to tell him where I was, where I was going and why. I didn't know what I'd find when I got here. Now I was desperate to phone him again. But I couldn't leave her and my mobile didn't work inside her room. What chance was there even if I called him again, what chance had he to come, what chance that time would allow?

Joy lay so quiet, her hand cold and featherweight. I kissed her forehead, bent my ear to hear faint breath. I lay my head beside hers. 'Joy, stay just a little longer.'

I had known for months her frailty, her shrugging off life as if it were another chore she'd completed. She'd said to me; 'Don't let me linger, will you? No drips, no drugs to keep me for longer than needs be.' She knew all about that. A nurse, even if auxiliary, with more experience than those with certificates. 'If I don't go out with a bang, like Jim, I don't want to hang around.'

I hadn't protested, rather ignored it as the inconceivable but inevitable. Before Paris, before Roger and me, Joy and I were sitting in her garden eating a feather-light Victoria sponge which she'd made; behind us a yellow rose climbing the pebbledash, fresh mown grass greening the air, the mower waiting to be put in the shed. And I said; 'I promise,' which was too half-hearted.

'You know, Greta,' she'd said, 'for all those years I wanted to know who fathered Lottie; it stuck in my craw that he could get away, no responsibility, and her with no opportunity of another parent. But I've come to think you must have been right. What if he hadn't cared?'

'Yes,' I said with relief and disquiet in equal measure. This was a subject we hadn't talked of for so long, one I'd thought done with.

A whisper of wind filled a silence, barely disturbing the garden's last burst of colour, a riot of mauve and magenta flowers, the names of which I'd forgotten. Reading my mind Joy said; 'Those were Michaelmas daisies till a few year's back, asters now. The bees don't know, don't care that it all changes.'

'Do you care, Joy?' The shift in topic a comfort.

'No, no, lovey. Everything changes, always does, always will. And, thank goodness. Lottie would have been a scandal fifty years back.'

'I don't think people were comfortable thirty years ago.'

'Perhaps, but it wasn't for us?'

'No, and you who were so good to me, you and Jim. I've asked so much and you've always given.'

We focused on the garden in front of us, the cake on our plates, each of us awkward with what we were saying, each mouthful easing the tension.

Joy said; 'Lottie asked me once if I thought her father was a good man.'

'You never told me.' I was shocked.

'It was only the once. Some child at school's dad had been to court for drink driving. Lottie wanted to know what'd happen to him and why. Jim explained. Everything was always black and white for her, wasn't it, good or bad.'

'What did you say?' The cake crumbs cloyed my mouth.

'That he must have been good to have made a little bit of her.' Joy was laughing, shaking her head.

'Was that enough?'

'Must have been. I remember Lottie grinned, that naughty grin, stole a biscuit that I'd made and was cooling on a rack. 'Course he's not really a dad,' she said. 'That's Jim.'

'Oh, Joy, I'd stopped thinking about it.'

'So you should. We've given up on reasons, the whys and whats we could have done, did.'

My heart scrunched tight, the tears too close, I focused on the pots of petunias we'd planted in May, pinks and purples; Joy scrupulously removed their deadheads with a pair of nail scissors, fooling them to flower, not seed.

'She was such a confident girl,' Joy said, 'going to Cambridge. So proud of her. Whatever it was we missed …'

'No, you, we, missed nothing, Joy. It was love that took her, a blast of overwhelming love, irrational love.'

She took my hand, caressed it, still looking out, didn't ask what I'd meant. Instead; 'We needed to say this again, didn't we? I wanted you to know.'

I nodded, not trusting my voice. That rift rarely expressed, was out in the open, resolved. She'd set me free.

'Whoever he was, he wasn't suitable and whatever she'd got from him, nurture's more than nature. And that was the end of it.'

I felt the catch in her throat. Lottie and end were two words we never wanted to put together.

'Thank you,' I said, 'it's so hard, so shocking, always will be.' Holding hands tightly we shared a look of knowing what we both knew, both suffered.

Now I think of this, my face close, breathing the last of her, that was the beginning of Joy signing out. 'I don't want you to go, as we didn't want Jim to go,' I whispered, 'but I'll believe when you have to leave me that you'll be with him.' I let the tears trickle to dampen her pillow; as my mother she'd allow me that.

A nurse knocked on the door and came in without waiting. 'How is she?' she said as if I'd know. 'A brave lady, your mother,' she added going to the other side of the bed leaning across to take Joy's pulse. 'A fighter too, I think.' She looked at me, a sweet smile. 'Can I get you anything? Tea, a sandwich, toast? It's too late for supper I'm afraid.'

'Nothing, thank you. But I need to make a phone call and …'

'Oh, yes, I'll bring a telephone through. I hadn't connected it before; I knew you were coming and she said there was no one else.'

No, I thought, as the nurse left us, there was no one else, but now there is.

'What shall we talk about?' I said to Joy. 'What about Jim making elder whistles for me, and then for Lottie? Do you remember? And her asking for them in different keys because she wanted "a whole orchestra"?' I smoothed the sheet and blanket covering her, pulled them up around her shoulders, crisp white laundered cotton, thin striped blanket, alien and as expected. 'Also,' I had to keep talking, 'there was that strange piano teacher who told Lottie that music went into your ears and came out of your fingers which was the cause of endless arguments and explanations. Do you know … '

But I didn't finish for there was another knock and the nurse was back with a telephone. 'And there's a gentleman in reception. He wanted you to know he's here.'

'Roger?'

She nodded. 'Shall I ask him to come in?'

I will always remember that room. The clinical quietness, the multi-functional bed with all the apparatus for sickness into death, yet the rest of the furnishings pretending something other. The curtains merged shades of pink, orange and red, sunset or dawn; walls hung with pictures of countryside where you could stride through fields of poppies or row a boat on a river dipped with willows and bulrushes; visit the fair with multi-coloured awnings smelling of toffee apples; or holiday in one of the cottages around a village green where the smoke of wood fires curl into a deep blue sky. Were these images of earthly paradise to keep us here or help us on our journey? But I wished I'd been there to keep her at home with the late August sun picking out the pink of her eiderdown, the double bed reminding us that she was one of a pair even if widowed, and I would have brought the old low nursing chair she'd re-covered in floral chintz to sit as I was sitting with her now. With the mother who saw no worth in coddling, the mother who considered brisk words and a big hug the best way to deal with hurt, the mother who never allowed boredom and misery to waylay any of us; tasks and hobbies were created to fill every hour of the day; the mother, who, even though knocked sideways by Lottie's death, shouldered Jim's grief.

'Are you sure?' Roger said, hovering at the door. 'Leo phoned. I wanted to come, be near, in case ...' He'd taken off his raincoat which was still dark from the downpour outside.

'Thank you,' I had to go to him, to kiss him briefly, a shyness overcoming us both. 'I was going to phone again but ...'

'Of course.'

I took his hand. 'I've told her there is someone. I wanted to tell her, for her to know.'

'She's aware that you're here?'

'We spoke before she slipped into sleep.' I pulled him towards the bed, stood over her to say, but I can't remember how I said it, the loving of Roger, how special, the one; I sounded like a teenager.

He said; 'I don't want to intrude.'

'No, just sit with me for a while,' I said, 'lets talk, I want her to hear your voice.'

And we did; he in the armchair and me on the bed. I kept hold of Joy's hand. 'We were remembering elder wood whistles,' I said. 'Jim made the best.'

Roger said; 'Really? I thought my Uncle Ted, was the expert. That's what he told me.'

'Did you hear that, Joy. A lie, of course.'

'Elder wood is poisonous, my mother always warned me,' Roger said. 'But then I'm not sure how much she liked Uncle Ted. She made elderflower cordial once, though not a great success.'

It was right to be lighthearted, this is what she would have wanted. Even when Jim died she'd said; 'He wouldn't have wanted any wailing and moaning. He chose the best way, leaving us to celebrate him, that he'd lived. And that's what I'd like too.'

And so we went on, reminiscing, Joy hearing us, I hoped. The nurse came with cups of tea and dimmed the lights as she left. Again she'd held Joy's wrist, the throb of a heart beat being measured by the tick of a watch. Outside the rain had stopped.

It was after 11.00 when Roger left. The nurse came back with blankets and a pillow for me, turning out the light as she went. I settled in the armchair, my hand laid over Joy's. There was no question of my leaving. The nurse knew, as I did, that Joy was releasing herself, the final letting go. The light from the corridor sneaked under the door, outlined my exit, not hers. I whispered the words which have come back to haunt me; 'Roger is the man who I would have wished to be Lottie's father. I love him, Joy.' I closed my eyes. Was this enough?

From the bed there was a sigh, a deep drag in of rasping breath; 'A good voice he had.' The words spaced out for me to arrange the punctuation. 'Jim had a good voice, Greta.'

'So peaceful,' they said. 'It was how she'd lived her life, so peaceful.' I couldn't contradict them. 'And how lovely that you were there with her till the end,' they said, kept saying. 'She was so proud of you.'

What would she be saying now? Joy who wasn't sweet and daffy, who turned a cynical eye on much of life's frivolities, tore strips off Jim for minor misdemeanours and had once savagely wanted a name for Lottie's father.

Joy was buried, beside Jim, and Lottie before both of them. As we stood at the graveside, it was for her I wept, for my daughter. The grass around her headstone dun, parched. The tree we'd planted thirteen years ago, the crabapple, bore few fruit that year, the leaves crinkled, brown splotched. The snowdrops beneath were resting, last year's progeny swelling to the tiny white bulbs which would push up to flower next spring. Now there was nothing.

We went to the Lake District, to his cottage, one of a row, two up and two down with a kitchen so primitive we were essentially camping. 'Come with me,' Roger had said. 'It's time I went up to do some repairs, make it more habitable.'

Was this meant to be a form of therapy, time to grieve or to test what we'd begun in Paris?

It was beautiful; the wide green valleys cut through by the urgency of water, bleak fells overshadowing, stone walls running up and along, barriers to keep out and in. Sitting outside the cottage when the birds were establishing the day's priorities, I was doing the same, except mine were for life. The sun misted the far trees bringing into higher definition those in the mid distance, as close by lavender bushes straggled for a low hedge. Cows moved in slow procession across a farther field cropping the grass on and on. Up here it was bare bar a few new shoots, the hay having been harvested weeks before. I saw the rolled bales of

265

straw as toys of the gods who frolic under the dark pricked sky, under the hollow moon. It was too idyllic.

Seeing Roger become a man on a mission, determined to make the place a home for us to play in, was exhilarating. And we did play amongst the chores. We hired a canoe, Roger convinced that this was a skill you never forgot. The lake was much wider and longer than it looked from the shore. An hour of paddling got us nowhere; two hours later we were back on shore, tramping up to a pub our arms and legs like jelly. 'I'm a city girl, from a small town upbringing,' I said.

Walking was not much better.

'We'll improve,' he insisted so that each day's challenge was a longer and higher walk.

That was all of it, a challenge to go from one to two, a pair. And it worked, astonishingly it worked. We were compatible, day and night. No one before had made me laugh so much or made me try so hard. We could walk in silence, read as if the other was not in the room, at ease. And yet there were words for everything, our whole life to explore.

Leo phoned when we'd been away for a week. 'Well, Greta, you sound like the cat with cream, positively purring, I'd say. I know he's a dish and I'm pleased your fastidious nature has come to the fore.'

He'd called to ask questions about publication of 'Calling You Foxy Baby' - it was delayed, therefore all the prearranged dates for signings and talks would need to be altered. 'Gives you more time with your dear man, I can call him that, can't I?'

I said; 'Why this approval, Leo? You've always been cool to frosty about my choice of men before I met Roger?'

'Instinct, dear Greta, trust me.'

And I did.

Roger brought me back to poetry. He'd recite from memory, a bit of Wordsworth here, Auden there, an eclectic range, never more than eight lines, sonnet length at most, and never in that preachy way which Gerald used, and I'd once admired. It naturally flowed as if part of the tea making, scything the grass. 'Where does this all come from?' I said one day.

'I did "a Wordsworth" when I was fourteen,' he told me, 'took a boat out on a lake by myself and decided if I couldn't write it I could learn it. My mother had a bookshelf of poetry anthologies; it's what she'd studied at university before she left.'

'What did she do?'

'Worked as a typist, as a childminder before I went to school, all sorts.'

'Do you have grandparents?'

'I did. But she was one of five, and going to university was odd to start with and then the pregnancy and giving up; there wasn't approval or much help.'

I thought of Dora, her plight, and again of Joy and Jim, their welcome of Lottie, their delight, their care of us both. How lucky we had been.

We were sitting outside his cottage, the tiny garden rolling away to meet open country. I'd already remarked; 'It's as if it all belongs to you.'

'Can I say 'us'?'

'A proposal of joint ownership? I'll have to consult my bank.'

'I think I was proposing marriage but perhaps it's too soon.' He'd looked at me, that long look, the frown that set his eyebrows askew.

We both laughed, leant in to kiss and then sat back to wallow in the perfection of it all. We weren't drunk; it was our first glass of the evening while the lasagne he'd made was cooking.

I was deliriously happy, that hackneyed phrase which is far beyond understanding.

It was while we were there, contemplating the foreverness that he asked about the meeting. I'd promised to go with Roger to meet his father when I was his friend before we were lovers. I'd joked about my role in accompanying him, understanding his embarrassment at having begun this proposed introduction, the confrontation.

'Where should we go to eat?' he said. 'I began thinking coffee but as I made the original overture I ought to buy the guy lunch.'

'Are you wanting to impress him?'

'No, definitely not. I want to go in, be polite and then out. I have no affiliation bar a few genes.'

I didn't say a few hundred thousand. He was unhappy enough but was in a 'I've started so I'll finish' situation. The man had written back suggesting a date. 'Says he'll be back from the States at the end of September. Sounds pompous, doesn't it?'

I shrugged.

'Somewhere anonymous and not posh.'

I said; 'What about a Pizza Express? Easy food, nothing pretentious. The one on the Strand?'

'Yes, good. I'll book. 12.30?'

'Do we meet inside or out?'

'Inside. I want to be there, in control. I'll wear a red tie so he knows who I am?'

I laughed; 'Is this an assignation, dead letter drop, spies?'

September

Is this tragedy or farce?

I see him first because, of course, I know the man. There's a woman with him. I turn away; I don't want to see him or, more importantly, for him to see me.

I am wearing a red dress, 'to match' Roger's tie. New, warm red, short and fitted, demurely matched with patent black pumps; wearing the right clothes for a particular occasion has always given me confidence. I have my persona for signing novels; dark dress, high heels, groomed as sharply as my detectives' minds, and there's a signature perfume. Today I want to spell solidarity, spirit, pride. I hadn't thought danger, blood on the carpet.

It is Gerald. He hovers at the entrance desk, clearly cross that there is no waiter to greet him. The woman trailing him makes me think roadkill; the squished thin body, smeared red lips, ragged orange hair, a foxy nose. Is this his wife? Not how I imagined the purse strings, the moral arbiter; but it can't be one of his pick ups even in his declining state. I think what a strange and awful coincidence that they're in the same restaurant until he appears to recognise Roger, or that tie, Roger's red tie.

My thoughts spin, wild.

Gerald is wearing a slouchy jacket in moleskin with cord trousers, his shirt unironed; he hasn't bothered to dress smart for the occasion. He looks Roger up and down, dithery; gone is the fake suave, superiority from height; they are face to face. 'Roger Harlow?'

Roger holds out a hand, expecting a polite greeting but Gerald has turned to the bizarre creature on his tail. 'It is him,' he says, 'do you want to stay?' She lifts one shoulder diffidently, bored.

He hasn't seen me. Could I escape? But Roger turns to his ally, holding my elbow to bring me forward. I can feel the tremor, his shaking. 'This is Greta Salway,' he says. 'Greta, Gerald Porter.'

'Oh!' Gerald steps back startled, 'I didn't see you, Greta,' he looks around as if expecting someone else to emerge, 'you're together?

I want to smile, to say; 'Yes, Roger's my partner. And am I at last to meet your wife, *the* Mrs Gerald Porter?' But my tongue is dry as leather, my face rigid.

Roger says; 'Yes, do you know each other?'

Gerald ignores the question; 'Hadn't we better sit down. You've got this table, have you?' Courtesy was never a talent he'd needed in the past when honeyed words with pathos were his hallmark.

Roadkill appears to be totally uninterested in our little tableau. She stands behind Gerald, picks something from the back of his jacket, examining it carefully before dropping it on the floor. A face without expression, she turns her attention to the table beside her, peering at the food on their plates. We're clogging the gangway.

Roger says; 'Is this your wife?' He turns graciously to the woman who shoots a look of disdain at Gerald, offers Roger her hand and says; 'Laura Porter.' She doesn't smile but at least the appraisal is frank, interested.

Roger ushers them in to the far side of the table, places her beside himself, pulling a chair out, sliding it in as she sits, the perfect waiter; stepson? A faint smile crosses her pinched face as she nods queenly gratitude for this politeness. Her leather bomber jacket cannot have been cheap, the fabric close up is silky, bronze; her fingers cluttered with rings. I hang back; Gerald and I will have to sit side by side. He shuffles in, stands behind his seat, pauses as if he has not decided whether to sit or to leave. I could say that I've already considered that option but we have no choice. Roger looks across at me, concerned; he must feel the added tension. How can I tell him? My bones are dissolving, breath stretched so tight across my throat that I think I am going to choke.

I sit before Gerald considers making the same gesture as Roger. I don't remember him ever behaving in such a mannerly way, but then, until that recent ridiculous lunch, we had never eaten together. The lunch where he wanted my opinion on a letter, the letter that must have been from Roger. And what did I advise, or did I? My mind is wool, my mouth devoid of any spit.

A waiter has appeared, thrusting menus at us, is asking what we would like to drink. Gerald scrapes back his chair, sits, folding his legs, nowhere near the table. Will he not be eating? I hear Roger asking what they would like to drink to which Laura - I can call her that - promptly replies; 'A vodka and soda, and Gerald will have red wine. Isn't that right, darling?' The 'darling' is a shock. Gerald, who looked grumpy and drained when they arrived, is now suffused with a red rash creeping up his neck.

I look away. This cannot be possible. It's a mistake. Someone is going to say; you're the wrong man. The restaurant is full, the hubbub which was annoying when we arrived is gone as if I've become part of a silent film. The only animation is the scene behind me. What does this all mean?

'And you, Greta? To drink?' Roger has put his hand across the table to attract my attention but my hands are in my lap, pressing down on my thighs, holding on to gravity.

I ask for white wine and he mouths, are you okay. I nod unconvincingly.

We all study the menu as if reading a foreign language; I order a risotto without seeing the ingredients while Gerald and Laura discuss the merits of the various salads, the heat, the health of them and I think I hear Roger order some sort of pizza. I look from one to the other. Is this possible? Is there any likeness? The jawline maybe, though Gerald has acquired jowls, his ears are much larger than Roger's, and the hair? Gerald's once tended towards baby curls, if left would have grown to ringlets. Roger is darker but I cannot deny the possibility of curls waiting to be allowed their way.

Laura is saying to Roger; 'So you think you're Gerald's son?'

'Yes,' he says. 'He and my mother were at university together, Durham. She named him on my birth certificate and in a letter she left with her will.'

Durham? I look at Gerald, remembering he'd said; 'I'm a Cambridge man'. The lie, of course.

'What year was that?' Laura says. Her voice is smooth as the vodka she is sipping.

'1955.'

'Ah, I was at RADA that year,' she says. 'I hadn't met Gerald.'

I want to ask what that means in this context. But she is, of course, disassociating herself.

Our food arrives and is sorted into who and what. Laura raises her glass; 'Buon appetito!' which I realise as the meal progresses is another sick joke. The food is picked over, titbits placed carefully between her teeth, nothing must touch those red, red lips, before the plate is pushed aside and another vodka requested. Who can blame her? I've stirred my risotto, pushed it around my plate, forced forkfuls down my throat.

Roger asks about Laura's career which is seized on with delight, though it is evident that any talent she possessed was bolstered by money. 'Mummy and Daddy' are referred to with an awe which we are supposed to acknowledge. 'Gerald swept me off my feet. A poet, how can you resist. Not that Mummy and Daddy approved even though he was published, working for his PhD. Penniless, weren't you, darling?' Again the endearment jars, pronounced without affection.

Gerald is eating with gusto, refilling his glass from the bottle which he is sharing with Roger; his life depends on being satiated with food and drink. At one point he turns to me with a wan smile, the pained frown, to make sure I am complicit; we do not know each other. This is so true, I want to say. I never knew you.

Roger is still playing the attentive host, listening, responding, observing Gerald. Our knees meet under the table, he glances across and I see a look of desperation. I have not spoken; fear, bewilderment, despair are bottled behind the questions or answers I daren't express. I watch his mouth, the shape as he speaks, and then look at Gerald who says nothing. Sympathy, empathy, which I want to offer are stifled; I am numb.

Gerald has finished the bottle of wine, requests another glass, calling the waiter over himself. I wonder if he will offer to pay the bill. Laura is talking about their 'latest trip to the States. We used to have so many contacts; Gerald taught there in the 80's. But they seemed to have lost interest in poetry, thank goodness. We could concentrate on my American connections.'

Gerald asks if anyone is going to have a dessert, obviously keen to bring the occasion to a close.

Laura ignores him, looks across at me, as if startled to find I am still there. 'What do you do? For a living I mean.'

Roger says; 'She's a celebrated crime writer, Greta Salway?'

'Oh,' Laura's finely drawn eyebrows rise, a smile of recognition barely creases her cheeks. 'I love your books. Well done you!' And she continues a monologue on the joys of reading, asking if I'd thought of writing for television.

Gerald intervenes with; 'We ought to address why we're here, Laura.'

Roger says; 'Yes,' looking utterly miserable.

I feel sick, daren't breathe, cannot breathe. We shouldn't have come. I don't want to know, I mustn't know.

Laura turns to Roger as if to a child; 'Gerald has no memory of your mother, you know. I think she must have latched on to a name, who can tell?'

'But why pick you?' Roger is addressing Gerald. 'Weren't you on the same course? The same degree? That's how I found you.'

Gerald shrugs. 'Is it important?'

Laura scowls. 'It must be or he wouldn't have bothered you.' She dips into her handbag to bring out a snazzy lighter and packet of cigarettes. She has one between her lips before asking Roger; 'You don't mind do you? Would you like one?' This is directed at me though the packet is already closed. 'And don't look at me like that, Gerald, all prissy.' The lighter flashes flame and she relaxes back into a cloud of smoke.

Gerald says to Roger; 'Do you want me to be your father?'

No, you bastard, I want to shout. It is what I should be shrieking for the whole restaurant to hear, if terror hadn't struck me dumb with a desperation to stop even thinking.

Roger says; 'No, if it causes you a problem.'

Laura half shuts her eyes, the smoke from her cigarette clearly out of control. 'We have two sons. They would be horrified at what you've proposed.'

'Why didn't you put this in a letter?' Roger says to Gerald.

'Because we thought it kinder to tell you in person,' Laura shoots a look of malice to Gerald. 'He wanted to ignore your letter; the easy option, of course.'

'I think he was right,' Roger says. He stares at Gerald. Is he also trying to gauge a likeness?

'Good,' Gerald attempts a smile, that wheedling smile, poor me. I ought to say something, though what? I want to agree, but I know this man. I could tell them exactly how it would have happened, the helpless adoration, the brush off.

But Roger is speaking, sharp, clipped; 'No, not good.' Sunlight has caught his spectacles, reflecting back, I can't see his eyes as he looks from Gerald to Laura. 'I have to say that there is no reason for my mother to lie or be confused. I take that as a slur. And I'm sorry that curiosity overcame my better judgement. You are clearly not my father.' He raises his hand to attract a waiter's attention. 'Or if you are, I'm doubly sorry.'

Gerald hangs his head, studies the hands he has placed firmly on his thighs, as if like me, holding himself down; smooth, elegant hands with long slim fingers, piano playing hands, exact replicas of the son he is denying. Lottie's hands.

'Well, that's over with.' Laura shrugs, stubs her cigarette out on her plate. She takes up her bag, slim clutch, sits up Meerkat style as if pulling her spine back into shape. 'Get your coat, Gerald. I'm going to the lavatory while you settle the bill.' And she is off.

I look from one to the other, Gerald to Roger, a fly caught in a spider's web, or am I the spider needing to construct a web to stop myself falling apart? Except it isn't only me. They are both hideously entwined; I know that. 'Roger,' I begin, but the waiter arrives with the bill. Gerald mutters something about splitting it but Roger has his card ready, is handing it to the waiter.

I stand up and while Roger is concentrating on entering his pin, I look down at Gerald, an expression that he must take for disgust. And he does; shaking his head he says; 'I can't admit it. What good would it do?'

'None,' I say. 'Though perhaps to honour her. Her name?'

'Stella.'

'You do remember?'

'Yes.' He looks at Roger. 'He doesn't need me. I'm not worth it.'

And it is said honestly, I hear the contrition. We, two people with secrets we won't admit, know his falsity; and he knows I know.

He pulls himself up from his seat, weary and wary, stands tall, all bravado and pretence gone. To Roger he says; 'I'm sorry. I did know your mother, Stella Harlow. The love of my life, I think, though you won't believe that. I was possibly a nicer person then, though too young.' There are tears on his cheeks. 'She didn't tell me. Just left.' He is defeated. The act that once fooled me.

Roger stands in front of him expressionless.

How long we stood there I don't know; another tableau worthy of paint. Time was unimportant, I didn't want anything to end or begin. Laura emerged, nodded a farewell, led Gerald from the restaurant, no backward glance.

Roger turned to me; 'That was hideous. What a bitch, what a bastard!' He picked up my raincoat; 'Come on, lets get out of here.'

We stood on the pavement. In front of us Nelson's Column and St Martin-in-the-Fields, familiar and alien edifices; a steady splatter of rain, cars slooshing past, a grey, grey day. Roger turned up his collar, he'd no raincoat. 'Shall we make a dash for it?'

Fate running amok

I left him in drenching rain, rain that should have been cleansing for what we'd experienced. But, no; I, stupid, selfish, stricken, left him standing hunched against the wet, without coat or umbrella. Not looking at him, I said I wasn't feeling well and had to go, would be in touch later. He called after me; 'Greta! Wait!' I heard him as I ran, oblivious to that rain falling as if to bring on a flood, the end the world. I ducked down into Charing Cross underground and leapt on to the first train going north. He didn't follow.

I should have stayed with him, told him the whole truth then and there but I couldn't. I wanted escape, to get away and think, or not think. How can I love a man who is my daughter's half brother? How do I continue a relationship with a man whose father I once loved, with whom I created a child, a child who never knew of his existence, or he of hers? Is this my final punishment?

He's rung my mobile and phoned here twice; I haven't answered.

It's dark, the curtains open, streetlights blinking on, a world of shadows outside, nothing wholly real. The radio is playing, Radio 3 which he tuned to when last here. I'd said; 'Put it back to Radio 4, when we've heard this.' A Beethoven sonata that was divine, music he tried to play himself. Those elegant fingers I'd seen moving effortlessly over the keys of his piano, a piano that is squeezed into the hallway of his minute flat.

'Why?' he'd said, a sideways glance, amused that I cling to a default setting.

'Talk,' I said. 'If there's a chance of loneliness, a human voice is what I need.'

He'd come to me, a shiny smile, arms wide as to enfold a child, hugging me to his chest, kissing the top of my head, and breathing in the scent of hair.

'Sweet shampoo, Greta.' He'd sniffed again. 'I can never be lonely now, nor can you.'

Oh, god, must I lose him? How will I tell him? What will he think, what will he say ?

What is a love that seemed so perfect, so all consuming this morning and for the past two months, if I turn away so quickly? Am I afraid of him, or for him, for us? Yes, for us. How do we go on? I look out to the small park beyond, leaves all gone from the silver birches; even their trunks are black silhouettes at this distance, branches weeping with the weight of the rain. People pass along the pavement, cut through the gardens; do I hope that one of them is him? The seats, three benches where Lottie and I have sat to watch the pigeons, pretending that the place was ours, our private yard, are deserted. As I am. A coward holed up in a flat that breathes memories of her and now him, of that short time when we found each other, the joy of being together. But why did I love? Was I latching on to some vague likeness, a resemblance to Lottie or even worse, to Gerald?

I am stiff and shivering, still wearing the dress, the blood red dress, my sodden raincoat flung on the chair in the hallway. The radiators are cold. I check my watch; half five, but too early for the boiler to light as it's still on a summer schedule. I could override, turn up the heat, make a cup of tea. Or I could override it all; pretend that Gerald never happened. Does Roger have to know? Could I ignore, forget? I go to my bedroom and pull on a dressing gown; fluffy, voluminous, down to my ankles, pink, a gift from Joy. 'You don't need all this glamour nonsense when you're cold; you were always a chilly little morsel, not like our Lottie. She was her own little hotspot.'

Oh, Lottie, my darling Lottie, what do I do?

'Roger?' I leave a message as his phone goes to record. 'I'm sorry not to have phoned before.' What else to say? 'Please, call me back.'

If only I hadn't left, had suggested going to the crypt, those few feet away, where I could have shared my secret, the one I'd half told months before in a park. *'Her father was my lecturer at university, married. We had an affair, par for the course, no pun intended.'* It had been a relief then to reveal, at last, Lottie's origins; but without a name, the name that was unnecessary then, that is now my blight. His too. Ridiculous, unbearable, irrational.

What would I say to Lottie? What would she think? 'That's odd. Spooky,' is what she'd say. She wouldn't have thought it impossible. 'Is that what they call serendipity?' Happy chance? She knew Roger, she talked to him, trusted him to write what she said, with her corrections. I've imagined that badgering of him, demanding that copy of his article for her approval.

I don't close the blinds but go to the kitchen and fill the kettle, plug it in. Doing something normal, going to automatic pilot, anything to ease the numbness, the torment. I have to talk to him. I go back to the phone and ring, no answer. How do I explain? Thirteen years ago when she died, there was no one to tell, no one to ask, who could understand or could bear to know the utter horror and loss, no one. Not even Joy. It is to Lottie that I turned, talked, imagined, she has been my strength; the memories of her, the belief in her wish to do what she did, her determination to make the world right. It is a kind of madness to think like this, as if knowing what she'd think or say, putting words into her mouth when she hasn't spoken for thirteen years. She, who couldn't live with the dice thrown in her path.

Nothing can compare to the shattering, broken times of Lottie's death. This is a mere hiccup, a nasty jolt.

I see my reflection in the window, lit up from inside against the darkness outside. Isn't this my life's pattern? Find a man, find the faults? I stare as at another presence, external, as if at a parallel world. These aren't his faults, nothing wrong with him. It's his provenance that is the problem. At which I know he'd laugh; 'I hope you're comparing me to a priceless antique.'

There are no teabags, 'truckers' tea' as Roger calls it. Boxes of peppermint, camomile, lemon and ginger, crowd the cupboard, fall out as I search for something stronger. 'Very refined,' he'd said, sniffing each open box, 'too delicate for a man from oop North.'

My mobile rings and he speaks before I need to say a banal 'hello'; 'Greta, I'm so sorry that was ...'

'No, I'm sorry, I ...'

But he's not listening. 'Crass. I should have known. My mother was right, she knew him, there was nothing ...'

'What did you call her?' I interrupt, I need to know. She is suddenly a real person, my doppelgänger, making the same poor choice.

'What?'

I walk from the kitchen, the neon light, my image too bright. 'Your mother, you always call her 'my mother'?'

There's a pause, and I can see the frown, his bunched eyebrows, for why am I going off the point? 'Mummy, Mum. Why do you ask?' he says.

'I'm sorry.'

Again a pause. 'Are you home?'

'Yes.' I clutch the dressing gown round my body pressing the phone to my ear. 'You've drunk all my tea.'

'What?'

'Roger, tomorrow. I'll see you tomorrow.'

'No,' he says; my chest tightens; 'remember, I'm off to Glasgow till Friday.'

Of course, I knew this before, before everything was distorted; 'Yes,' I say, a wash of relief allowing me to sink on to the arm of a chair. I ought to say something else. 'Roger, I'm sorry.'

'Stop saying you're sorry,' there's a lift in his voice, he'll be smiling as he says; 'It's an occasion to be forgotten, right?'

People glibly say 'sleep on it' but I haven't slept. I drank coffee as there was no caffeine infused tea, and have eaten nothing, couldn't eat, I wandered from room to room as taut as a strung puppet. Wine was out; memories of Gerald slurping glass upon glass of red, or Roger and I savouring Sauvignon Blanc on the side of a valley as the sun slid orange fire behind the Fell leaving a blushing sky; both are excruciating in different ways.

What is this confusion of coincidence, fate running amok through my life? That letter, Roger's to Gerald, which has taunted those dark hours. And I've distinctly remembered my advice to Gerald was to do nothing. If only he'd ever been on my side, valued my opinion. Or is this what happens with all men? Did I venture any such advice to Roger? Was I asked? It's all a tangled blur.

This morning is no better. I need to get out, though a meeting with Leo and my publicist isn't what I'd have chosen. A proof of the dust cover for 'Calling You Foxy Baby' is grotesque, bordering on the pornographic. I know how little say we authors have in cover design and I've only voiced small objections in the past. This one though has to be fought off.

'It's eye-catching, Greta, you have to admit that,' my publicist says awarding us both a jolly smile. I know whose side she's on, who pays her to do what she does, in her view.

'Yes,' I say, 'and what does it tell a reader about the content, huh? Porno crap.'

'I'm with Greta on this one, Caroline,' Leo says though I register his wince at my profanity. He 'd already commented on my 'distraught look' before we even entered this Covent Garden coffee house.

'Are you using a new illustrator?' he asks her.

He knows perfectly well this is exactly what they've done. 'A young turk they're trying out; cheaper, and someone they'll say has their finger on the latest trend,' he'd already told me on the phone.

'Yes, Charley's right up there with the new zeitgeist,' the girl is aglow. 'We're thrilled with what he's doing; readers have so much choice these days, the internet, eBooks flooding the market, paper books need to shout their wares.' She's triumphant. ' You have to stand out on a bookshelf, make a can't-look-away statement.' The marketing team in her mouth.

There is a long pause in which the hiss of milk being steamed and frothed for someone else's cappuccino expresses so accurately my acknowledgment of her explanation that I shouldn't need to respond. And if I hadn't been so stressed, bound up like a trussed turkey with what else I needed to worry about, I might have been more conciliatory.

'Utter bollocks,' I say. 'Whatever your latest wunderkind believes will make my readers pick up and pay for this novel, he's not met them, or read it or any of my back catalogue, as they say.'

I see Leo visibly shrink and glance severely in my direction before saying to the girl; 'Again I have to agree with Greta.' His tone is gentle and gracious, inclining his head submissively. 'I was equally shocked and, although I know you have our best interests at heart, somehow your young man hasn't picked up the right vibes.' He smiles at me, a pixie look to indicate that he's in control. 'And by the way, Caroline, zeitgeist *is* new, that's the meaning, the spirit of the age.'

'Yes,' she pulls at a stray lock of hair, winds it behind her ear, an irritating habit. Sighing exotically, she places her hands on the table to say; 'I don't know what we can do at this late stage in ...'

'Late stage?' I begin. 'This is ...'

'Yes, Greta,' Leo interrupts, 'you're right. Caroline, these are the first proofs you've shown us. It's never too late to get things right.

'But ...' she draws back, sits up as if reprimanded.

'We are in no hurry. You have Greta's final proofs of 'Calling You, Foxy Baby'.'

'But,' she tries again, 'the budget doesn't ...'

'Pardon?' Leo assumes the position of a priest, palm to palm, fingers on his lips. 'Who's running this one? Hugh or Derek?' One eyebrow raised. 'Just tell whoever it is that we don't like it. And we'll wait for you to get back in touch. This time next week?'

Caroline sits for a moment not knowing what to do but then presses the cover images back in her briefcase and pushes back her chair. 'I'll do my best.' She sounds desperate, poor girl, and looks deflated, the plump cheeks, pouty lips diminished, as she gets up, giving a brief and uncertain wave to say goodbye, and is gone.

I draw a deep breath. 'Thanks, Leo.'

'No, it's my job,' which sounds far too curt. But then; 'Are you all right, Greta?' he says. I don't know how I look, what he sees. 'You're not, are you?' He peers at me over his new spectacles, whips them off to sit back and contemplate me, a specimen. 'What is it?' But then he spreads his hands out, palms up on the table as if expecting me to place mine on top. And I can't even shrug, but shake my head, demur with a half-hearted smile. I am torn apart, an old Teddy bear, the stuffing leaking from my back. 'You're not well?' If the caffeine hadn't bolstered me I'd have burst into tears. 'You know I'd do anything for you, Greta. So what else can I do for you now? What's wrong?'

On the edge is such an apt expression, a chasm yawning at my feet. 'It's too complicated, Leo.'

'It always is.' For a man who presents himself as finely strung, fussy, pernickety, he radiates, at times like this, a rock-like strength. He looks at me, the patrician expression with a gentle upturn to his lips. Not amusement, a fondness which is like an infusion. We look at each other, old comrades, with other battles won. 'If you'd like me to help unpick your problem, unravel a lover's knot, if that's what it is, dear Greta, you know I'm your man. Life has thrown most of its muddy water at me and I've learnt how to come out sparkly clean.'

I smile a real smile though rigid fear has fused my spine, or that's how it seems. I'm not able to even think what I'd tell him; the words would never come out right. I'm unable to absorb this new reality myself so how can I start picking it apart with him. Dear Leo.

'Life's like a lone surfboard that some fool has left for another to unknowingly step on,' he's saying. 'Wham! it flips up to hit you, flat on the forehead, senses knocked for seven.'

I laugh a pathetic huff; the image of Leo with a surfboard is impossible, far too energetic. 'Six,' I say

'Whatever you want, Greta.'

'And you're right, Leo. Slap bang. But I'm the one to sort it out.' I put a hand into his still open palms. 'Thank you; one day maybe.'

'Is it Joy? Such a huge loss.' He looks so concerned, all polished veneer put aside. The suit is impeccable, the shirt cuffs linked discreetly, but he has somehow shrugged into the guise of a mother himself. 'Have you given yourself enough time, whatever that's supposed to mean.' He is the one to huff, shake his head, not knowing.

'Yes, what does that mean?' We assume deep frowns, playful now, for he can see that I've pulled away, putting on the bright false face.

Outside we part with a promise to pursue the cover problem. I wander back past the Royal Opera House, posters for the perennial Christmas ballet, 'The Nutcracker' and am reminded of the time I took Lottie when she was ten. Impressed as she was with the plush seats, the sumptuous red velvet and gold flounced curtains sweeping aside to reveal the spectacle of a huge Christmas tree, she was fidgety. 'It's all so spikey, so contrived. And it must hurt horribly, standing on their toes, bloody too, flipping round like that.' 'Well,' I had begun, 'it's ...' But she'd shaken her head, given me a little nudge of reassurance. 'The music is ace. I'm just closing my eyes and it's bliss.'

How bright and resolute she was; her golden hair, the generous smile, a smile like Roger's. I stop abruptly, thumped to earth in another moment of recall, causing the band of three walking arm in arm behind to fall into me, pushing me off the kerb and into the path of a bicycle who swerves to be missed minutely by a passing van. One of the three, scarves flying, all woolly knits, big boots, grabs hold of me. 'Are you okay, lady?' she says. The cyclist has stopped and is staring back, sheet white, hard black stare. 'I'm so sorry,' I say to any of them. I straighten up, force an apologetic, pleading smile and back off to stand, catching my breath in front of a shop selling glittery dresses, fake fur. 'You'd look fab in one of those,' Lottie had once said of a sequinned dress she'd wanted me to buy. 'That and a fluffy white boa would be perfect. Sooo yoou!' I had almost succumbed, the Twenties and Thirties fashions appealing to my face and figure. Short dark curly hair begged a bandeau, the tendency to skinny rather than plump, I'd be a shoe-in.

Overhead is a muffled grey sky, a nothingness that promises neither sun nor rain. I take out my phone to find a message from Roger. 'Will be back by 7.00 tomorrow evening. Can I come straight to you?'

I walk up to the British Library where I'd originally planned to do some research, a thread to lead me to the next crime.

The books I've requested are brought to me. Tomes which would, two days ago, have looked like treasure troves, mind-absorbing knowledge dug up by experts. It may have been a Celtic practice to throw metal tokens into the River Wallbrook but what I'm working on, at least John Aynsley Howden is investigating, is corruption in the city where the old river is buried, deals spreading across Europe. And I'd thought how good it would be to travel to the cities of Europe in the way of research. We, Roger and I, would have loved that. Except now my life is the tattered myth.

How to tell him, where? Neutral ground where he can walk away as if from a casual meeting, not overlaid with what we have become, lovers and more. Neither my flat nor his? Our recent associations mustn't get in the way of his reaction, the disgust for what I'm to reveal. Is that what he'll feel? Disgust?

It's three o'clock. I haven't eaten, need coffee, and every sentence I read is blocked with the words; 'where can we meet?' I give back the books and request them for Monday. I have to believe that life will go on; those ideas, that research is of centuries back. Mine is another small cog in this relentless wheel. I hear Lottie; 'Mumma, what fishy philosophy!'

I phone.

   'Dora, are you free tonight?'

   'Greta angel! Where've you come from?'

   'Sorry, I've been so busy. I should …'

   'Course, no, it's doesn't matter. Great to hear you.'

   'It's ridiculous, short notice, but I'm here at King's Cross and …'

   'I'm at work, love. Lucky you caught me. Just popped out for a fag.'

   'Of course, I …'

   'We need to catch up. My new job, Johnny's prostate, it's all happening. And you?'

   'Okay.'

   'Hum, that sounds like not.' I can hear the drag on her cigarette. 'You must miss Joy. Sorry I couldn't come to the funeral.'

   'Yes, and I didn't expect you to. Lovely card, thank you.'

   A silence follows where I question my ability to nurture friends.

   But she's back with; 'Can't manage tonight, sweetie, though I'm not ringing off without we set a date.'

   'Yes, yes,' I say almost relieved. I couldn't have told her, spilled so many beans, which was one of her expressions. 'When would be a good evening for you?'

We fix on the following Tuesday, which seems like another era for by then all hell will have swallowed me up.

'Johnny, you said? Is it bad?' I say.

'A bloody nuisance, and let's face it, we don't know yet; cancer's not anyone's best friend.'

'God, Dora, I'm sorry. Give him a big hug from me.'

'Huh, don't know about that. He's always had a crush on you, your plush posh friend is what he calls you.'

'Bless him! Not so plush today, I'm afraid.'

There's a long pause, neither of us knowing how to go on or how to end.

'It's going to be all right. Johnny's found this saying, something like, "Life's crap when seen in close-up, but a comedy seen in long-shot."'

'Yes, that sounds about right.'

'Take care, Greta,' she says, 'keep your pecker up.'

The café is on the station concourse. The coffee is in a cardboard cup but the sandwich is what he would call, 'a bacon butty', the vowels distinctly Mancunian. 'Proud, I am, of what's left of my roots.' I'm here for the next train to Cambridge. A night and day in Waterbeach is the answer; my first home, Lottie's real home, my roots.

The sky is clear when I reach the house. It's cold and damp inside, the heating having been left to switch on only in the event of frost. I light a fire, a reminder of Jim, firelighters of rolled newspaper, stiff and coiled. If I had told him about Gerald, if I had told them both, would it have made a difference? No, no, not to their estimation of me, of that I've always been sure, and am still certain. It was for me that Gerald is my shame; I knew it then and now that knowledge is significantly magnified. How would they have borne this?

I phone Roger to tell him I'm in Waterbeach and will meet him at Euston tomorrow evening.

'Why don't I come and join you there?' he says.

I explain that I'm coming back to London, ask what time his train will come in. A rush of words, an attempt to sound normal, but I don't fool him.

'What's wrong, Greta?'

The silence before I say, 'tired, a difficult day,' is too long.

It's as if someone has opened a door, another person is hovering, and I cannot speak with them, with this, there between us.

'What's worrying you?' he says.

'I'll tell you tomorrow.' I say and then, 'take care,' which sounds even more false.

His silence is vast.

I'm standing outside, the moon full and aloof. Wisps of cloud veil and unveil, fragments covering and revealing, as if embarrassed at its stark beauty.

'The sky here is marvellous tonight,' I say, 'and with you?'

'Yes,' he says, 'of course.' But I know that 'of course' which means he doesn't understand or agree. 'I look forward to tomorrow.'

'Me too,' I say, aching to share words of love, unable to turn from the nightmare.

Is this the end?

Again it rained as I walked to Waterbeach station this afternoon. November rain, wet, incessant, gutter dripping, puddling up, slooshing down drains, pavements mirror black. Miserable, dank leaves, once bright with autumn colour, fallen to a slew of brown mush, mounded on street corners.

Last night I huddled in front of the fire, trying to focus on what I need to do with the house. Will I keep or sell? Joy's clothes are still hanging in the wardrobe, the half and half wardrobe; Jim's side empty. 'He wouldn't want them gathering moth and mildew,' she'd said, and rushed them off to charity shops and a local jumble sale. But her loss of him was maintained in the open space where no dress, blouse or skirt would trespass.

And even here, there was no distraction. I stared at the hearth, the familiar red brick modest fireplace, the stand of plated brass tools, brush, shovel, poker and tongs, flames curling and the hiss of the coal, giving off minimal heat. Even there, amongst the magic of fire-licking life, was the assault of guilt and despair. How can I hurt this man I know and love? How do I give him up? The language of romantic novels but, of course, there's truth in the banal, churned-over words.

Before Roger, I was myself, a person safe in her own space, needing no one. Independent, secure, unhindered by the whims of other people, for I could always write them out. Angus was the first to know that he might become a cypher for a character; 'Make sure I'm a villain, Greta, not a man of the law, a goody goody.' Max was vain enough to believe he'd have been the hero, and Paul, if he'd realised, would have been unable to find himself. Michael, the temporary prop, as I was for him, has been the prototype for several 'officers and gentlemen'. Then I was done with men. To be loved was what I was given as a child, as an adult I was on my own, responsible, without the clamour for affection or of giving part of me. That was Lottie's gift. I needed nothing more.

Or so I fooled myself, for that isn't a normal state, is it? I constantly stitched shut the rip, the hole, that impulse and hunger to be loved and to love another, other than my child. I can remember the first time I drew back from allowing the pain of association. After reading Shakespeare's 'The Rape of Lucretia', I found a picture that didn't disport her naked body for a lustful audience. Rembrandt's image is of a numbed and desolate girl, alone in the act of suicide. To die was to expunge the hideous act of others. Dying she stands before us, fully clothed in this one; the gash of blood seeping through her white shift where the dagger she holds has torn flesh, stabbed her heart, moved me to tears. If I was to be that young woman I would hide my wound. Being alone, careful to take men superficially, no more heartbreak; can I blame Gerald?

The train from Cambridge to London was packed. I huddled away from the chatty weekenders, up and out on Friday night. I stared from inside the neon lit carriage at the dark beyond. Late afternoon, lights from anonymous windows, street lamps as sentinels, flashes of car headlights running past, all happening elsewhere and I was excluded. Cold, alone, in a trough of self-pity.

'Greta,' Joy once said, 'there is no point in misery, sulking, waiting for some fairy wand to make your happiness. You have the world at your feet and a bolster of love; self-pity is a sin against your soul.' As a grumpy teenager I'd muttered; 'Soul? What's that? A churchy construct.' She'd heard, I'd gone too far and for a split crack into another life, I expected her to slap my face. 'I'm sorry,' I said, to which she replied; 'Think what you're sorry for, never for yourself.'

Joy's garden, her world where love was strong, is going to sleep. Three weeks ago I'd taken down the runner beans, bundled and tied the poles, stacked in the shed, Roger beside me gathering the debris on to the compost heap. He'd cooked supper. We'd walked around the town on Sunday afternoon where I'd pointed out the landmarks of my childhood, and Lottie's. My single bed was too small for both of us, we'd decided, and he'd insisted it wasn't right to sleep in Joy and Jim's double bed; the sofa would be fine. In the morning I stood and watched as he lay asleep on his back, one arm raised above his head, a leg abandoned to rest on the floor, a crease chiselled in his cheek from a cushion's piping, the slow rise and fall of his chest. And then his eyes opened, the slow smile, the stretch; 'Didn't sleep a wink last night,' he'd said.

Roger was my enigma; too precious with what I knew and wishing to know so much more. How fatal.

I walk along Euston Road to King's Cross, the wind and rain buffeting my umbrella; how am I going to convince him to eat in a nearby restaurant rather than go back to my flat, less than a taxi ride away? I pass a man sitting with dog and rug, a sign announcing that he is homeless. 'Bad night, lady, got any change?' I stop. Bad, change, homeless; I give him a fiver, a fellow traveller.

The surge of passengers coming from the train transfixes me; running, pushing, skirting around each other, dodging to be the first through the barrier. And then out of the crowd he appears, the only person I see, coming towards me smiling a happiness that's impossible to fake, a tartan scarf muffling his neck. He strides, wide steps, a purpose but there is no hurry. Time should stop.

'Hi, you.' He's put down his briefcase, enfolds me and I cannot draw back. One last moment, I think.

'A new scarf?' I say, raising my face to give and receive the kiss that I need, before the end.

'You like?' and he lifts the tassels to caress my cheek. 'Soft Scottish wool from sheep hardened for a rough climate, stripped of their coat to give comfort to me.'

'How selfish!' I say, and I don't want to move.

We stand close, looking at each other. I know he is, like me, assessing when 'what is wrong' can be brought out for examination, a subject equally difficult to broach. But he will have no idea of the bombshell; he has accused me before of being 'a bolter, a thoroughbred spooked by the slightest change in the wind.' This is a hurricane, a tornado tearing up to destruction.

'We don't want to eat out, surely?' he says. 'Lets pick up something from a store here, on the forecourt. Then a taxi home?'

'Home?' I say.

'Your flat?'

'I thought ...'

'Do you mind?'

'I ... can we have a coffee first?'

'What, here?'

'Just ... I need to tell you something.' But I don't break away. The warmth of him, the solid body; I want to stay, I don't want to tell.

'If we must,' he shrugs and it's he who pulls back. Picking up his briefcase he takes my hand as if I'm a child, an awkward child to be kept in order. He makes me stand with him at the counter. I ought to be the one taking charge saying 'shall we share a pot of tea?'

but I'm too agitated, irresolute even at this point, to make a decision. We are obviously the last customers and they are about to close. I sense their exasperation. They also think why did we stay, why didn't we go home; it's too late to make amends.

At a table, sitting side by side, he says; 'So? If this is about that lunch, you know it should never have happened.' He takes my hand. 'Can you really hold it against me? If he is my father, I'm sorry, but it was good to have you there. Thank you for that.'

I look down at the hand he holds, my left hand, the one with the ring on my fourth finger, which I've worn since Lottie started school. Joy and Jim bought it for me, a wide and twisted silver band, gold seeds nestling in the one of the cracks; expensive, avant garde for the time when they bought it. It's beauty, without the appearance of a wedding ring, their care of my good reputation, or Lottie's, touched me. There was no insistence, it was a gentle gesture. 'To stop any silly speculation,' Jim'd said. I wore it, wear it, for love of them but as I see it now, the connotations of marriage, what Roger and I might have had, my stomach shrinks.

'No, not your fault,' I say. 'It's what I discovered.'

'What, that a man with such an amoral attitude, self-serving and ill-bred might be my father?'

'He is your father,' I say. If only I could leave it there.

'You're that certain?'

Wind funnels in through the door as the last customers leave, a chill reminder of what I'll soon have to face.

I close my eyes. 'Yes, I am, and I wish he wasn't.'

'How? Does it alter your opinion of me?'

'No, no. You're nothing like him, only some features, some likeness in looks, your hands.'

He spreads his other hand, looks at it as if new. 'That's a relief. Or is it?' He places it on mine, both hands, a firm grip; 'You're not going to do a runner again, are you?' his voice coaxing, inviting me to look at him.

'No, but I think you'll want to.' And I have to face him. 'I'm sorry.' Why am I stuck with mere phrases for answers? Me, the storyteller, ought to have set it all out in one; clear, over in one.

A girl is working her way round the tables, wiping them and the chairs, rearranging, she'll soon come to us. We will have to go.

'Greta, whatever this is, just tell me.' His scarf unwound, hangs on either side of his neck, the red stripe in the plaid echoes his sweater. I see the shadows under his eyes, the tight lips. He hasn't slept either. It's not just me.

I say it slowly; 'Gerald Porter is Lottie's father', each word emphasised. A grenade thrown but it hasn't exploded. He looks at me as if waiting for something else.

'Gerald is the lecturer,' I say, 'the one I had an affair with, par for the course, remember?' He has to see it, he must understand. 'Lottie is your half sister.'

'What?' There is no shock in his tone, curiosity is all.

A man comes over to lock the door, looks across at us, assessing how long he'll be stuck, how long before he can chuck us out.

'I know it's impossible to take in,' I say, 'the stupid, uncanny coincidence. But I know, you and my daughter, are related in blood.'

'Are you serious?'

'Would I joke about something like this?' What I look like, the grey pleading of my face, the grim lines of certainty, I know without a mirror. 'I'm sorry.'

Roger holds on to me, tighter. 'Stop the 'sorry', Greta.' He looks around at the rest of the café. 'I'm not sure what to say, but we can't stay here to say it.'

'I suppose you're right, I just thought …'

'What?' Sharp, annoyed, did I have to make him angry?

'Distance, somewhere neutral,' I say.

'Why? Are you expecting argument?'

'No, it's just space, for you …'

'You're not making any sense, Greta.' He pushes back his chair. 'We're getting out of here, they need to go home. I'd suggest the same for us.'

'Where?' I say.

'I don't mind. But please, you've kept this from me all these days. It needs out. Why didn't you tell me then, after the lunch?'

We take a taxi, the rain a deluge, bright threads against the street lights. We hardly speak on route, apart from a comment about sheep and the smell of wet wool as if from strangers. A uneasy rancour circulates around us.

My flat is warm, familiar, as we scrub our feet on the doormat, slip out of our sodden shoes, hang our coats on the hooks behind the front door. Roger sets down his briefcase, takes out a bottle of wine. He collects glasses from the kitchen, unscrews the cap and pours us each a full glass, white wine, a Viognier, a favourite of mine. We each taste without a toast. Is the wine for support or oblivion?

We stand as if at some drinks do. It's my home, I'll need to take the lead but to sit means to relax, to stay. Yet I indicate that we ought to be seated as if interviewing a researcher. I wish I was.

We sit on my new armchairs, bought with a matching sofa, at right angles to each other, the soft shade of green a slurpy grey in the dim lamplight. We are both perched forward on the too plump cushions; their firmness, the perfect seated posture style so carefully chosen and delivered after our Lake District love affair, are all wrong. Why do I have to think in the past?

'So,' Roger says, 'you knew Gerald from the moment he walked into the restaurant?'

'Yes,' I say.

'That's why you were behaving so oddly.'

'Is that surprising?'

'No, but you could have told me.'

'So could he. He could have said, yes, I know Greta, but he wouldn't, would he, with her there.'

'Couldn't you?'

'No, what was the point and I wasn't sure ...'

'Of what?'

'That you were his son.'

He's shaking his head, wipes his hand across his forehead. 'I don't understand why you didn't expose him. It might have ended the whole thing before it started.'

He's right but; 'It's all very well now; not then ...' I should be taking control rather than this interrogation.

'It's the dishonesty,' he's saying. 'You and him? Were you colluding?'

'Oh, for goodness sake! I was shocked, appalled, stunned by the whole thing. Can't you see? Roger, I know, I should have told you then. I was wrong but I couldn't think, admit, the ridiculous impossibility of it ...' I don't want to sound angry. I want this over.

'Yes, but I thought we were ... I'm disappointed.' he says. 'I'm sorry.'

We're both clutching our wine, each take a gulp, in odd unison.

'But afterwards?' he says. 'Why not tell me then? The weekend, when I rang?'

'Over the phone?'

'Yes, at least better than this.'

'Would it have been?'

He says nothing, looking at me as if I'm the one beyond comprehension. 'Cowardice.' I shrug like some vapid teenager. 'I don't know, I've thought over and over since, but at the time it seemed ... well, it was a pathetic knee jerk reaction.'

He doesn't agree or look mollified.

'I even wondered if I needed to tell you,' I say; 'I was scared. Still am.'

'That?'

'Us, how can we go on?'

'Really?' He's genuinely baffled.

'It's cruel, unbearable, but it's a reality.'

'I can't take this in.' He finishes his wine and gets up for a refill. Lifts the bottle in my direction, but I mustn't be lulled back to where I want to be.

I say; 'The awful thing is I knew about the letter, your letter to Gerald.' It has to come out, the whole truth. It's easier with him standing. 'A year ago he asked me to meet him for lunch. I'd not seen him since we chanced to bump into each other in Cambridge and then at that Literary Festival in Warwick, just after I'd met you. He'd wheedled my address out of my publicist. Wanted my opinion on whether he should answer your letter. I had no idea who it was from, no name. His whole attitude was unpleasant; I was cross, rude, dismissive, and I thought I'd told him not to get in touch. But ...'

'You didn't tell me any of this?'

'It wasn't relevant. It was before we were ... I wanted to forget anyway. An incident in my past that's been written out of my script.' He again takes a large gulp of his wine but I've put mine aside; you don't drink in the dock, and that's where I feel I am. 'I was ashamed that I'd ever loved him.'

'Like my mother? What am I to say? You both had poor taste?'

We stare at each, me looking up and he looks down, those words between us. Is he beginning to see, to realise what it all this means?

I say; 'It's impossible, isn't it?'

'What?'

'You and me. Us?'

'I don't see why? We're not blood relations. I don't remember anything that the church decreed about ...'

'No it isn't that.'

'Then what? All of it was years, years ago. How old were you when I was born? Maybe six or seven? And me, when you and Gerald ...?'

'Nine. But that doesn't alter genes.'

'Genes? What's that got to do with it?'

'You, Lottie, each of you, half that man?'

'So what?'

How do I convince him? I know he hasn't comprehended and he must.

'Can't you see?' I say. I have to stand up, face him fully. 'How could we honestly be together, as we were?' The buzz of the wine on an empty and sleep deprived stomach is making me feel dizzy. 'You'd regret it. Think, I'm Lottie's mother. Like your mother, I had a child with that man.'

Is he at last seeing it, understanding? I don't want to breathe. His frown, his clenched eyebrows, his dark eyes trying to read me, trying to make sense of what I've said, and I want to smooth his cheeks as he did to me with his scarf and say, we'll put it out of our minds, it's nothing.

But he's saying; 'That was so long ago,' his voice less certain.

'Yes, but look what it's given.'

'What, me, your lovely daughter, you and me. What does it matter?'

'It matters because …' And I know defeat. I want to take hold of him, hug him, shake him; even the shadows on the ceiling press down on me. 'Because we're not just friends,' I say, 'are we? How could we go on?'

'Go on?'

'Roger, please!'

'Are you asking me to leave?' I hear only disbelief, a gentle questioning, not the disgust that I expect. Why won't he see? I'm desperate; why do I have to be the one to break us apart? A flare of anger runs through me, plain, hot spite.

'Yes, look, you've got to see it!' I can't stop, my voice is loud and cracked. 'If we go on you'll be fucking with your sister's mother and I'll be …!' I stop, the words in my ears all wrong, but for a moment there is relief.

He looks as if I've hit him, which I have; I feel that metaphorical blow myself. I can't take it back. His eyes are screwed up and he opens his mouth as if to say something but shakes his head. I was right; the horror, at last he's comprehended. Quiet and cold he backs away and is gone. I hear him putting on his coat and shoes. I hear the door open and shut, exit, the end.

I wish we could talk

I look up to see the moon is a ball of pure, cool light, reflected rays of a sun that's disappeared from our horizon. Lottie and I always fought over the full moon, a competition for who would see it first, never through glass. 'Not that I'm superstitious.' she'd say. 'It's only silica, whether transparent or not, but it's a barrier to the true magnificence.' I'd told Roger. So easy to share with him.

He's left a message on my phone. 'If you ever want to talk …' Just that. I do and mustn't.

The sky is sluggish today, smudged clouds, grey plumes, uninterested in the drab scurrying creatures below, always in a hurry, purposeful. The books are waiting for me at the British Library. I have a reason to walk into that other world of what went on before us. I'm either sticking my head in the sand or moving on. Either way I'm not ready to talk.

Leo tells me that my publishers have come up with a more suitable cover for 'Calling You, Foxy Baby'. He'll send a hardcopy for my approval, but he's confident I'll like it. Of course, I say, though if I tell the truth I care about nothing; it's all one.

We, Roger and I, fitted like the perfect dust jacket.

'Looks like we both need the whole bottle,' Dora says that evening as we push our way to the bar.

'Johnny? Tell me. It's definite, is it?'

'The big C? Yeh, and an op. Wasn't given a choice but he likes to pretend it's his idea. Like he's in control.'

Her hair is prettier than before, shorter, flattering her face.

'Better isn't it? Johnny said it takes years off me. Needs to, what with him to worry about.'

'I'm so sorry,' a distracted and useless phrase which is lost as I stretch my arm out to pay and retrieve the change. But I repeat it; 'I'm so sorry.'

Loaded with our bottle and glasses we find a table up a corner, tucked in beside each other on a banquette. The wine, a Chardonnay, her favourite, gleams and swirls pale gold as I fill our glasses.

'It may be risky,' she says, 'but you've got to take your best chance - any chance.'

The best chance? Control? That's what I've lost. Both. And here I am absorbed again in my own vacuous dilemma.

I hold up my glass; 'To you, Dora,' I say, 'and to Johnny.' We clink our glasses; 'Here's to the NHS,' she says, 'it better be the best.'

We sit looking out, seeing the other bodies, words unheard, all anonymous, unimportant to us.

I say; 'They've smartened this place up.' Inconsequential talk, but true, everywhere looks different, even the Library was intimidating, hostile this morning.

'You've not changed,' she says. 'The same lost soul.'

'What?'

'Without a decent man.'

I try to laugh, a distorted bleat.

'Serious, Gret, it's like you're holding back. Even when you were with that man and the boat, not connected.'

'Too right, Mrs Freud. He went ages ago.'

'And?'

'Complicated.'

She sips her wine, puts the glass down as if about to deliver a sermon which I suppose it is. 'Losing Lottie was enough to pull the heavens down on anyone.' Her pencilled eyebrows askew, fragment into a frown which brings a pathetic raggedness to her face. The music around us is a jazzy mix, a trumpet squeals and soothes, voices a blur. She shakes her head with a huffing sigh; 'It's still too much, isn't it?' She puts her arm around my shoulder, and I put a hand up to hold hers, as if to absorb the hurt that comes with admitting it out loud. 'I don't want to think about it with Johnny, but I'm terrified, and daren't say it to him.'

Death, the bond between us is pulled tight. There is nothing for me to say. The lights are a sulky glow.

She says; 'Riding the storm, each day as it comes, giving it your all.' We're still holding hands. 'Sodding all comfort, yeh?'

'No, but ... somehow, life has to be ... oh, sod it too!'

'Huh!' She brightens, her eyebrows perfect their arch and we both smile.

'I'm a rotten friend,' I say.

'No, you're the best. Here we are, haven't seen each other for what, six months, more? And it's like we're snuggled safe, I can tell you anything, have a good cry with you. If I want.' She gives my hand an extra squeeze and unwinds her arm from my shoulder. We sit back and sip our wine eyeing each other, amused that we are women who've said all that needs to be said. The trumpet or is it a saxophone bopping around us, sways into a lilting rhythm, a woman's voice smooching along to its call.

Dora picks up the bottle of wine, checks and refills our glasses. Holding hers up to the light, she stares into it as if expecting wisdom to float up to the top and is waiting to fish it out. 'I saw you with someone the other day,' she says.

I begin to protest that I hadn't seen her, and where was it, why hadn't she called out or something, but she ignores the cheery flow.

'You looked sort of linked up, you were laughing, arm in arm, and I thought it's happened, maybe he's come.' She looks at me, sad expectation. 'I was wrong, was I?'

'Complicated.'

'Gret! What am I to do? Isn't he worth sharing?'

Roger has sent a text; 'This is madness.' I agree but don't reply.

The cover copy's come and I laugh out loud. There she is, Foxy Baby, the brazen lift of the chin, the nose, a flow of red hair; Laura Porter in her prime. The blood drooling from her lips an added feature; wishful thinking.

Roger would be amused, I think.

A day so clear, the sky a slab of blue, buildings outlined, pencilled and painted in. Sitting in Leo's office, the sash window high enough to afford a view, I fold out of my coat, discarding my brittle self.

'It's good,' he says. 'Do I see approval?'

'You do,' I say. 'Did they find someone else or is it the same new guy?'

'No, a woman, one of their old school. Safe hands.

'Thank you. I know I was rude when …'

'Your prerogative, Greta, even if I find profanities coming from your mouth a tad shocking.'

The sun streaks a shaft of brightness above my head to raise the leather surface of his desk to a glossy sheen. He toys with a propelling pencil, the silver catching and throwing Tinkerbell flickers of light around the ceiling. I ought to be happy.

December has arrived. Christmas decorations sparkle, stream false festivity. Mornings dark, afternoons cut short, buses, taxis grinding to a halt, traffic blocked.

Shopping, a frantic charade, circles the streets and I stand like Scrooge sneering at their profligacy. Who do I buy presents for?   In front of Selfridges shop windows, staring in at a glorious fairy tale ride of glamour, I see reflections at my back, as if taking me into their group. Instinctively I look round.

A girl in a black leather jacket says; 'Amazing, isn't it? So gorgeous it makes you want climb in there with them. Don't you just love this time of year?'   She's addressing me, drawing me into her excitement, her joy. I nod. 'Of course,' I said.

A text from Roger. 'I miss you.' I wait before messaging back; 'Moi aussi.'

'Johnny's got a date,' Dora says. 'End of January. Is that quick enough?'

A phone call.   But I have no intelligent answer to give. All those months with no contact; now there's an urgency in keeping close to this friend.   Friendship is effort times affection, in equal portions.

'He says it's best to enjoy Christmas and the New Year, have a big bash.   Like before they come at him with the big knife, is what he says.'

'There'll be lots of tests beforehand, I expect,' I say.

'What, sharpening that knife!'   Her bravado not matched by the wobble in her voice.

'We need a hug, Dora,' I say.   How true, how true!   I blot the memory of Euston Station.

The routine has returned.   A strict timetable.   Check yesterday's work after breakfast; coffee after satisfactory progress on redraft; the rest of the morning on new work.   No meetings or research or phone until after lunch.   A walk to somewhere whatever the weather, and back for the long haul.   It'd been essential when I had Lottie, to keep focus, every portion of time accounted for productively. And fame, or whatever the constant sale of books adds up to, meant that I had to ride the bandwagon. It is too easy to get pushed off. That dread, as it used to be, is as nothing with Roger gone.

Dora's on my back; messages. 'Wot u doin at Xmas? Cum 2 us?' But I'm not ready for kindness.

Do I need to avoid people, would it aid my recovery? Out there I see assembled together on seats, couples, old and young, comfortably disposed, as we were, sharing long looks into the future and sideways to note and appreciate each other. A pair, linked by the act of sitting down united, a held hand, a word passed, the notion that there will be reassurance, together taking life on as one. That is what I see constantly, my eye caught as if called to observe. Is this what I might have had?

Leo says; 'You're as pale as a plaster cast, Greta. What's this all about?'

'Exaggeration on your part,' I say with what Joy would have called a goose grin.

'If you must,' he sighs extravagantly. 'If you're not eating enough greens … now that's a point. Christmas, darling, what's happening for you at our blessed festive season?'

Leo has always purported to hate 'all this simpering flummery', declining any of my invitations to Waterbeach. 'I'm deeply honoured, can imagine how heart-warming and delectable the feast will be, but it's head under the duvet time for me and my sweet man,' he'd always said.

In this reversed situation I tell him of Dora's request without saying that I've not as yet accepted.

'Well, I'm sorry,' he says. 'This year I'm having a sumptuous soiree. Finlay and I have been together for twenty years from that very day, 25th December 1993. Met in my local off licence - I bless Islam for their openness to trading when the rest of the world shuts up shop and leaves we miserable atheists to the dreariness of an empty larder.'

He rarely tells this story, Finlay being his best kept secret.

'You have to come, Greta, three line whip on this one.'

My diary is open as, before his interjection on the state of my health, he'd been giving me dates for book signings, literary festivals which had asked for my presence in 2004. This was the distraction I wanted.

'Mark it down this minute. I insist,' he says. 'Finlay will be there. He's promised not to be off on one of his 007 missions.'

Where Finlay works, and at what, is a mystery. The allusion to work for MI5 is one of Leo's constant ploys to shroud him from the public eye. Could I resist the chance to meet him once again face to face?

'You will won't you, Greta?' Leo says as if beseeching a child. 'And that nice man, Roger.'

I shake my head. 'No, that's one too far.'

He doesn't press me further.

A text from Roger; 'Are you OK?'

No, I want to reply but instead write; 'Sorting myself out. You too, I hope.'

My input and output at the British Library is poor. The danger of blind research with no focus, aimless meandering down lines of enquiry with lack of inspiration, is real.

A full diary must counter the inertia. I have accepted Dora's invitation for Christmas Eve only; I will go to the service in St Martin in the Fields on Christmas morning to enjoy the music and in memory of Joy who kept close to her sociable and undemanding God. Leo's party in the evening will be where I prove that a solo life is attractive and fun before I flee to Waterbeach to lick my wounds. I will gift myself books that I never find time to read and will do so in front of the fire. It is my bolt hole and I have decided not to sell.

I am convincing myself that the shock of finding the relationship between Roger and Lottie, the sudden and uncomfortable exposure of our situation, encountering Laura and Gerald together, is what has caused me so much grief. Out of all proportion, really. He was merely another man I'd found, thought I loved, who would have gone the way of all the others, eventually. The timing of our end was merely not of my choosing.

Johnny's operation had been brought forward. A week before Christmas. I sit with Dora in the hospital while he's in theatre. Inside the curtains drawn around his temporarily vacant bed, cut off from the rest of the ward by the flimsiest means, we feel alone and private.

'Who was he?' she says, returning to the subject we'd left in the wine bar. A cunning ruse to challenge me at a vulnerable moment when I know that to talk of anything other than what is going on in the operating theatre, is vital.

'He's Roger Harlow, an economist,' I said. 'We did like each other a lot. Perhaps I did think he was the one, after all my ... dalliances.'

'So? Why did he go?'

I look at the empty bed, white sheets pulled back, the pillows still showing the imprint of Johnny's head. All the paraphernalia for medical procedures on show; the metal sides of the bed, cage-like to enclose, levers to raise and lower, apparatus on the walls to fix oxygen

310

cylinders, a drip feeder abandoned in the corner, the slot into which they'll slide his notes at the end of the bed, the saga of his bodily health.

'He didn't,' I say, 'except he would have done when he'd thought about it.' Is this good for me, I think, because I know it's good for her. How strange amongst all the angst to use this as a means of distraction. Hidden for all those years, the secret secret, recently exposed so drastically. 'It's a hideous coincidence,' I say, 'more than that, it's fate gone mad. He's Lottie's step-brother.'

'Wow!' Her eyes sparkle. She's dressed in 'tracky bottoms', her hair tied back, strands escaping to straggle across her face. A face where the sharp lines of her eyebrows and the purple shadows under her eyes are the only prominent features, brightens. 'How come?' She's ignored my obvious distress.

I explain; 'You remember all those years ago when I asked you for advice on how or whether to tell Lottie about her father? The father who I dismissed, or perhaps he dismissed me. Anyway that's irrelevant.' Yes, what did my secret liaison matter any more? How trivial it's become in all the rest of the chaos. I tell the tale.

Dora says nothing, her expression of expectation fading, being involved in my juicy gossip gone. I can't read her.

'It's impossible,' I say again. 'How could Roger and I go on?'

She still says nothing, looks at me as if assessing whether I've completed my story or whether there's a need to respond.

The voices around us become more acute, nurses or doctors pulling aside other curtains, the rattle of metal hooks on rails, the odd words of medical procedures prominent, protestations from somebody on the other side of the ward.

Finally Dora says; 'My dad's the father of my brother's father.' She smiles. 'Work that one out, Greta.'

I can't, don't, it's not what I'm expecting her to say.

'I've never told you that 'cos it wasn't important. I was brought up with it, no big deal. Lots similar.'

My revelation, which I thought would shock, is eclipsed.

Still smiling she says; 'My Mum fell pregnant with Ali when she was sixteen. His dad was the same age, no chance he was going to stay round and marry her. Says she didn't want him to. A fun bloke who grew into an overweight berk.'

The lights in the ward suddenly seem incredibly bright, white light that saps the brain. Fatigue drags me to wish that I could climb into that bed but Dora's determined that I hear her out.

'His dad, my Dad, Eric, was only in his thirties, divorced, fell for Mum and the rest is a piece of cake. Happy as two bath buns, they've been together for the last twenty years.'

I look at her wanly, not knowing where that takes me.

She has her head cocked to one side; 'So, what's your problem, ducky?'

An email from Roger; 'I wish we could talk.' I don't reply.

A sprinkling of snow; eerie silence as soft flakes float and fall effortlessly, layering a thin line of white on the branches of the birch trees beyond my window. There is a lightness in my lungs, of waking from an illness with a wish to get up and walk outside. I put on boots and anorak and go to stand and let snowflakes fall on my head. Icy cold, dissolving as soon as they touch, these star-like structures are so frail. I think of Lottie, her fine hair splayed out on those cold dark rails. Her soft skin, the fragile beauty of her complexion, the brightness in her blue eyes, the expectancy of life being good. 'Snow's for kids, Mum,' she'd say. 'Enjoy!'

Grief is the last gift we give to the dead; the expression and proof of love.

Dora phones to say that Johnny is out of hospital, 'Doing good, driving me mad. Bring a bottle 'cos I might need to smash it over his head.'

A Christmas card from Roger. A scene reminiscent of Russia, a mix of pine and birch snow clad, the blush of a dawn or twilight sky. Inside he has written; 'I don't see a problem. I want your friendship above all. I rattle the bars of the cage which are of whose making? Should Gerald win?'

There is nothing else.

How will I respond?

On Christmas Eve morning I meet with one of the private investigators I use for 'the low down', Leo's expression. My lack-lustre approach to this next novel is immediately dispersed by his dismissal of all my ideas. It costs me an expensive lunch and a fair bit of boasting on his part; but the anger I feel towards him is a spur. I email Leo afterwards; 'Is their lifestyle so shabby, their need to blag so inherently nasty, that they have to bolster themselves with vainglory? The new title will be 'The Vainglorious Blaggers of the Wallbrook Sewer.''

There is no response.

I text Roger. 'Thank you for your card. What can I say?' Which is pathetic and unkind, I know, but every contact, every thought of him, brings a turmoil of doubt and doom.

Christmas Day dawns though it is hard to tell. No sun, grey scudding clouds, rain. The candles in church flicker nervously, the music rises to the beams and arches, but there is nothing to brighten the stained glass windows. I am underwhelmed; a bad daughter. Jim would say; 'It strikes us all in different ways. For our Lottie life's about making things better. We don't all need prayers.'

Leo's flat is a total contrast. Red and gold lanterns, sizzling candles, Madonna, Kate Bush and others I don't know, piped through all the rooms. I say to Finlay; 'I'm surprised that with your contacts I don't find these super songsters here in person, and Kylie Minologue.'

Leo comes up behind us to say; 'No, afraid not. He'd prefer to bring Putin to serenade you on his horse, bare chested.'

Finlay and I both groan.

Leo says; 'I need to talk to you for a moment, Greta, private. Finlay will keep everyone else happy.'

He takes me out onto the balcony, his party mood eclipsed as soon as he closes the French windows behind us. The overhang keeps us dry but the chill damp attacks despite the amount of wine I've already drunk.

'Greta,' Leo looks out over the murky streets below. 'Roger Harlow came to see me yesterday.'

'What?'

'He tracked me down at my offices so not a casual call. I might say he was good enough to phone me before arriving, a courtesy'

I stare at the back of Leo's head.

'He told me your story, his and yours. I was astonished at the passion of the man. Although he apologised for revealing your secret as well as his, I was soon attuned to his desperation.'

'When was this?' I say, the dank air clogging my throat.

'Yesterday morning, before you emailed with your assessment of private detectives.'

I want to sit down. My body is too heavy for my legs, the weight of whatever is afflicting me crushes my lungs.

'You need to talk to him, Greta, ...'

'I did ...'

'No, I think you threw your ideas at him without giving him a chance to discuss, argue, or persuade.'

'But ...'

'But what?' He's turned back to me, the steel sheen of his hair, his haughtily raised eyebrow viewing me as a disagreeable child. 'You know me, Greta, I talk as if love is a wild commodity to be grabbed and discarded as the whim takes me. But you also know it is pretence; lust yes, but not love, the happy accommodation of the other to oneself. It seemed to me you had it with him, seeing you together, and then hearing him yesterday I was even more convinced. Call me an old romantic, Eros in disguise if you wish, but I'm fully advocating the warmth of a held hand, the ear of a trustworthy mate and the sweetness of shared suffering.' He puts a hand on my shoulder; 'Give him a chance.'

Tears have welled in his eyes and mine in response, or was it the other way round. 'At my age?' I say.

He gathers me into a careful hug. I'm aware that I might be creasing his black silk shirt which makes me weep and giggle at the same time. I push him away, worried that my makeup and tears will stain his princely exterior. I say this to him.

'It'll come out in the wash, darling,' he says which makes me laugh even more.

The rest of the party is a blur; Finlay called a taxi at two in the morning. By then the rain had cleared and a few stars glimmered through the lit London sky.

'This letter is from Roger. Read it when you're home, or as soon as you are capable, in your right mind.' Leo presents this to me as Finlay shrugs me into my coat. 'I've arranged another taxi for you tomorrow morning. Meet the man, at least do that.' I look from one to the other, such good friends, the pair escorting me down to the pavement and into the cab.

'Please,' Leo says as he opens the car door. 'Chance brought you two together, good people, shared experience, Lottie too. All the best of credentials. That other man was a mere footnote of no consequence. Happiness is hard to find if you doubt your ability to be worthy of it.'

'Such wisdom,' I say, 'and at this time of night!'

Roger's Letter

Dear Greta

In desperation I am using Leo as my courier. I've never confided in a third party before, wished to take advice in such a private matter, but I need help. Electronic messaging is not the way to conduct this conversation, one which I want to have with you in person.

I hope that you'll read this, a letter that sounds far too formal, I know, but it's the best I can do in the circumstances. I hope that you'll then meet me so that I can understand how you feel about us, on reflection. I hope, perhaps in vain, that your final utterance after telling me that you knew Gerald and that he is my father - I still cannot believe it's him - was flung at me in a moment of distress.

You also said that I might wish to 'do a runner' after I'd accused you of doing just that. I therefore need to state, before I go any further, that I don't. I wish to stay, not to go back to where we were before, but to discover where we are now, and go on together.

I know that I could never comfort your grief at the loss of Lottie, a grief that won't diminish. I can't fully comprehend your feelings for Gerald, the distress he must have caused you in the past, and I suppose still does. You will not know the intricacies of my childhood loss. But we were, and can be, in sympathy.

My two adult relationships, one a marriage, ended with little love lost. Sometimes I wondered, before I knew you, whether I was capable of passion, an abiding desire for another person, a genuine joy in their presence. Was I a cold fish? Was I scarred by my mother's depression, being fatherless, her suicide? All that vanished when I met you.

I've spent these last weeks - in fact it's over a month - trying to put together the aspects of what we've just learned which might make our life together difficult or impossible as you suggested. I can find none.

This is not a love letter, per se. It is a plea from a hopeless man for a hearing. If you are able to consider a meeting, I will be waiting for you as Leo has arranged.

I will always love you, whatever your decision,

Roger

Letting music out

The taxi dropped me off on Duncannon Street, beside St Martin-in-the Fields. 'This is as close as I can get you,' the driver said. 'It's old Nelson's Column you want.' He thought me a stranger to the city, my fare prepaid.

At first I thought of it as a Bruegel painting. True, there was no snow, the peasants were not skating or fighting or struggling to make a living. The buildings surrounding us were not cosy in appearance, the red against the frozen grey water, the stark brown trees. This place was all white stone, tall elegant blocks, a range of roofs, the famous column and opulent blue pools refreshed by spouts of water. The tree was a Norwegian spruce, unlit and the darkest green against the sky, a sky white with a promising gleam of sun. It was the bustle of people that surprised me, milling around, bolstered in winter coats, dark figures out for the Bank Holiday, youngsters climbing on the bronze lions, chasing pigeons, a scene of gaiety.

Roger was standing below the column as if unaware of anyone else around him. He was wearing the scarf, that soft warm scarf, his knitted beanie hat, and was as upright as the man above him. I came down the steps from the National Gallery slowly, determined to take in the scene. I wanted to see his face when he saw me.

It was then that I heard the man with the accordion. Not a concertina, but the same principle. Bellows squeezed tight, expanding to pull in air, letting music out.

Roger saw me and came to where I stood. I smiled; 'I saw this as a Flemish scene when I arrived but we could be in Paris, don't you think?'

'We could,' he said, and took my hand.

ACKNOWLEDGEMENTS

My thanks, as always, to my writer friends who give me constant advice and encouragement, proofread both the copy and the characters for veracity. And especially to Sandra Horn who did the final check to eliminate anomalies.

It is to Drew Westcott, my designer and publisher, that I wish to give particular thanks for his skill in designing the cover, as well as the whole book.

And I am grateful to the many coffee houses we have frequented in the months of bringing this production to completion.